"What [...] with him?" Ryan demanded

Mildred didn't answer. She turned away and rammed two stiff fingers down her throat, trying to induce vomiting. It took Ryan only an instant to understand. With a curse he tossed away the canteen. Poisoned. The whole bastard lake was poisoned!

Dropping the Steyr, the man clumsily cut his arm with the panga, hoping the pain would keep him awake as his world started to go dark. But Ryan barely felt the passage of steel through his skin and knew that it was already too late.

Enraged over his failure to recognize the trap, Ryan felt an adrenaline surge course through his body. But the brief respite vanished quickly, and, still fighting to remain conscious, the one-eyed man slumped to the ground and went still. The rest of the companions joined him moments later.

Soon, there was no movement at the crystal lake other than the steady rush of the waterfall and the bright sunlight reflecting off the gentle waves.

Other titles in the Deathlands saga:

JAMES AXLER

DEATH LANDS®

Tainted Cascade

A GOLD EAGLE BOOK FROM

WORLDWIDE®

TORONTO • NEW YORK • LONDON
AMSTERDAM • PARIS • SYDNEY • HAMBURG
STOCKHOLM • ATHENS • TOKYO • MILAN
MADRID • WARSAW • BUDAPEST • AUCKLAND

Recycling programs
for this product may
not exist in your area.

First edition May 2011

ISBN-13: 978-0-373-62608-3

TAINTED CASCADE

Printed in U.S.A.

Slavery as an institution that degraded man to a thing has never died out. In some periods of history it has flourished: many civilizations have climbed to power and glory on the backs of slaves. In other times slaves have dwindled in number and economic importance. But never has slavery disappeared.

—Milton Meltzer
1915–2009
Slavery: A World History

THE DEATHLANDS SAGA

This world is their legacy, a world born in the violent nuclear spasm of 2001 that was the bitter outcome of a struggle for global dominance.

There is no real escape from this shockscape where life always hangs in the balance, vulnerable to newly demonic nature, barbarism, lawlessness.

But they are the warrior survivalists, and they endure—in the way of the lion, the hawk and the tiger, true to nature's heart despite its ruination.

Ryan Cawdor: The privileged son of an East Coast baron. Acquainted with betrayal from a tender age, he is a master of the hard realities.

Krysty Wroth: Harmony ville's own Titian-haired beauty, a woman with the strength of tempered steel. Her premonitions and Gaia powers have been fostered by her Mother Sonja.

J. B. Dix, the Armorer: Weapons master and Ryan's close ally, he, too, honed his skills traversing the Deathlands with the legendary Trader.

Doctor Theophilus Tanner: Torn from his family and a gentler life in 1896, Doc has been thrown into a future he couldn't have imagined.

Dr. Mildred Wyeth: Her father was killed by the Ku Klux Klan, but her fate is not much lighter. Restored from predark cryogenic suspension, she brings twentieth-century healing skills to a nightmare.

Jak Lauren: A true child of the wastelands, reared on adversity, loss and danger, the albino teenager is a fierce fighter and loyal friend.

Dean Cawdor: Ryan's young son by Sharona accepts the only world he knows, and yet he is the seedling bearing the promise of tomorrow.

In a world where all was lost, they are humanity's last hope....

Chapter One

Moving low and fast, the six sweaty horses galloped across the blazing plain of the Great Salt desert, the grim-faced riders hunkered low in the saddles, their hands desperately reloading weapons.

"We're not gonna make it!" J. B. Dix shouted, glancing over a shoulder.

"Yes, we are!" Ryan Cawdor yelled back, pointing straight ahead with his bolt-action longblaster.

Squinting hard against the wind and the airborne granules, the six riders could only make out a blur in the distance. Then as they crested a low sand dune, an oasis came into view, a tiny patch of blue water smack in the middle of the scorched hell of the vast salt desert. A few palm trees grew alongside the shimmering pool of water, their abnormally long fronds bending all the way down to hesitantly touch the surface as if trying to sneak tiny sips when nobody was watching. Bizarrely, a predark mailbox jutted from the damp sand alongside the pool, the metal sandblasted to a mirror-like sheen over the long decades, but the shape was unmistakable.

"Thank Gaia!" Krysty Wroth exhaled with a grin, reining in her mount.

In the far distance, a large black cloud crested the horizon. Skimming low and fast over the salty sand, the cloud moved with singular purpose, heading straight for the six companions, as unswerving as a laser beam.

"Here they come!" Mildred Wyeth yelled, bringing her horse to an abrupt halt alongside the pool.

"Into the water!" Ryan commanded, sliding off his stallion and dropping into the water. The man grunted with annoyance as the water only reached the top of his combat boots. Fireblast, he thought, this wasn't going to offer us any useful cover. No other choice, then.

"Ace the horses!" Ryan shouted, firing a single 9-mm round into the left eye of his mount. The horse recoiled from the trip-hammer blow of the copper-jacketed lead and reared high on its hind legs, whinnying loudly. The big brown eyes stared accusingly at the man, then the horse collapsed onto the damp sand, twitched and went still.

With grim expressions, the rest of the companions followed suit, arranging the bodies in a crude barricade around the small pool. Wary of where they put their boots in the shallow water, the companions put their backs toward one another to stand in a defensive circle. Now, they were covered up to their chests, which gave them a fighting chance for survival. That still wasn't much protection, but it was better than nothing.

Reaching out, Mildred took J.B.'s hand, and he squeezed back, the couple savoring the touch for a single precious moment, the gesture saying in volumes what no words ever could. Breaking free, J.B. slid the S&W M-4000 shotgun off his shoulder and passed it to the woman. Mildred nodded her thanks, removed a fat red cartridge from one of the loops sewn into the strap and slid it into the belly of the scattergun.

"Never heard of stingwings hunting in a pack before," J.B. stated, working the arming bolt on his Uzi machine gun. Short and wiry, the man was wearing a battered old leather jacket and a fedora that had seen better days. Wire-rimmed glasses were firmly tucked into place on his nose, at his side hung a leather satchel, home to various bits and pieces of munitions in addition to several sticks of dynamite.

"If this is our last day, so be it, my friends!" Dr. Theophilus Algernon Tanner stated in a deep stentorian bass, cocking back the hammer on his massive LeMat revolver.

Dressed as if he came from another century, which he had, Doc wore a long frock, a frilly white shirt and cracked knee boots. His hair was a silvery white, but his thin face was lined.

"Not dead yet," Jak Lauren drawled in forced calm, a Colt .357 Magnum blaster clutched in his right hand, the left fist holding two throwing knives by the blades. A true albino, his hair was the color of fresh snow and his eyes as red as rubies. Sweat poured off his face to disappear into the collar of his camo jacket. More knives were sheathed on his gun belt, and the handle of a stiletto jutted from his left combat boot.

"Too true, Mr. Lauren. Vini, vidi, vici!" Doc declared boldly, even while trying to control his pounding heart. Moving with exaggerated grace, as if he had all the time in the world, the old scholar tucked the blaster into his gun belt and drew his ebony walking stick. Twisting the lion head of the stick, Doc pulled out a long steel sword, the razor edge glinting in the harsh desert sunlight. He drew the blaster again and stood

ready, his shoulders hunched, his eyes riveted onto the
ever-approaching cloud.

"Stuff it, ya old coot," Mildred growled, hefting the
shotgun along with a Czech-made ZKR target pistol.
Short and stocky, the predark physician was wearing
a red flannel shirt, blue jeans and a U.S. Army jacket
and combat boots. Slung across her back was a patched
canvas satchel bearing the faded lettering M*A*S*H.
Fear was a metallic taste in her mouth, and Mildred
tried to spit it out. Then the physician recoiled at the
sight of the blood from the chilled horses oozing off the
bank to spread out in a crimson cloud across the pool.
She prayed to heaven the sight was not prophetic.

"Must have gotten thirty or forty of the bastards,"
Krysty said, replacing the round in her S&W Model
640 revolver spent acing the horses. Her animated red
hair flexed and curled around her face in response
to her heightened emotional state. A truly beautiful
woman, the redhead was nearly as tall as Ryan with
a well-proportioned figure. Krysty was dressed in a
khaki shirt with the sleeves cut off and patched denim
pants that were tucked into the top of her blue cowboy
boots.

The cloud was noticeably closer now, and the companions could once again hear the flapping of the leathery wings of the muties. There were so many of them
that the flock of stingwings was as black as pitch, a
patch of midnight flying fast through the noontime sky.
The companions had escaped once before, but their
horses soon became exhausted, forcing the companions
to make a last-ditch stand.

"Let's see what I can do about thinning them out,"

Ryan stated, lifting his Steyr longblaster and working the bolt to chamber a fresh round. Tall and leanly muscled, the man radiated a sense of raw physical strength that was almost palpable. His long black hair was tied off his face with a rawhide thong, a leather patch covering what had once been his left eye. Ryan was wearing a ripped denim shirt, military camo-colored pants and combat boots. A SIG-Sauer pistol was holstered at his hip and a curved knife known as a panga was sheathed on the other.

Ryan held the Steyr in both hands and looked carefully through the cracked telescopic sight, delicately adjusting the focus. It took the one-eyed man a moment to locate the roiling flock of muties, then he chose the biggest creature leading the flock and gently squeezed the trigger. The 7.62-mm copper-jacked hollowpoint round plowed into the head of the hideous mutie and came out its rear, carrying along a wealth of blood and organs. As it fell, several of the other muties dived to the ground to start feasting on their fallen member, but the rest kept coming, as unstoppable as the tide.

Again and again, Ryan carefully aimed and fired, slamming home rotary clip after another, trying to chill as many of the winged monsters as he could before they arrived in force.

"Not bad, old buddy," J.B. growled, releasing the Uzi to hang by its canvas strap while he rummaged about his munitions bag. "But watch this!" A moment later, the Armorer unearthed a pipe bomb and a precious butane lighter.

Flicking the flame to life, he lit the fuse until it began to sizzle. Tucking the lighter into a pocket, J.B.

then whipped the pipe bomb forward at the end of a rope. Soon, the man had the explosive charge spinning around his head in a blur, steadily building speed as the fuse burned down quickly. When it had almost reached the bomb, J.B. released the rope, and the pipe bomb sailed high to gently curve back to the ground and violently detonated in the air.

Half of the flock vanished in the fireball, several more dropping from the sky, their leathery bodies riddled with shrapnel.

"Well done, John Barrymore!" Doc boomed, slapping the man on the back. "Once more, sir, and with vigor!"

"Can't, no more rope," J.B. said, swinging up the Uzi again, his fist tightening around the pistol grip.

Instantly, Jak turned to the nearest horses and started cutting off the reins.

"Too late. Here they come!" Ryan growled, louder than he expected, triggering the Steyr twice more, then shouldering the longblaster to draw the SIG-Sauer from his gun belt and jack the slide.

Screaming their wild keen, the stingwings spiraled down from the sky toward the huddled companions. Instantly, J.B. and Mildred aimed skyward and cut loose with their weapons, the Uzi and S&W shotgun blasting a huge hole in the flock. But the rest of them kept coming, the inhuman faces distorted in a feral rictus of savage hunger.

Then the smell of fresh blood reached the stingwings, and the slavering muties flowed away from the huddle of people to attack the dead horses, plunging in their needle-sharp beaks and nosily slurping the warm blood, their wings beating so fast that the air hummed. Taking advantage of the brief distraction, the companions ruthlessly gunned down as many of the muties as they could, firing and reloading with frantic speed.

Nothing stopped a stingwing but death, so the huddled people made every bullet count, taking an extra half second to aim and placing their shots with desperate accuracy.

Unable to reach a horse through the feasting of its brethren, a young stingwing dived for the nearest companion. Firing from the hip, Ryan blew off a wing, and as the mutie tumbled, he swung out the panga. The long curved blade neatly severed the mutie's head, pale blood gushing out to sprinkle into the salty pool.

But at the death cry of the nestling, the rest of the muties turned their deadly attentions from the cooling mounds of flesh to the living, breathing companions. Screaming, the stingwings surged forward, eyes as bright as diamonds, mouths full of needle-sharp teeth.

In a ragged cacophony, the companions cut loose with every blaster, mowing down the first wave of the muties, the riddled bodies splashing into the pool, their lifeblood tainting the water a cloudy pink.

Triggering the second barrel of the massive LeMat, Doc annihilated four of the muties with a shotgun blast from the oddball weapon. The gun smoke was still pouring from the barrel when Doc started to move the selector pin to fire the main cylinder. He caught a blur of motion out of the corner of his sight. *Cowardly dastard!* Smacking the Civil War blaster across the head of the inhuman thing, Doc heard the breaking of bones, but unsatisfied, he slashed out with his sword, the razor-sharp steel removing the head of the creature like blowing the foam off a beer.

Blaster and knife moving in determined patterns, Jak wailed at the air, pale mutie blood sprinkling the teenager constantly. One stingwing landed on his collar to try for the albino youth's vulnerable neck, then the mutie shrieked as its legs came off, severed by the cluster of razor blades hidden along the collar.

Kneeling down to reload the shotgun, Mildred heard a flutter of wings from behind and shoved the buttstock backward as hard as she could. There came a satisfying crunch of bones, and she rose, firing the weapon just in time to annihilate another stingwing, its deadly claws just missing her face by the thickness of a prayer.

Triggering her blaster several times in rapid succession, Krysty heard a creature scream in rage, and jerked to the side just as a mutie dived straight for her back. Smacking the blaster across the back of the mutie, Mildred sent it spinning away, then blew it apart with a perfectly aimed discharge.

"Flare!" Ryan bellowed, dropping the spent clip from his blaster and shoving in a fresh one.

Still firing the Uzi, J.B. reached into his munitions bag and unearthed a waxy cylinder. Thumping the bottom of the military flare on a raised knee, he saw the top erupt into a hissing rush of magnesium flame. Instinctively, the stingwings moved away from the fire, and J.B. waved the flare about, the sizzling stiletto of chemical flame clearing a good yard of space above the pool. The companions reloaded fast, trying not to think about how little brass was left in their pockets.

Unexpectedly, the flare sputtered and died. Casting

it away with a curse, J.B. rummaged for a replacement.
A small stingwing streaked low across the still water,
coming in at groin level. Dropping the flare, J.B. swung
up the Uzi, knowing he was a nanosecond too slow,
when the scattergun roared. The muzzle-blast pounded
his eardrums and almost dislodged his glasses. But the
stingwing was blown into its component parts, blood
gobbets soaring everywhere.

"Thanks!" J.B. shouted, over the stuttering machine
gun.

"Anytime!" Mildred replied, unleashing hot lead
death.

Firing the SIG-Sauer nonstop until its clip was
empty, Ryan holstered the blaster while he swung up
the deadly panga. The wicked blade took the creatures
apart, removing wings, legs and heads with ruthless
efficiency. Pale blood splattered everywhere, and soon
the man's clothing was soaked. A gush of intestines
caught him full in the face, blocking his sight. Fireblast! Taking a deep breath, Ryan threw himself into
the shallow pool, the salty water stinging every cut and
abrasion on his body. Rising from the water, rivulets
streaming down his face, Ryan braced for a new attack,
but the stingwings now arched around the man as if he
were invisible.

"Get underwater!" Ryan yelled on impulse, sheathing the panga and quickly thumbing loose brass into
the empty clip for the SIG-Sauer in case the ploy faded.
"Do it now!"

Although they had no idea what he was planning,
the others trusted the man with their lives, and Krysty
went first, then Jak and Doc, closely followed by J.B.

and finally Mildred. Surrounded by a screaming cloud of the deadly muties, Ryan tried to watch for an attack from every side, but the creatures were no longer interested in him. In fact, several of the winged muties landed brazenly on the dead horses and noisily began to feed once more, ripping away chunks of the warm flesh to reach the juicy morsels deeper inside.

Rising from the bloody water, the other companions shook their faces clear and watched for the next rush. But the stingwings were paying them no attention, almost as if the companions weren't there.

"It's the blood," Krysty whispered in astonishment. "There's so much of their blood in the water they can no longer smell us!"

"Not smell, not find," Jak stated confidently, brushing back his sodden hair. "How long last?"

"Probably until the first time we sweat," Mildred muttered, as if the volume of her voice could reveal their presence to the feasting creatures. "Only primates have isotonic traces of ammonia in their sweat. They must zero in on that."

"Good," Ryan grunted, and ducked under the water once more and came up sopping wet. "Then chill them all!" he growled, and started firing, carefully putting a single round into the gore-streaked heads.

Using blades only to minimize the noise, the companions slashed a bloody path of destruction through the feasting muties, until every one was gone, and the salt water swirled thickly with their life fluids.

"Any more?" J.B. asked, adjusting his glasses to scan the dunes on the horizon. The lenses were dripping with pale blood, his shirt and pants drenched to the skin.

"That last," Jak stated with a somber note of pride, swishing his blades in the filthy pond to clean the steel.

"Thank Gaia," Krysty added, her soaked hair flexing limply under the accumulated weight of the blood and gore. "We haven't been this close to getting chilled since the Anthill!"

At the mention of the nightmarish military base, everybody grimaced, then continued with their crude ablutions.

"Okay, anybody hurt?" Mildred demanded, looking over the assemblage. Everybody had been slashed a dozen times by the talons of the deadly little muties, but they all appeared to be only surface cuts, nothing deep or dangerous, and there was no telltale flow of red human blood.

"Fine, just low on brass," Jak complained, emptying the spent brass cartridges from his blaster and thumbing five fresh rounds into the 6-shot cylinder. If the fight had gone on for only a few more minutes, they all would have ended up inside a stingwing, looking out.

"Alas, I have plenty of ammunition," Doc rumbled, looking forlornly at his Civil War–era blaster. Black powder was dribbling out the side of the massive cylinder from the constant dunking. "But I fear my LeMat will not be useful until thoroughly cleaned and dried."

"Can't leave you naked. Here, take this," Ryan said, passing over the SIG-Sauer and a handful of loose rounds.

Eagerly, Doc accepted the weapon and worked the

slide, keeping a suspicious watch on the dead muties. If life had taught the time traveler anything, it was to always be prepared for betrayal.

Going over to her horse, Krysty used her knife to flick aside a couple of tattered stingwings and inspected the chewed remains of the beast. Sweetcheeks had been a fine horse, not particularly intelligent, but bridle-wise, trail-smart and very strong. The woman silently said a prayer to Gaia to treat her friend well in the next casement of existence. Death was merely a part of the cycle of life, neither the beginning nor the end.

Ryan finished reloading a spare clip for the longblaster, slung the weapon and reached into a pocket to withdraw a squat black object about the size and shape of a soup can. With a snap, he extended the antique Navy telescope to its full length and swept the horizon in every direction.

"Nothing coming our way yet," Ryan told them, lowering the optical device and compacting it back down again. "But with this much blasterfire and fresh blood in the air, you can bet your nuking ass we'll soon have lots of company. Tanglers, stickies, hellhounds, you name it."

"Maybe even some of those big wendies we've heard about that have invaded the desert from the far north," Krysty added grimly.

"Wendigos," Mildred corrected. "They were just a myth in my time—Canadian folklore—but they're sure as hell real enough now. The bastard things patrol along the border of the desert to attack anybody coming out."

"Picking off the weak and tired," J.B. said, tilting back his dripping-wet fedora. "Pretty smart."

"Pretty deadly," Ryan stated.

"And, alas, we shall be walking thirsty from this point onward," Doc rumbled, scowling in displeasure at the sight of the ruined water bags draped over the saddle of his own deceased mare, Buttercup. Most, if not all, of their leather water bags had been savaged by the stingwings and torn to shreds, the precious contents soaked into the bastard mixture of sand and salt crystals. Their U.S. Army canteens were dented, but still intact. However, the adjective *great* hadn't been a misnomer in conjunction with the dreaded noun *salt*. The scorched desert was large and arid.

"How far away from clean water are we?" Mildred asked, squeezing the excess brine from her beaded plaits. Hanging at her side, the canvas med bag sloshed and felt as if it weighed a hundred pounds. All of her primitive medical supplies were safely sealed inside plastic bags, and the canvas satchel itself was waterproof. Which made it a perfect catch basin for the contents of the brackish pond.

"Tell you in a tick." Using the minisextant hanging around his neck, J.B. checked the position of the sun and did some fast mental calculations.

"Any chance we're near Two-Son ville?" Mildred asked hopefully, tilting the med bag to pour out volumes of excess water.

"No, that's a thousand miles to the south. Unfortunately, we're close to the eastern edge," J.B. said glumly, tucking the sextant away again under his shirt. "So we've got about a gazillion little salt ponds like this straight ahead of us for a good forty miles before reaching Clearwater Springs."

"Forty miles?" Jak frowned.

"As the stingwing flies," J.B. added, trying to smile at the weak joke, but could see that his words had fallen hard on the others. Forty miles through the searing, nuke-blasted heart of the desert on foot. That was tantamount to a death sentence.

Sloshing through the bobbing swamp of bodies, Ryan climbed onto the muddy shore and stomped his combat boots to dislodge some sticky entrails. "Okay, take only the essentials," he directed, tugging a water bag free from the pommel of his nameless stallion. "Water, food and brass. Leave everything else."

"Even the cyclo?" Jak asked with a scowl.

Strapped to the rear of three of the horses were bulky objects securely wrapped in heavy canvas. The companions had journeyed long and far to find an undamaged library and recover an encyclopedia. That had been Doc's idea to give the books to Front Royal in Virginia and help them with the rebuilding of civilization. Front Royal was one of the very few well-run baronies on the East Coast. The ville was still a long way from reclaiming predark technology. The encyclopedia could provide invaluable information.

"Indeed, it seems that we must, my young friend," Doc muttered, drying the sword on a sleeve before sliding it back into the ebony stick. "For while knowledge is indeed power, in this particular case it is only a millstone about our all-too-frail necks." The blade locked into place with a hard click.

High overhead, a lone vulture was starting to circle the killing field. The first of the scavengers to arrive.

"Might as well start walking," Krysty stated, pulling

a candle from her pocket and rubbing the wax with a finger before applying it to her lips. The old trick eased thirst and could help keep a person alive for a full extra day.

"I'll fill a spare canteen with dirty water in case any more stingwings come hunting for us," Mildred said, removing the cap and plunging the container into the reeking pool.

"A hellish perfume, indeed, madam," Doc said, sniffing in disdain. "But then, it is always advisable to use a long spoon when supping with the devil."

Washing as much gore as possible out of their hair and clothing, the companions then plunged some rags into the relatively clean mud along the banks, getting the cloths nicely damp before tying them over their heads as crude protection from the sun. Rummaging through the saddlebags, they took everything useful and left the rest of the supplies behind to start walking in a single file with Ryan in the lead.

Saving their strength, the companions didn't talk as they marched through the shifting sand, each lost in his or her own private thoughts. They were fighters, survivors, victors in a hundred battles, but the Great Salt took its toll. In many villes, the name of the desert was a euphemism for death.

Slowly, the long miles passed under the monotonous trudge of their heavy boots. The sun beat down on the companions without mercy, and the hot air stole every drop of moisture from their parched mouths. Using more wax on their lips, the companions licked the sweat from their arms to help stave off dehydration and wondered if this was the day that they would die....

Chapter Two

"I said, out!" McGinty roared, throwing the outlander through the Heaven's doorway.

Tumbling across the wooden porch, the man hit the brick street and his head cracked loudly on the stonework. With a low groan, the outlander went limp, and the giggling children descended upon the unconscious norm to rifle his pockets and carry away anything small of value. The knife and shotgun holstered at his side they avoided like a rad pit. Stealing a weapon was a hanging offence in the ville, even for children.

"Anybody else wanna try to buy a drink with brass filled with dirt instead of powder?" McGinty snarled, tapping a lead pipe into his palm. But the challenge from the barkeep went unanswered in the tavern, and everybody studiously turned their attentions to drinking or gambling.

After a moment, McGinty grunted in satisfaction and went back behind the counter to continue serving drinks and swapping lies with the regular patrons.

"Should have aced the bastard and taken his boots," Petrov Cordalane muttered, taking a sip of the shine in his cracked mug. Waste not, want not, his mother always used to say. A trader visiting Delta had suggested that his ancestors were probably Russkies. Born and raised in Deathlands, the man took that as an insult and slit the outlander's throat with a broken bottle. Then Petrov took his belt knife and zipgun. It had been his first chilling, and the weight of the blade made him see the common sense of acing folks only for a profit.

Nowadays, Petrov owned two knives and a working handblaster called a Webley .44, with fifteen live rounds. His mother would have been pleased to see how far her son had gone from such a simple beginning. What his father thought about the matter Petrov neither knew nor cared.

"Boots and gun belt. That's what I would have taken," Rose DeSilva said with a sneer, chewing on a hard piece of waxy cheese rind.

The slim woman had yellowish-blond hair, the bouncy curls almost childlike. Rose was covered with scars and missing the pinkie on her left hand from tangling with a stickie in her teen years. The woman had aced the mutie with a rock, but it took her finger first. Afterward, Rose had left the stickie alive while she tied it to a tree, and built a huge stack of dry branches around the creature. The fire had lasted long into the night, and she still remembered the agonized hooting with great pleasure. The big crossbow hanging from the back of her chair had been carved from that same tree, her first crude arrows glued together with the sticky resin harvested from the aced mutie.

Drinking shine, Thal Dagstrom merely grunted in agreement. Whenever possible, the huge man preferred not to speak. A hulking giant, Thal was a good foot taller than anybody else in the tavern and heavily muscled to the point that some folks thought there had to be a little mutie blood in his veins. But nobody was stupe enough to ever ask. His entire body was bear-like, covered with thick black hair. Only his head was naturally bald. His hair had started thinning when Thal was a teenager. These days, he wore a black wool cap, no matter the temperature outside. A tiny Remington .22 automatic blaster was tucked into his rope belt, the worn silvery finish carefully blackened with a pumice stone. The clip held only four live rounds, two of them homemade varieties of unknown quality, but at his side hung a stout wood club, the tip bristling with rusty nails. In close quarters, it was a formidable chilling machine.

"Soft, the locals are soft," Charlie Bernstein added, using a piece of bread to mop up the last vestiges of gravy from his bowl of gopher stew.

His appetite was legendary, and the angular face of the gaunt man showed the starvation of his childhood, but his arms were thickly cabled with muscle. His clothing seemed to be composed more of patches than original material, but the overall effect was a sort of camo pattern that allowed him to disappear in a forest. Even his boots were pieced together from an assortment of other shoes and such, mostly to hide the short nails sticking out of the toes. More than once, Charlie had kicked a man to death while hooting and laughing. For some reason, he enjoyed pain, giving and receiving, and sometimes, in the deep of the night, Charlie wondered if he was insane.

The big bore blaster holstered at his side was home-made, just a hunk of steel bathroom pipe reinforced with coils of iron wire. The wire was applied red-hot, and when it cooled, the coils tightened, reinforcing the old pipe enough for it to take the blast of a 12-gauge cartridge. The wooden stock was carved from an apple tree and bore the crude design of a naked woman, the notches along the top showing the number of chills he had done. The actual number was only half as many, but it still represented a lot of folks on board the last train west.

"Delta is an odd town, that's for sure," Petrov countered, taking out a worn deck of playing cards and beginning to shuffle. "But that's why I like the place. Strange suits me fine."

The rest of the crew could find no fault with that. Delta ville sat alongside the Whitewater River that flowed out of the Great Salt like a slashed artery of blue life. The muddy banks were lined with reeds, bamboo, flowering bushes and even a couple of stunted trees bearing tiny bitter-tasting apples. But the farther the river got from the desert, the more the greenery expanded until only a day's ride away the plants spread across the landscape in a true forest of real trees, bushes and green grass. The ville did all of its hunting and farming out there, both groups accompanied by heavily armed squads of sec men as much-needed protection against the muties that lived in the trees and, sometimes, under the ground.

However, never in the history of the ville had a single mutie gotten past the front gate. The defensive wall around Delta was huge, made of rocks hauled out of the river by decades of slave labor, the mortar between the layers said to be liberally mixed with blood, sweat and tears. It was probably true, but old Baron Cranston had died a long time ago, and his wife, who'd succeeded him, hadn't tolerated such brutality. Nor did her son. If you were caught stealing food, a person got twenty-five lashes at the post, every time, no favors or leniency. Rape a woman or a child and that got you beaten by the women in the ville with clubs, whipped by the men and then sent to the gallows—if you were still sucking air. The only crime that got a person sent to the wall was disobeying the orders of the baron. That put you in chains to work and labor on the ville wall, expanding the barrier, making it higher and thicker until a full moon had passed, then you were set free and tossed outside the ville gates. Alone and weaponless, the person would be easy prey for slavers or muties, but at least still alive.

Most of the old folks considered the baron too damn soft on coldhearts, especially those operating a salve trade out in the Boneyard, but they never said it out loud. Only Petrov Cordalane knew the truth of the matter, and since he lived in Delta, the man said nothing about it to anybody, not even his gang. Secrets held power.

Besides, Petrov had a good thing going here in Delta, and he wouldn't ruin it. Heaven was the main tavern in the ville, boasting food, drinks, an actual working piano for Sunday, a gaudy house upstairs and a still out back. The local brew was made out of rotting fish guts, an acquired taste, to say the least, and it was also burned in lanterns to make light and to degrease machine parts. But the locals sang its praise, claiming that the river juice would cure all manner of ills, from the black cough to the shakes, along with a dozen other ailments that had once ravaged the world since skydark.

Petrov liked the food in the tavern, so he didn't do biz in the ville. This was his haven, a safe place to run if trouble came snapping at the heels of his crew, the Pig Iron Gang.

It was cool inside Heaven—the walls were made of stone. The rafters in the ceiling were black with age and the smell of the accumulated fumes of the fish-oil lanterns was reminiscent of a smokehouse.

Over by the window, a young woman was sitting at a battered piano playing remarkably well, a large group of outlanders and travelers listening with rapt attention. Some of them had never heard of such a thing as a piano before. Dozens of other folks were eating fish stew, gambling or drinking shine. A few of the ville oldsters were caging smokes from travelers in exchange for fantastic stories about the muties in the woods, or even better, the hot sluts upstairs. Those were always popular, and the more details, the better.

Positioned near the wooden stairs leading to the second floor, five gaudy sluts were eating bread and smoking cigs. Their assorted dresses were some velvety material cut and stitched together from the safety curtains of a ruined movie theater; the material couldn't be set on fire. Amazing stuff. The low-cut blouses and short skirts displayed an amazing amount of flesh, and on a regular basis, a man would shuffle over to talk some biz. Then the man and woman would go upstairs for fifteen minutes or so and come back down. Smiling wide, the man would be buckling his belt.

One large gaudy slut named Post seemed to be a particular favorite this night and was constantly chosen by customers to go upstairs.

"How does she know what they want?" Rose asked in idle curiosity. "Isn't she deaf?"

"Bitch can read lips," Petrov answered, then added, "She also has the best tits I ever seen."

Across the tavern, Post smiled at the compliment, then pulled down her blouse for a moment to flash the man a peek at both of her highly prized assets.

"Pretty nuking good," Charlie agreed, gnawing on a heel of stale bread. But nobody was sure if he meant the slut or the food.

Most of the bottles along the wall behind the counter were made of plastic and filled with water. After one too many bar fights, McGinty had decided not to risk his stock by putting it on display. The real shine was kept safe under the counter, right alongside a working predark scattergun, a pump-action monster called a Neostead that held eight fat cartridges. All of them were homemade these days, the black powder purchased from a traveling trader, and then the base was packed with bits of broken glass, small rocks and bent nails. The combination opened the belly of a person like stomping on a fish.

"Another round!" Petrov bellowed, waving his empty plastic tumbler.

An old woman wearing an apron shuffled out from behind the bar, carrying a clay jug with a cork in the top. The waitress was an oldster, barely able to walk anymore because of the misery called the bends, her back hunching over to make her almost appear to be a mutie. But she was a gene-pure norm and once had sold a night in her bed for a round of live brass. Now, the former beauty ferried dirty dishes and slept in the corner near the fireplace, kept warm by the glowing embers and her lost dreams of youth.

"I hear tell you're called the Pig Iron Gang," the waitress said, pouring drinks into the glasses and mugs. "How come?"

"Shut up," Petrov snarled, not willing to admit that he had no idea what pig iron was, he just liked the sound.

With a shrug, the waitress turned and went away, looking for more empty glasses to fill, her long day only just starting.

"Enjoy the shine, this is the last round," Petrov said, sipping the acidic brew. "And we'll be sleeping outside the wall tonight, so try and steal some blankets."

"We broke already?" Rose said out of the corner of her mouth, dealing a new hand of cards.

"Shitfire, that seems to happen faster every month," Charlie mumbled, watching the deal as he picked his teeth with a sliver of wood. He found something interesting and chewed the unidentified morsel briefly before swallowing.

"You eat too much," Thal rumbled in a surprisingly gentle voice. Then the giant scowled and clawed for his Remington.

"Fragging, mutie-loving bastards!" the outlander snarled, staggering back through the doorway. There was blood dripping from the back of his head, chilling in his blurry eyes and a scattergun held in his shaking hands. "Gonna ace ya all!"

Instantly, Petrov and his people cut loose with their assorted weapons, the barrage of arrows and lead blowing the outlander off the floor and sending him sailing back into the street.

"Nuking hell, you boys are fast!" a sec man gasped, his own blaster only halfway out of his holster.

"The way that idjit was waving his blaster around it was him or us," Petrov said, the smoking Webley still tight in his fist.

"Well, you boys got yourself a free round on me," the sec man stated, slapping the other man on the back. "And feel free to take anything that outlander owns."

"That include his blaster?" Rose asked, nocking a fresh arrow into her crossbow.

"Yep, the scattergun is yours now."

"What about his horse?"

"That too, if he had one." The sec man nodded. "Now I know that seems kinda hard, so I'll tell you what. Baron Cranston gets half of any brass recovered from a fight, that's the law." Then the man paused. "But I won't be counting it very closely. Savvy?"

"Yeah, we savvy," Charlie replied, already cutting a fresh notch into the stock of his own blaster.

Gathering the loose cards, Rose stuffed them into a shirt pocket. Only a feeb left their belongings unguarded in Heaven. Rising from the table, Petrov walked outside and found a crowd gathered around the body, but nobody was closer than a few yards. The accuracy and speed of his gang were well-known in the ville and much respected.

Rifling through the warm, bloody clothing, Petrov unearthed a dozen rounds for the scattergun and passed three of them to the waiting sec man, then one more. Pocketing that extra round, the sec man gave the gang a brief salute and walked off toward the brick house on top of the hill in the center of the ville, a former

National Guard armory that was now the castle of the baron and what remained of the Cranston family.

Divvying up the rest of the belongings with his crew, Petrov gave the gun belt and scattergun to Rose. She beamed in delight over finally owning a blaster and tested the action on the weapon several times before loading in two live cartridges. The weight perfectly balanced her crossbow and made the diminutive woman feel more dangerous than a shithouse rat.

"Short barrels mean a big spray," Thal stated. "And watch for the kick. That scattergun is gonna rise up hard. A lot more than your crossbow."

"Just cause there wasn't any iron on my hip doesn't mean I'm a fragging virgin," Rose answered curtly, tucking her thumbs into the gun belt. Then she smiled up at the giant. "But thanks for the advice anyway, Bear."

Unsuccessfully, the colossus tried to hide a grin at the use of his private name. They had been bed partners for years, and it amused the other two men to pretend that they didn't know about the raucous nightly coupling.

"Pity the outlander didn't have a horse," Petrov said, turning away from the body to head back into the tavern. "We could have sold it for a week of hot food and clean beds here at Heaven, or just slaughtered the beast and lived off the jerky for a good month."

"Fragging son of a bitch cost us a fortune in brass," Charlie muttered angrily. "The shine and blaster help, but we're still coming in low on this."

"Mebbe we could go check the traps," Rose suggested, pausing at the open doorway. At her appearance, a cheer came from the patrons and staff.

"This soon?" Petrov said with a scowl, scratching the back of his head. "Only been a week or so."

"Mebbe we'll get lucky," Thal rumbled, patting the new cartridges for his blaster. "It feels like a lucky day."

"More lucky for some than others." Rose laughed.

Hitching up his gun belt, Charlie frowned. "Think Big Joe will mind us…?" He left the sentence hanging.

"What he doesn't know won't kill him," Petrov said, smirking, and he walked into the cool darkness.

TRODDING UNDER the merciless sun, time seemed to stand still for the companions, the hot day lasting impossibly long. Or so it seemed, anyway. A dozen times over the past few miles, they passed more of the shallow saltwater ponds, the sight of the water a growing ache in their throats and bellies.

Pausing to take a tiny sip of warm water, Ryan sloshed it around in his mouth before swallowing. The urge to take a big gulp was strong, but he knew the foolishness of that. Drink too fast when you're that hot, and it could come right back up. And that was moisture he couldn't afford to waste.

"What's that sound?" Krysty asked, glancing around, a hand going to her blaster.

Immediately alert, the rest of the companions drew weapons and scanned the vicinity. But there was nothing in sight except the endless shifting dunes and the sparkling vista of dried salt.

"What did you hear?" Ryan asked, then paused as he caught a faint whisper over the desert wind. It was gone in a heartbeat, but just for a split second, it sure as nuking hell had sounded just like a—

"Waterfall!" J.B. shouted, pointing a trembling hand straight ahead.

Hesitantly taking a step forward, Ryan scowled at the vague sight of something blue in the distance. It seemed to be coming right out of the side of a rocky escarpment that rose from the baked sand like an island in the sea. There was even some ragged green tufts of grass on top, a tiny touch of life almost lost amid the rolling sand dunes and windswept salt.

"Is…it…a mirage?" Doc asked, his normally booming voice reduced to a hoarse whisper.

"No, I smell water. Clean water!" Jak croaked, rushing forward, only to stop after a few yards.

"Good place for ambush," the albino teenager added, drawing the Colt and thumbing back the hammer. The metal was so hot under the sun, he thought it would burn his finger, but he pushed aside that minor consideration. Better pain today, than death forever.

"Standard formation, on me," Ryan muttered, swinging down the Steyr and working the bolt. "And watch your bastard flanks!"

Moving in a tight combat formation, Ryan and the others advanced upon the waterfall. Gushing from the side of a small hill, the clear water pooled around the turbulent base to flow off toward the east, directly away from the sizzling desert. The delicious smell of fresh water filled the air like a healing balm, easing their itchy eyes and the pain in their throats.

Doing a complete circle of the escarpment, Ryan and the companions looked hard for any signs of tracks or spoor, but the ground was smooth and undisturbed, pristine and perfect.

"Okay, we're alone," Ryan said, holstering his blaster. "I'll take the first watch, and—"

Whooping in delight, Jak rushed forward to dive bodily into the water. He came up a few seconds later sputtering and grinning. "Cold!" he shouted, waving an arm. "No salt!"

"I should think so," Mildred muttered, going to the edge of the small lake. Sitting, she eased off her boots and dangled her bare feet in cool water, washing away the sweat, and then proceeded to wash the salt and sweat from her boots.

Wading into the water, Doc cupped his hands to daintily wash his face and neck. Then on impulse, the man ducked below the surface and came up laughing. "Never before have I extracted so much joy from simply not being thirsty!" he boomed, his words echoing slightly along the outcropping.

Krysty walked into the shallows, then dived under the water. She stayed submerged for a long time, then rose again like a modern-day Venus. Her soaked clothing clung enticingly to her figure, and her hair spread out in a wild corona as the living filaments tried to dry themselves.

"Thank Gaia, I needed that!" She laughed, opening the canteen at her side. Filling the container, she tossed it to Ryan. He made the catch with one hand, the other filled with the Steyr. The man used his teeth to twist off the cap again, then liberally poured the water over his head and face before taking a small sip, then a much larger swallow.

"Thanks!" He exhaled. "I needed that bad."

"Anytime, lover!" Krysty called back, starting to remove her clothing.

"Madam, please!" Doc gasped, turning away quickly.

"You can wait until we're done," J.B. said, easing off his munitions bag. "But we're going to be swimming here for quite a while."

"But…b-but…"

"Go ahead, Doc, I got your six," Ryan said, sitting on a flat-top rock and taking another long swig.

"I see." Pursing his lips, Doc acquiesced to the logic of the matter and stripped to his underwear, which was as far as decorum would allow the man to go with ladies present.

"Crazy old coot. We've all seen each other without clothes before." But in deference to Doc's modesty, everyone left on their undergarments.

"Indeed, madam, but not in quite such intimate proximity!" Doc countered.

In short order, the companions were swimming around the pool. J.B. still wore his glasses and fedora.

"You're going to wash that, too, I hope?" Mildred asked, sidling closer to the wiry man.

Smiling wide, J.B. started to answer when a strange expression swept across his face, and he started to hack and cough.

Stumbling to the shoreline, J.B. almost didn't make it out of the lake when Ryan grabbed him under the arms and hauled the unconscious man onto the dry ground. Only steps behind, Mildred scrambled out of the water and rushed to his side. Looking inside his mouth for any obstructions, the physician quickly checked his pulse and removed his glasses to look into his eyes. No, it couldn't be! she thought.

"Son of a bitch!" Mildred gasped in horror. "Everybody, get the fuck out of the water!"

Startled by her tone, the rest of the companions needed no further prompting to slosh out of the lake as fast as they could.

"What's wrong with him?" Ryan demanded, every instinct honed in a thousand battles suddenly alert.

But Mildred didn't answer. Instead, she turned away from everybody and rammed two stiff fingers down her throat, trying to induce vomiting. It took Ryan an instant to understand, then he threw away the canteen with a curse. Poisoned. The whole bastard lake was poisoned!

While the rest of the companions frantically tried to do the same thing, they noticed the waterfall was starting to sound muted, as if in the distance, and soon their movements took on a vague dreamlike quality.

With his own vision failing, Ryan tried to help, but having drunk so much water, the effect seemed to be hitting him the hardest. The world was already going dark, his strength dwindling fast. Dropping the Steyr, the man clumsily drew the panga and cut his arm, hoping the pain would help him stay awake. But Ryan barely felt the passage of the steel through his skin and knew that it was already too late. Enraged over the failure to recognize the trap, Ryan felt an adrenaline surge course through his body. But the brief respite vanished almost as quickly as it had come, and, still fighting to remain conscious, Ryan slumped to the ground and went still. The rest of the companions followed suit only a few seconds later.

Soon, there was no movement at the crystal lake, aside from the steady rush of the waterfall and the bright sunlight reflecting off the gentle waves.

Chapter Three

Lost in a dreamy world of muzzy thoughts and sensations for an unknown length of time, Ryan awoke sluggishly, feeling as if he was going to be sick. His stomach ached fiercely, and the world was rocking back and forth. Dimly, the man wondered if he was inside a redoubt suffering through a bout of jump sickness, which always hit the companions after using the mattrans unit.

The redoubts were the greatest secret of the predark world, and even more so now. Built before skydark, they were military underground bunkers, constructed to withstand a direct hit by a thermonuclear weapon. The secret bases were safe havens of clean water and sterilized air, equipped with hot showers, washing machines, storerooms full of food, medicine, vehicles and weapons of every type imaginable. At least, they were originally. Sometime after the atomic holocaust, all of the military personnel assigned to the redoubts left, taking most of the supplies with them. Nowadays, the companions considered themselves lucky to find a single dented can of stew forgotten in the kitchen, or to scavenge a handful of live bullets that had rolled under a shelf. But sometimes they hit the jackpot.

Much more important were the mat-trans units. These fantastic machines were able to transmit the companions from one redoubt to another in a few seconds. Unfortunately, the knowledge of how to control a jump had been lost over time, so every journey through the machines was now blind chance. Even then, the redoubts and the mat-trans unit gave the companions a chilling superiority to everybody else in the world—mobility.

It was a fact that Ryan was starting to appreciate more as he slowly began to notice the splintery wood under his cheek. The floor of a mat-trans was smoother than silk. So, where the frag am I? he wondered.

Suddenly, the events at the waterfall came rushing back, and Ryan sat up, clawing for the blaster at his hip. But the weapon was gone, along with everything else he owned, including his outer clothing. Even his eye patch was missing.

Trying to focus his good eye against the constant bouncing, Ryan glanced around to see that he was inside some sort of a wooden cage. The floor was covered with dirty hay, the bars were thicker than his wrist and the door was set into the ceiling a good ten feet high. The man had to grunt at that. Smart. It would be triple-hard for any prisoner to escape when they couldn't even reach the bastard door.

Outside the cage, a rolling grassland stretched to the horizon. A few trees were scattered around, along with the occasional stand of cacti and bushes, but the grass itself was a deep emerald-green. There was no smell of salt in the air. Wherever this was, they were a long way from the desert. Just how long have I been out, Ryan wondered, rubbing the stubble on his chin.

Scattered around the squalid cage were the rest of the companions, clad only in their undergarments and clutching their heads as if in pain. The bouncing came from the fact that the cage was in the back of a large buckboard wag. Ryan could dimly see the two drivers sitting in the front seat, one of them holding a crossbow, and the other man working a set of reins. As he gave them a shake, several horses whinnied and the bouncing got worse.

Slavers. Ryan cursed quietly. The sons of bitches had to have dosed the water and then simply sat back to wait for parched fools to come racing out of the Great Salt and straight into their waiting chains. The man felt like a feeb, but pushed those thoughts aside to concentrate on how to escape.

There came a rustle from the largest pile of hay.

"You okay, lover?" Krysty whispered from inside the pile of loose material. Both shapely legs stuck out from the green hay, her full breasts just barely concealed. Her face was calm, but her hair flexed wildly, showing that she was furious.

"More importantly, are you?" Ryan countered, studying her for any sign that she'd been raped while they'd been unconscious.

"Nobody rode me," Krysty answered softly, casting a glance at the fat men in the front of the wag. "Nor Mildred, either. But I don't think we're likely to stay that way for long."

"Not likely," Ryan agreed grimly, rubbing his unshaved jaw. There were two other wags in the convoy, the cages in the back jammed full of scrawny people. However, Krysty and Mildred were the only adult females with some flesh on their bones, and all of the slavers were men, not a single woman among their ranks. Yeah, come nightfall, things would get ugly.

"I am glad to see you back, my dear Ryan," Doc rumbled, wiping his mouth on the back of a hand. "I had feared that your consumption of the tainted water may have taken you across the River Styx."

"Not aced yet," Ryan stated, flexing his hands, feeling the strength slowly return.

"Got a plan yet, buddy?" J.B. asked, reaching up to adjust his glasses. With a start, the man frowned when his fingers only touched bare skin. Dark night! the Armorer thought. Without those I'm nearsighted to the point of being blind! About as useful as a dick on a cactus.

"Working on it," Ryan murmured, studying the cage and wag.

"Work faster," Jak whispered, picking up an old piece of string and using it to tie back his long hair. Although only a teenager, the albino youth was covered with a wide assortment of scars forming a rippled pattern caused by being caught in acid rain, knife cuts, laser burns and the circles showing a healed bullet wound.

Deep in thought, Ryan merely grunted in reply. If this had been an iron cage that would have been another matter. But these wooden cages were generally the providence of slavers. Cannibals used iron cages because they didn't really care if the prisoners banged their heads against the bars and took their own lives. They were going into the cooking pot either way, and beating themselves up only made the meat more tender. However, slavers used wood, sometimes with canvas padding wrapped around the bars, because they needed the merchandise alive and relatively undamaged.

Carefully, Ryan studied the other two wags, noting their positions in the caravan, then he turned his full attention to the two men in the front of their wag. Both were fat, but with broad shoulders and wide hands, suggesting that some of their girth came from being large men. The driver had a mustache, the gunner was bald, and each was armed with a machete, a club and a bullwhip—but not any of the blasters taken from the companions. Fireblast! He had been counting on the slavers carrying the weapons on them.

Unfortunately, aside from the green hay, bits of string and some old yellow straw, there was nothing else in the cage but the companions. Slowly, a plan began to unfold in his mind, and Ryan briefly told the others. They nodded and moved to the appropriate positions. They would only get one chance, and failure meant worse than death.

Briefly, there was a tickling sound along with the smell of fresh urine.

Abruptly rising from the hay, Krysty and Mildred loudly yawned and scratched themselves, the women spreading their arms to display their figures to the fullest advantage.

"Well, well, looks like we got a couple of gaudy sluts this time." The gunner leered, glancing over a shoulder. "Keep it up, sluts! I likes me a good show!"

"Then how about some dinner theater?" Mildred snarled, throwing forward a gob of newly moistened dung. The drek hit the wooden bars and splattered across both of the slavers.

"Stupe move, bitch," the driver snarled, the back of his shirt speckled with the material.

"Yeah, tonight we're gonna make you eat that." The gunner smiled, rubbing his crotch. "Along with some other stuff, too!"

"Without first having dessert?" Krysty asked, and flung a second wad. The dripping drek sailed through the bars to smack directly into the gunner's face, catching him in the middle of a chuckle.

Hacking and choking, the fat man bent over the side of the wag to loudly wretch, while the driver howled with laughter.

"She got you good, Billy!" The man guffawed, slapping a knee.

"Shut up, Henry," the gunner panted, using a sleeve to wipe the bile and drek from his face. Pursing his lips, the man spit filth from his mouth, then stood to uncoil the bullwhip at his side. "Fuck the bounty! I'm gonna skin that bitch alive!"

"How very odd," Doc said in a cultured tone of voice, sitting upright amid the hay. "Because that was exactly what I said to your mother before I raped her."

"Wh-what did he say?" Henry gasped in genuine shock, almost dropping the reins.

"My, my, you should have heard how she squealed like a little piggy." Doc grinned amiably. "It was most amusing. I bet that you can squeal like a piggy, too, if you try. Come on, squeal, my fat little piggy. Squeal for Daddy!"

Sputtering obscenities, Billy turned a bright red in the face and lashed out with his bullwhip.

Expertly, the knotted length shot between the bars to score a bloody furrow across the old man's chest.

Gushing crimson, Doc was thrown backward from the brutal strike, but Jak and Ryan dived on the whip and pulled with all of their strength. Caught off balance, Billy was hauled forward to smack his face hard against the wooden cage. Rising from the hay, J.B. thrust his hands through the bars to grab the slaver by the ears and bang the man's head repeatedly against the cage until blood poured from his slack mouth and his eyes rolled back into death.

"Son of a bitch!" Henry yelled, and clawed for a wooden whistle tucked into his belt. But before the slaver could sound the alarm, another gob of dung hit the whistle, and it tumbled out of sight.

"Mutie fuckers!" Henry snarled, reaching for his machete.

Moving fast, Ryan lashed out with his stolen whip, slicing open the slaver's forehead. Blinded by the flow of blood from the minor wound, the driver flailed about with the machete, hitting nothing. Ryan rushed to the front of the cage and shoved his arm through to lash the whip out sideways. The knotted length coiled around the slaver's throat, and Ryan yanked back with all of his strength. There was an audible snap of bone as Henry flew out of the seat to crash into the bars. Gurgling horribly, the man could only feebly twitch as Krysty held him hard by the hair, and Mildred grabbed the machete to chop down twice and end his misery.

Freeing the whip, Ryan tried to get the reins and failed, the leather straps having fallen over the side of the wag in the tussle. Knowing that time was short, the companions dragged both of the corpses closer and looted them of anything that could be used as a weapon: both machetes, the other whip, a massive flint-lock blaster with a barrel large enough to serve as a gren launcher, a canvas pouch filled with black powder, shot and cloth wadding. Plus a big iron key.

Using the long handle of a whip to snatch the reins, J.B. shook them gently and whispered soft words to the team of horses, making them maintain an even speed. If this wag fell behind, or the companions tried to make a break, they would be spotted instantly, and the other slavers would slaughter them with those longblasters. Meanwhile, hauling the dead men up against the cage, Krysty and Jak held them in place to make it look as if they were still alive. The trick wouldn't fool anybody paying close attention, but all they needed was a few minutes. Speed was their best chance at survival now. Speed, and some triple-savage chilling.

Still bleeding, Doc passed the flintlock and ammo pouch to Mildred, and she started to quickly reload. The physician longed to help the wounded man, but this wasn't the time or the place.

Going to the middle of the cage, Ryan went down on his hands and knees. As the strongest person there, he would be the foundation. Climbing barefoot on top of him, Doc reached up high and just barely managed to ease a hand around the bars to start fiddling with the key in the lock.

"John Barrymore, it will not fit!" Doc whispered, his legs trembling from the effort of standing. His face was pale and sweaty, the blood still flowing freely from the deep laceration across his torso.

"Probably just rusty!" J.B. whispered back tersely, furious over not being able to do the job himself. "Lube it up!"

"With what?"

"Piss, blood, spit—anything ya got!"

Having no other source of lubrication, Doc spit on the key and tried again, with an equal lack of success. Suddenly, raised voices came from the other wags, and a shot rang out, the wood near his fumbling hand sprouting jagged splinters. Jerking back in surprise, Doc cursed as the key went flying to clatter off the bars and land in the hay below.

"Here they come!" Krysty shouted, releasing the corpse.

"Yee-haw!" J.B. bellowed, shaking the reins hard, and the horses obediently took off to a full gallop. But even pressing himself against the bars, the man could just barely make out the grassland before the animals and had to rely upon the innate good sense of the horses.

Letting go of his own corpse, Jak dived for the key just as the racing buckboard jounced through a dried gully, and the key jumped into the pile of hay.

"Krysty, Mildred, cover fire!" Ryan shouted, rocking to the wild motions of the rattling transport.

Going to the side of the cage, Krysty grabbed a bar tight and leaned far to the left. Resting the long barrel of the flintlock handblaster on the stable platform of the other woman's arm, Mildred clicked back the hammer, gauging for wind and droppage.

Clawing the green hay aside, Jak revealed the old straw and the key sticking out of a small pile of drek.

Without hesitation, the albino teen grabbed the key and spit on it twice before wiping it clean and passing it up to Doc.

Holding her breath, Mildred braced for the recoil and gently squeezed the trigger. The hammer moved downward, scraping the flint along a worn piece of steel throwing off bright sparks that ignited the loose powder in the flashpan. There was a brief hiss, then the primitive blaster roared so loud that Mildred thought it had exploded in her hands. Then the physician saw with cold satisfaction the driver of the second wag fly off the buckboard to be trampled under the pounding hooves of the horses pulling the third wag.

"Hell of a shot," Krysty grunted, shaking her hair to ease the sting from the fiery discharge of the weapon.

"I was going for the horses," Mildred growled, already starting the laborious process of reloading the big bore blaster.

Shots rang out from the third wag, several of them smacking into the wooden bars of the cage with remarkable accuracy. Krysty grunted at that. Clearly, somebody over there really knew how to shoot. With no choice, the redheaded woman stepped in front of the frantically busy physician to offer what protection her body could.

Steering around what sort of looked like a pile of boulders, J.B. grimaced to see it had actually just been a stand of cacti. Dark night, he thought, I'm going to get everybody aced unless I get this nuking thing under control!

A flurry of gunshots rang out from the second wag, and Krysty flinched as a miniball scored a hot line across her thigh. Jak was thrown backward into the loose pile of hay, his arm gushing blood.

Trying the key once more, Doc was delighted when the spit proved sufficient lubrication and the lock clicked open easily. But the hatch was incredibly heavy, and try as he might, Doc couldn't get it to budge an inch.

Shaking the reins for more speed, J.B. could see a couple of longblasters tucked into a gun boot along the side of the buckboard. But trapped inside the cage, those were completely unreachable at the moment, so he simply concentrated on trying to control the horses. Dodging the cacti was easy, as the horses knew better than to run through it. But there was a forest coming up fast, and J.B. would soon have to turn left or right. That would slow the wag, making them an excellent target for the furious slavers. It all depended on whether the slavers wanted to try to recapture them alive or wanted to chill the companions to recover the stolen wag. Either option wasn't very good. Nearly naked and trapped in a cage was not the way to survive a fight. Especially if you only had a single working blaster.

Rising again, Mildred placed the flintlock on Krysty's strong arm, the other woman's animated hair coiling away from the expected pain of the muzzle-blast. Aiming through the roiling dust clouds, Mildred lost sight of her target for a moment, but as the horses charged back into view she instantly fired. The lead horse of the third wag screamed as the soft lead plowed into its neck, crimson squirting out in a high arch. The other horses in the team reared in fear at the terrible smell, almost tearing loose from the wooden yoke beween them. The buckboard wag shook hard from their reaction, and the gunner went off the side to land in the stand of cacti, his high-pitched wails of agony cutting through the rattling wags, clattering wheels, pounding hooves and blasterfire.

Suspiciously fingering the jamb of the hatch, Doc gave a humorless smile when he found a second bolt. Clever bastards! Tearing it aside, Doc then easily swung the hatch open and it hit the bars with a hard crash. Now holding on for dear life, Doc braced himself against the pain in his chest as Ryan moved out from under his feet and started climbing the old man like a ladder.

Finished reloading, Mildred began to aim when the wag jounced through a weedy gully and the entire supply of black powder and wadding went flying away, briefly forming a dark cloud in the air before vanishing behind the escaping prisoner.

"Last shot," Mildred said in forced calm, commanding herself to be cool in spite of the situation. It was like performing emergency surgery on a friend.

Reaching the top of the cage, Ryan helped Doc over the jamb, and together they started to crawl along the cage.

"Easy does it," Krysty said in a soothing voice. "There's no rush. We have loads of time."

Thankful for the calming lie, Mildred still had trouble aiming against the constant jerks of the wags, then a white hand grabbed the bottom of the flintlock in an iron grip.

"Nuke 'em," Jak muttered, panting heavily.

With a grimace, Mildred wordlessly stroked the

trigger, and the driver of the second wag threw back his head with most of his throat gone. Clutching his neck with both hands, the reins dropped and the gunner tried to make a save, when a slave poked a skinny leg through the wooden bars and kicked the man hard in the ass. Pitching forward, he landed on the yoke, struggling to hold on, but his fingers slipped and he went under the hooves of the horses and then the wheels of the wag. What was left behind in the dust could only barely be recognized as human anymore.

"Power to the people!" Mildred shouted, raising a clenched fist. Incredibly, the other slaves repeated the cry, now pelting the remaining slavers with wads of dung.

Reaching the front of the cage, Ryan and Doc dropped into the buckboard seat.

"Blasters to the right!" J.B. shouted, giving the reins to Doc.

There were two longblasters in the boot, crude flintlocks over a yard long and more suitable as clubs than firearms. Snatching up the first, Ryan was pleased to find it loaded and ready to use. Useless for dealing with prisoners in their own cage—the things were just too long—the long-range weapon was just what Ryan needed at the moment.

Speaking soft words to the horses, Doc began easing the wag to a gentle stop. Obviously realizing where this was heading, the two remaining slavers began to arch away from each other and head in different directions.

"If get away, back soon with friends!" Jak shouted, a pale hand tight over his wound.

"Not gonna happen!" Ryan bellowed, clicking back

the colossal hammer. Standing, the man rested the flintlock rifle on top of the cage and pressed his body against the wooden bars for additional support. Then several pairs of arms wrapped around his legs and torso.

"Got your back, lover!" Krysty shouted.

Ryan took careful aim at one of the remaining slavers and fired. The blaster almost tore itself loose from his grip. With a strangled cry, the first slaver doubled over, clutching the red ruin of his flopping belly.

Switching longblasters, Ryan aimed once more, and the other slaver stupidly tried to put the cage full of slaves between himself and Ryan for protection. But the man angled the horses too sharply, and one of the animals tripped, then another. Suddenly, the entire team was entangled in the reins and yoke, flailing helplessly, their combined weight pulling the wag sideways. As the buckboard started to dangerously tilt, the driver tried to jump clear, when the dirty hands of a dozen slaves grabbed his clothing and held their former master firmly in place.

Pulling a knife, he wildly slashed at them when the wag passed the point of no return and thunderously slammed into the ground. Dirt and leaves exploded from the shattering wreckage as horses screamed and people shrieked in unimaginable agony.

Chapter Four

Walking through the predark ruins, the Pig Iron Gang kept in a tight group, their new blasters held up and ready.

The remains of the ville were mostly crumbling brick and cracked pavement, thickly covered with a lush blanket of foliage from the nearby jungle. Here and there, oak trees and birch were starting to appear among the banyan trees, the branches reaching out to mingle overhead, forming a sort of canopy over the ancient highway. Slowly, the jungle gave way to a proper forest, the creepers becoming ivy, and the Spanish moss replaced with mulberry bushes and laurel.

"I remember when this was a swamp," Charlie said, adjusting his new glasses. The hammerless S&W Model 640 was tucked into the pocket of his bearskin coat, the Czech ZKR held tight in a fist. The man was delighted over the find of the wire-rimmed glasses. He had just assumed that everybody saw the world in a kind of foggy blur, but with these he could see things hundreds of feet away as if they were at arm's reach. It was nuking amazing!

"Yeah? Well, my daddy said he was alive when it was a desert, and my granddaddy said he swam in it as a lake," Rose retorted, hefting the compact Uzi rapid-fire. "That don't mean drek to me or mine."

A camouflage jacket hung loose on her shoulders, the collar heavily festooned with feathers and bits of metal, perfect for a nightcreep in the ruins. Rose had discovered the hidden razor blades just in time to keep from losing another finger, and now the woman slept in the jacket, she liked it so much. A minisextant dangled between her pert breasts, the purpose of the thing completely unknown. But Rose liked how it shone golden in the sunlight.

"It is good to know what has happened, so that we may prepare for what will occur," Thal rumbled, shifting the med bag to a more comfortable position. A rad counter was clipped to a knife sheathed on the canvas gun belt of the huge man, and he was carrying a Colt Python .357 Magnum blaster in his right hand, a .44 LeMat in his left. His pockets bulged with spare brass, spare socks stuffed in there to keep the ammo from jingling when he walked.

"Shut up and watch for jumpers," Petrov commanded, clicking off the safety on the Steyr longblaster.

A battered old fedora was perched on the back of his head, and fingerless gloves covered his hands. A frock coat swept out behind the man like soaring wings, the silver toes of his cowboy boots glinting in the cathedral light streaming in through the dense foliage overhead. The ebony cane was thrust into his gun belt on the side, and the S&W M-4000 shotgun was slung across his back.

The outlanders at the waterfall had been carrying a baron's treasure of blasters, brass and tech, a lot of it unknown to his crew, but Petrov made them take it all anyway. The poisoned waterfall was one of Big Joe's best traps. He had them laid out all over the countryside to gather in a steady supply of prisoners to sell to the slavers. Petrov and the others had been poaching the traps for years. They hit the traps every now and then, never very often, and only took the belongings of the unconscious victims, but otherwise leaving the people unharmed. They didn't even rape the women because that would have lowered their value to Big Joe. Slavers liked fresh meat. Petrov knew that Big Joe wanted them aced something fierce, a man could load that into a blaster for damn sure. Nothing pissed off a thief more than getting robbed himself. But so far Big Joe and his bone troopers had never been able to find out who was jacking the traps, and so the Pig Iron Gang lived a comfortable life, stealing a little, staying low and staying off the radar. Ghosts in the fog. Masters of the nightcreep.

Reaching the outskirts of the ville, the gang found the roadway covered with leafy vines, which made them wary of a puppeteer hidden inside one of the buildings. But Charlie identified the plant as just a form of kudzu, and the gang happily plucked some leaves to chew upon and ease their thirst as they probed deeper into the ancient metropolis. There were plenty of pools of cool water among the trees, but the moss on the rocks tainted those, making it a hundred times more potent than shine, or even jolt. The mossy water was what Big Joe used to poison the waterfall near the Great Salt, and a score of artisan wells. In this part of the Deathlands, nobody sane drank water until it had been boiled for longer than a man could hold his breath, and most folks did it twice, just to make sure.

Rising no higher than five stories, the buildings were

neatly sheered off at exactly the same height, a sure sign that a nukestorm had swept across the land, the flying bridges, and warships and megatons of debris simply annihilating anything they encountered. However, the town of Trevose had been built inside a sort of depression in the ground, not quite a valley, and not quite an arroyo. So the thundering maelstrom merely passed by overhead, cutting off anything that reached above the height of the surrounding hills.

"Do you really think that we can do this?" Rose asked, hefting the Uzi. "Hit at Big Joe on his home turf?" It had taken her hours to figure out there was no safety switch. The handle of the rapid-fire had a sort of lever along the back that was depressed when making a fist. When it clicked, you could shoot, but not before. It was the damnedest thing she had ever heard of.

"We've never had a better chance," Petrov stated, working the bolt on his longblaster.

Turning a corner, the gang moved past a church covered with thick moss, and abruptly stopped in their tracks. Unexpectedly, the streets were clean of any ivy or kudzu, even the leaves had been swept away. The lush greenery on the sidewalks was chopped neatly off at the curb. A wide, smooth boulevard extended directly to a large brick building that dominated the rest of the ruins, even though it was only four stories tall.

Encircling the building were old, rusty pikes topped with the decaying heads of the people and muties who had been stupe enough to cross Big Joe and so had paid the ultimate price. The walls had been painstakingly patched with different color bricks from a hundred buildings until the outside was a strange mosaic of conflicting colors, and rumored to be thicker than the defensive wall around most villes. There were no windows. Those had also been bricked shut until there were tiny slots where the people inside could fire out with blasters and crossbows.

The only visible door was solid bronze, heavily decorated with eagles, flags and other totems of power. The metal was covered with countless small dents from blasters. Flanking the door was a wooden catapult and an iron cannon so old that the metal had turned green in color.

However, the truly terrifying aspect was the intact USAF jet fighter perched on the rooftop. Angled downward, the sleek skykiller looked as if it was about to do a bombing run and unleash untold horror on the denizens of the Deathlands.

Easing back around the corner, Petrov and the others moved back into the shadowy foliage before daring to speak. The sight of the aircraft disturbed the four people more than they wished to admit.

"So, that's the Boneyard, eh?" Charlie said in false bravado. "I've seen better."

"In your dreams." Petrov snorted. "That fragging—" he paused before saying the ultimate curse word "—that…that *plane* scares the ever-loving drek out of me." The man tried not to shiver, and failed. Death from above. During the past nuclear war that had been more than just a colorful phrase: it was a painfully accurate description of how the world had ended.

"So, how are we going to handle this?" Thal rumbled quizzically. "Nobody's ever gotten inside and out again alive. Except for Big Joe and his troops."

"I have," Petrov said unexpectedly.

At that, Rose gasped in shock. "You used to run with Big Joe?"

"No," the man replied, turning away from the Boneyard to zigzag deeper into the greenery. "Now, here's the plan…"

"WHOA, GIRLS! Whoa!" Doc commanded the team of horses in a gentle tone, loosening his grip on the reins to bring the rattling wag to a ragged halt. "Easy now, girls! Easy, there."

As the exhausted horses stood sweaty and panting, Ryan quickly reloaded the stolen longblaster while the rest of the companions hurriedly climbed out of the cage.

Taking the other flintlock rifle, Jak loaded it with sure fingers, then hefted the bulky weapon, only to switch sides to his undamaged arm. The rifle was in poor shape, nowhere as clean as it should be, and there were notches cut into the stock to show the numbers of chills the previous owner had done. Jak scowled at that. Notches only damaged the wood, making it vulnerable to water damage. A wise man counted his friends, not his chills.

"I don't see anybody moving," Mildred said cautiously, ramming powder, ball and cloth wad down the muzzle of the flintlock handblaster. There was only the soft rustle of the wind through the trees and a distant rumble of thunder.

"Only one way to be sure," Krysty growled, glancing upward. The clouds overhead were mostly orange and purple, which meant a storm was on the way. But there was no telltale reek of sulfur announcing an acid rain.

Crawling under the front seat, J.B. unearthed a pair of heavy crossbows and a quiver of arrows, the crude iron tips slightly rusty, but still lethally sharp. Without his glasses these were useless to him, so the man gave one to Krysty and the other to Doc. The arrows were shared equally. There were a lot more supplies tucked away in the shadows, including a rolled-up tent, blankets, pot and pans, bags of grain for the horses and what looked like a cardboard box of .22 cartridges coated in a thick layer of wax, but there were no predark blasters in sight.

"We must be a long way from their home to storage this sort of stuff," Ryan noted, resting the heavy long-blaster on his shoulder. The Steyr weighed only seven pounds, while the flintlock monster was about twenty pounds, if not more.

"At least it means there'll be no more of the bastards," Krysty replied, testing the balance on her new weapon. The wooden stock was expertly carved and well balanced, the bow made from the steel leaf-springs of a predark car. She had seen something similar many times before and knew the limitations of the homemade weapon. If blasters weren't available, this was the standard weapon of the Deathlands.

"Better let the horses rest for a moment, then we'll go over and do a recce," Ryan stated gruffly. Common sense dictated that the companions grab some water and clothes if possible. Cutting a deal with the slaves over the horses and wags would be a lot easier to negotiate if the companions were armed and dressed.

Locating a couple of leather sacks slung underneath the wag, stashed there to keep them out of the sun, J.B. deduced one was a water skin and popped the top to take a long swig before passing it around to the others. It was gratefully accepted, especially by Krysty and Mildred, who wasted some by washing off their sticky gun hands.

The other bag was securely tied, and J.B. broke a fingernail in the process. Hoping for his glasses, the man was sorely disappointed to find only hard rolls of bread, a lot of smoked fish and a couple of plastic bottles of shine. But there was no sign of their blasters, med bag, grens or any other of their missing possessions.

Stripping the two corpses of their clothing, Doc found most of it too befouled to be of any use. So taking a knife from the belt of one of the fat men, he cut the man's shirt and pants into ribbons. After tying one around his chest as a crude bandage, Doc handed another to Jak so that he could do the same. Krysty and Mildred declined the proffered strips.

Feeling ridiculous, Doc layered several strips around his loins as a crude kilt. Born and raised in a time where a man or a woman showing an inch of bare skin was considered the height of vulgarity, almost wanton, the scholar was horribly embarrassed to be nearly naked among his friends. He knew it was ridiculous, but the wisdom of childhood often formed the templates of adulthood.

Ryan and J.B. took the shoes of the dead men, but left behind the reeking socks. Personally, neither of them gave a nuking damn about being half-naked, as long as they had a blaster in their hand.

From the second buckboard, the wind began to carry over the shouts from the prisoners in the cage. Ryan couldn't clearly hear any of the words, but guessed it was merely them begging to be set free. He would do that soon enough—after the companions had first searched the other wags for their missing belongings.

Slinging a bag of ammunition over a shoulder, Krysty jumped off the wag and did a little dance, allowing her bare feet to get used to the hot dirt under the grass. "Wish there was more cloth to make moccasins," she growled.

"Lots of aced slavers over there," J.B. said, jerking a thumb toward the toppled wreckage. "Should be enough to get all of us shoes and blasters."

"Some pants would be nice, too," Mildred said, tugging her bra to a more comfortable position. Then she frowned, catching a tiny piece of what the imprisoned slaves had been shouting for the past ten minutes.

"Outriders!" Krysty cursed, spinning fast to bring the crossbow up to her shoulder.

Just then, a group of large men on horseback galloped over the horizon, each of them carrying a longblaster, with a brace of blasters tucked into their belts.

Quickly, the companions moved behind the wag for some cover.

"By the Three Kennedys!" Doc cursed, hefting his own crossbow. "The dastards weren't running for their ville, but to their compatriots! We should have known there would be more guards than these pitiful, plump patrons!"

"Let come," Jak snarled, ramming a fresh load of powder down the hot barrel of a longblaster.

Wordlessly, J.B. scrambled up the side of the buck-board and took the reins in hand, ready to run or charge, whatever needed to be done. The other companions would have to do the chilling, but even blind he could plow the wag through the newcomers to break their charge. A disorganized enemy already had one boot in hell, as Trader always liked to say.

Lifting his flintlock, Ryan aimed between the wooden bar, sweeping the longblaster through the group of outriders for a target. A big man with a beard seemed to be shouting orders to the others, which marked him as the leader. Good enough.

Bracing against the numbing recoil, Ryan fired, and the discharge of gun smoke masked the results for a few seconds. When the breeze cleared the air, Ryan cursed to see he had missed. The damn flintlock was about as accurate as throwing dry leaves! Just for a microsecond, the one-eyed man wished the bolt-action Steyr was at his side. Then he shook off those kinds of thoughts and concentrated on the here and now. Six against six, with the newcomers mobile and the companions armed only with two longblasters, a handblaster and a couple of crossbows. He'd been in worse situations, but not by much.

Whooping like lunatics, the outriders charged over the lush grassland toward the companions, their weapons throwing smoke and flame.

"No way they can hit us at this range," Mildred said, a hand blocking the sun from her eyes. "They must be trying to scare us into submission." The flintlock pistol was in her other hand, the hammer cocked and ready.

"No nuking chance of that happening," Krysty stated,

lifting her crossbow high and releasing an arrow. It soared high to arch back down and slam into a juniper tree just behind the outriders.

Contemptuously, the outriders opened fire again, scoring more furrows along the side of the wags, smacking out a chunk of wood from the bars of the cage.

"What in the...the bastards aren't going for us, they're trying to ace the horses!" Mildred shouted in comprehension.

Using the nimrod to ram down a fresh load of powder, ball and wadding, Ryan cocked back the hammer and took aim. "Then we'll just use theirs, instead," he growled, and squeezed the trigger. The longblaster loudly discharged, a dark cloud of smoke gushing from the wide muzzle with a bright stiletto of flame extending through the center like a lightning strike in the night.

The hat flew off the head of the leader, and the other outriders openly laughed. Then red blood began to trickle from his hair, and the man limply toppled over sideways from the saddle to disappear in a clump of thorny bushes.

Shouting curses, the remaining riders bent low behind the heads of their mounts for protection and started wildly shooting their blasters. Then Jak fired, scoring one man along the leg and tearing off the blaster from his gun belt.

"Well done, lad!" Doc proclaimed, releasing an arrow. It flew straight, then a gust of wind made it veer off wildly and impale a tall cactus. Under his breath, the scholar muttered a word that normally he pretended didn't exist.

Pressing the handblaster against the bars of the cage, Mildred triggered the weapon, the recoil almost knocking the flintlock out of her grip. Oddly, the blaster sounded louder than the rifles, and as expected, she hit nothing. The range was simply too great for the short-barreled weapon. But she dutifully tried again anyway, determined to go down fighting. If nothing else, she forced the outriders to divide their attention.

"Dark night, if only I had my bag," J.B. muttered, rubbing his bare shoulder. Then the man grinned wide and dived under the buckboard seat to come out with the wax-covered box of .22 cartridges.

"What do?" Jak asked, quickly reloading.

"Watch and see." J.B. laughed, emptying out the leather sack of smoked fish, then reaching through the bars to start packing it full of clean straw.

Meanwhile, Ryan and Jack alternated firing and re-loading their weapons to maintain a steady barrage. However, they were going through the small reserves of black powder at a prodigious rate and would soon be unarmed.

Just then, the team of horses started kicking and bucking, becoming frightened by the approaching outriders. "Millie, keep them under control!" J.B. yelled, adding a handful of loose black powder to the straw.

Triggering the blaster one last time, Mildred then sprinted to the front of the wag and seized the reins to try to calm the frightened team. "Easy, boys! Easy, now." The physician chucked gently, her heart hammering inside her chest. Out in the open, she was a sitting target for the outriders and was gambling they wouldn't want to chill a woman unless absolutely necessary.

Using both hands to draw back the steel cable for her crossbow, Krysty nocked another arrow. This one was tipped with a wicked piece of black volcanic glass, the razor-sharp edge of the basalt glinting like polished death.

Ignoring the people, this time the woman aimed for the much larger horses. She fired again, and a black stallion reared high to paw the air, the tuft of fletching sticking out of its heaving chest. Somehow, the rider managed to stay in the saddle. However, as the other outriders charged past, his animal slowed to a halt and simply stood there, gasping for breath, reddish foam dripping from its slack mouth.

Whipping the animal, the rider dug in his spurs to try to get it moving again, to no effect. Slowly, the beast lay down and went still. Crawling off the horse, the outrider kicked the dying animal in the head with a boot, and it lashed out with a hoof, cracking open his skull like a rotten egg. His head stove in, the faceless rider staggered about for a moment, blood squirting from the pulped mess of teeth and eyes, then he toppled over alongside the horse and they died in unison.

Stuffing in the box of cartridges, J.B. lashed the bag closed with a knotted length of rope. Yanking out the cork with his teeth, he opened a plastic bottle of shine and liberally soaked the entire bag. "Who's empty?" the man demanded urgently.

Quickly, Mildred tossed over her exhausted blaster, and J.B. awkwardly held the firing mechanism of the weapon close to the bag and pulled the trigger. The flint threw off a spray of sparks and the leather sack burst into flames.

The heavy miniballs of the outriders hummed past the wag. One lucky shot, or perhaps a superior marksman, scored a furrow in the wood alongside Mildred, splinters flying out to pepper her face. Cursing, she knelt to try to clear her eyes.

With a snarl, J.B. swung the crude bomb around his head, building speed while estimating the range, then he let go. The flaming sack sailed away to land in a bush near the outriders. Immediately, they separated to ride around the smoldering greenery, when the box full of .22 cartridges started cooking off. Banging away, the tiny rounds went in every direction, kicking up loose leaves and knocking a bird's nest out of a tree. Then a horse whinnied in pain, rearing high to dump its surprised rider, and another man clutched his face, blood gushing between his spasming fingers.

"Three down, three to go," Mildred stated, hunkering down low in the front seat. Her lips were dry, and the leather reins were tight in her sweaty hands.

As if suddenly realizing that they were the last living members of the group, the remaining riders reined in their horses and forced them to lie down. Taking refuge behind the living barricade, the slavers hidden inside some bushes began steadily firing at the companions, the miniballs now slamming into the grass underneath the wag with noticeably better accuracy.

"Okay, this is our chance," Ryan stated, yanking out the worn flint and shoving in his only spare piece. "Mildred, set the horses loose! Jak, set the straw on fire!"

That caught Mildred by surprise, but she reached

down to yank out the kingpin holding the yoke to the crossbar. As it fell loose, she lashed the horses with a whip. "Yee-haw! Yee-haw!" Already fidgety, the nervous animals needed no further prompting to take off at a hard gallop, leaving the companions and wag behind.

Once the horses were safely away, Jak thrust his flintlock inside the cage and dry-fired the empty blaster, the spray of sparks from the flint setting the rest of the straw and hay ablaze. Soon, thick plumes of smoke rose from the conflagration, the breeze wafting the fumes directly toward the crouching outriders. No longer able to see the companions, the slavers slowed in their assault.

"Nice move, but it won't last for long," J.B. growled, opening and closing his empty hands.

Unfortunately, Ryan could see that was true. The fire was already starting to die in spots, the meager amount of bedding nearly half-consumed.

"What now, my dear Ryan? Are we to abscond?" Doc asked, a note of disbelief in his cultured voice.

"Not yet," Ryan retorted, and took off at a full run toward the second wag. The rest of the companions stayed close behind, their movements covered by the billowing smoke.

The naked prisoners in the wooden cage stopped yelling advice as the companions came their way. But they promptly began again as Ryan and the others ignored the cage to rummage under the front seat for any stores of black powder and shot. There was plenty, along with a couple more flintlock handblasters, another crossbow, arrows and some boomerangs.

Grimly, Doc and Krysty grabbed blasters and ammo, while Jak took the boomerangs, as well as a small hatchet. The boomerangs had a rounded nose, with tufts of human hair embedded into the wood. Obviously, these were used to capture runaway slaves alive. But Jak had a very different use in mind.

"Don't leave us!" a woman pleaded, reaching out with a dirty hand.

"Take us with you!" a scrawny man added. "We can help fight! Please!"

Wordlessly, Ryan tossed them the iron key from the pocket of a fat corpse. A woman made the catch, but a man tried to snatch it away and a fight started inside the cage, the naked prisoners yelling and punching one another like lunatics.

"Work together or you'll get chilled!" Krysty yelled in annoyance, slashing the reins. But the caged slaves seemed to be beyond reason, scrambling and crawling over one another in a mad attempt to get the key first, or die trying.

Turning away from the growing madness, the companions each chose a horse, then cut it free from the brace and yoke.

"Stupidity is its own reward," Doc growled in disgust, painfully climbing onto the back of a roan horse and kicking with his bare heels. Well trained, the horse immediately broke into a gallop, nearly tossing the scholar off its rear end. Grabbing a double fistful of mane, Doc held on for dear life and wrapped his pale legs around the mare's powerful chest as best he could.

With Ryan and Krysty in the lead, the companions

headed away from the battleground and toward the rocky hills. But when a rise in the grasslands took them out of sight, they immediately changed directions and headed toward the setting sun.

Splashing into a shallow river, Ryan saw streaks of glass ribbons in the mud, the marks of a nuke crater. Without thinking, he tried to listen to the clicks of his rad counter, then cursed himself for a fool. Gone. Everything he had gathered so painfully over the long years was gone. A blind rage filled the man, and Ryan swore a blood oath to seek savage retribution on the cowardly thieves.

"We better get out of this triple-fast!" J.B. warned, the hooves of his mare throwing out a constant spray. More of the glass ribbons were coming into view, the risk of getting aced by rad poisoning rapidly escalating.

"Okay, back we go!" Ryan agreed, sending his stallion onto the grassland. He had hoped to get behind the last couple of outriders, but now that was impossible. There was no other choice but to charge at them headlong.

Returning to the second wag, the companions saw the fight was still raging inside the cage, and they rode past the fools at a full gallop. They were sickened by the stupe actions of the slaves. But then, most folks were dumber than muties. That was how the fragging world got destroyed in the first place, Ryan thought, greedy fools fighting over things they should have been smart enough to share.

Racing into the thinning smoke, the companions primed their weapons and waited for the first sight of the enemy. In spite of its grim purpose, there was an almost dreamlike quality in their charge, their speed through the billowing smoke softening the grassy landscape into a greenish blur.

At the sound of the approaching hooves, the slavers hidden in the bushes began to wildly fire their weapons into the smoke. Wisely, the companions spread out to avoid offering a group target. Then the smoke cleared, and there were the outriders, crouching low in the bushes, their longblasters sticking out like the quills of a porcupine. Instantly, everybody fired.

With a start, Ryan actually felt the passage of a miniball as it hummed past his head, and Jak was thrown off his mare as the animal unexpectedly bucked, blood erupting from her muscular neck. The teenager hit the ground hard, losing his longblaster, but he came up in a run, waving the hatchet and throwing the boomerang.

Spinning fast, the weapon skimmed across the bushes and slammed into the chest of a slaver, sending him toppling backward. Before the man could rise again, Jak arrived and whacked him with the hatchet, the blade rising and falling in crimson fury.

Bringing his stallion to a stop, Ryan slid off the back end and ran into the thorny bushes in a crouch, uncaring of the cuts and scrapes incurred. There was a rustle to his left, and Ryan almost fired when he spotted Krysty, racing low to the ground, her blaster and machete at the ready. Doc fired his longblaster into a tree, hitting nothing. Dropping the weapon, he swung around the crossbow and continued onward.

A stand of cacti bellowed thunder and dark smoke, a miniball just missing J.B. to ace the horse behind the man. Popping up into view, Jak threw another boomerang. Dodging to the left, Ryan fired his blaster, scoring a horrible shriek. Then the bushes exploded with activity, the cloud of smoke strobing with the muzzle-flashes of blasters shooting in every direction. The big mini-balls hummed through the murky air. Horses screamed, men cursed and something exploded with stunning force, wildly shaking every bush, tree and cactus. Then there was only a ringing silence, and nothing moved for a very long time.

Chapter Five

Gradually, the smoke cleared, and the companions stiffly rose from the bushes, their bodies covered with dozens of tiny scratches from the thorns and brambles. Their weapons already reloaded, Ryan and the others carefully surveyed the field, dutifully counting the assorted body parts until reaching the correct number. Six outriders, six heads. Check.

"That's all of them," Ryan declared, resting the heavy longblaster on a shoulder. That's when he noticed the clusters of splinters sticking out of his arm, some shrapnel from the cage. Gingerly, he plucked out the slivers, then did the same to his hip. Fragging things were everywhere! Even his back itched something fierce.

"Hold still a sec, lover," Krysty said, stepping behind the man. He did, and there came a sharp pain from between his shoulder blades, followed by blessed relief.

Grunting his thanks, Ryan motioned for the woman to turn around. She was free of slivers, just dirty, bruised and streaked with blood. Luckily, none of it from her.

Going to a corpse, Jak looked hard at the body, then smiled and pulled off the boots. Slipping them on, the teenager stomped the leather into place, then went after the rest of the clothing. His pale skin was already starting to get sunburned, and Jak needed some cover fast or else he'd be in real pain for the next week.

In short order, the companions looted the aced men, taking random items of clothing, gun belts, ammo pouches, flint, knives and everything else that was useful. The boots were old leather, but still very strong, while the oversize clothing reeked of sweat and other things the companions tried not to think about.

"Oh, great god Laundry Soap, where are you when I need you?" Mildred said to herself, fighting the urge to scratch everywhere.

Going to investigate the dead horses, Ryan and the others found a couple more flintlocks, a couple of .22 zipguns, plus a great deal more ammunition and food. But none of their missing belongings.

"Must be in one of the other wags," Krysty said, not really believing the words. "Or on the horses that ran away?"

"Nuking hell," Ryan growled. "The weapons are gone. If these fat fools had our rapid-fires they would have used them in the fight." Brushing back his long hair with stiff fingers, Ryan exhaled deeply. "Somebody else has our things now."

"The dastards who poisoned the water?" Doc postulated, draping a saddlebag of food over a shoulder.

"Now I'm sorry we aced all of the slavers," J.B. said, slinging a pepperbox rifle across his chest. "I knew a nasty little trick I learned from a Hun once that would have gotten one of the bastards talking fast enough." His new cumbersome weapon had a dozen small chambers that each had to be individually charged with powder and ball, but they fired together with the pull of one trigger. The combined effect was devastating to anybody standing within a couple of yards, and generally harmless to anything a yard past that. But still, it was better than nothing.

Tucking a zipgun into a holster designed for a much larger flintlock, Mildred frowned at the idea of torture, then suddenly went cold inside when she again remembered what was hidden inside her med bag. Oh, my dear God, she thought. We have to get my bag back at any cost! She started to tell the others, then paused, unsure of how to inform them about her colossal blunder.

"Mebbe slaves know," Jak stated, sliding a knife into his new belt. "They probably see trade."

"Let's go ask," Ryan stated, heading that way.

Along the walk, Mildred decide to keep quiet for the moment about the journal. If she got it back, or it was destroyed, no problem. She would only have to inform the others if the med bag became permanently lost, and she was a long way from that yet. Pushing the matter to the back of her mind, Mildred inspected the wounds on Doc and Jak, and decided they would also keep for the moment. Neither was particularly deep, and both men knew how to tie a field dressing almost as well as she did.

Going to the crashed wag, Ryan went to check the bodies of the slavers, while Krysty and Mildred went to free the prisoners. Meanwhile, Jak went to look for the weapons of the companions under the buckboard seat at the front of the wag, and Doc inspected the horses to see if any of them could still walk. Sadly, all of the animals were crippled, so he solemnly drew a knife and began to mercifully slit their throats.

Keeping a safe distance from the group, J.B. stood

guard with the pepperbox, a hand curled around the huge hammer.

The body of the first slaver was in such ragged condition Ryan had no need to check for any sign of life. The man's head had cracked open on a rock, and his brains were lying in the dirt, covered with scurrying ants. Upon closer inspection, the driver of the wag turned out to be a woman; she was so fat that her huge breasts sort of merged with her belly to round out her shape into a blob.

She also didn't have any blood on her clothing, and Ryan kicked a stone in the dirt to send it tumbling into her side. Instantly, the fat woman rolled over and fired a hidden blaster. The miniball hummed past Ryan, punching through his hair it came so bastard close, and he shot back, blowing a ragged hole in her arm. They needed her alive.

Staggering back from the explosion of blood, the slaver turned and whipped out a boomerang. The spinning wood went straight for Ryan's face, and he just barely managed to block it with his longblaster, the boomerang smashing into pieces on the iron barrel.

Snarling, she draw a hatchet and started lumbering forward when an arrow slammed into her leg. With a cry of pain, the fat slaver turned to stare in raw hatred at Doc, holding an empty crossbow. Low and fast, Jak was running closer, a boomerang held in a raised hand. Dropping the longblaster, Ryan pulled a flintlock handblaster and cocked back the hammer.

"Surrender!" J.B. shouted, aiming the massive pepperbox.

"Nuke you! Never gonna put me in chains!" she growled, and pulled a machete to hack again and again at her own neck. As crimson fluids gushed from the self-inflicted wounds, the companions could only watch as she slowly sagged to the ground and expired.

"Damn fool," Doc muttered, nocking in another arrow. "She thought we would do to her what she had done to so many others."

"Makes sense," Jak said, tucking the boomerang into his belt. "Do unto others, all that."

Never having heard the message of peace from the Bible twisted in such a manner, the old man gave no reply, not sure if he should be offended or bemused.

Just then, Krysty got the cage hatch unlocked and the prisoners crawled out of the box onto the soft green grass. Ten people exited the cage, with two more staying inside. It was readily apparent from the impossible positions of their bodies that the slaves' dream of freedom had been granted early by the cruel gift of death.

"Thank you, mistress," an old man croaked, holding an arm that was clearly broken in several places.

Leading the man to the front of the buckboard, Mildred got some supplies from under the seat and commenced washing the arm with water and shine.

"You a healer?" the wrinklie asked in wonder.

"The best in the world," Mildred stated truthfully, wrapping the arm in a dirty shirt before lashing it tightly to a broken spoke from the busted wag wheel. "This'll itch like crazy in a few days, but don't take this off!"

"Pain is life," the old man said as if he had heard the phrase often.

"For a couple of months, at least," she answered back

with a grin. Hesitantly, he smiled back, then inhaled sharply as she tightened the ropes even more.

The rest of the freed slaves remained standing in a loose group, looking greedily at the food and weapons at the front of the wag. Some of them started to move toward the aced slavers, but then glanced at the weapons held by the companions and nervously stayed where they were.

Frowning, Krysty looked over the forlorn people. Starved nearly to death and buck naked, they looked ready to keel over and buy the farm. What baron would ever want to buy a workforce like this?

Reloading the longblaster, Ryan ambled closer. "Any sign of our…boots?" he asked, stressing the last word.

"Not here," Jak said meaningfully, looked sideways at the undamaged wag. The fighting in the cage had finally stopped, and several of the prisoners were stretching their arms between the bars to try to reach something on the ground. Obviously, during the ruckus, the key had accidentally dropped into the grass.

"Anybody see who sold us to the slavers?" Ryan asked in a loud, clear voice. Walking closer, the man lifted an ammo pouch from his belt, hefting it in a palm. "There's a reward."

Unfortunately, nobody had seen the transaction.

Getting the water skin from under the wag, Doc passed it around, making sure that nobody had more than a sip the first time, but then allowed them to drink freely the next. "There's a river just that way," Doc said, indicating the direction with his chin. "Plenty of clean water."

"Lots to eat, too," Jak said, thrusting a spare knife into the rump of a dead horse. "Long as you don't mind raw meat."

Mumbling excitedly, the freed prisoners expressed their sincere opinion that raw meat would do just fine.

"Mister, I could eat the ass off a swampie if it held still long enough," a tiny wrinkled woman said, her flowing hair silvery-white with age.

Snorting in amusement, Jak tossed her the knife. She made the catch and started for the animal.

"Before that, which one of you is the skinny guy that kicked the slaver off the wag?" Ryan asked, looking over the assemblage.

"That was me," a burly man stated, stepping out of the crowd.

Only a split second behind the man was a skinny woman, her breasts flaps of loose flesh on her bony chest.

"Nuking liar, I did it!" she shot back defiantly. "Me!"

"Shut up, bitch," he growled, raising a clenched fist.

Moving fast, Krysty pressed the muzzle of her long-blaster against the side of his throat. Instantly, he froze in position.

"Best to let her speak," Krysty stated, thumbing back the hammer with a loud click.

Casting a glance at the muscular legs of the naked man, Ryan then looked at the skeletal woman and rammed the wooden stock of his longblaster into the stomach of the man. Air exploded from him in a wheezing gasp, and he collapsed to the grass softly moaning.

"He eats last for lying," Ryan stated, resting the stock

of the weapon on a hip. "But you get a blaster, water and food from the stores of the slavers, plus a pair of boots for helping. But we keep any of the live horses. Savvy?"

Her eyes wide in astonishment, the woman nodded her understanding, her pale tongue licking her chapped lips.

After a moment, Ryan jerked a thumb. "Take whatever you want, then start walking."

Hesitantly, she started forward, then scurried to claim her prizes from the dead and took off for the trees with amazing speed.

"Anybody that goes after her will get an arrow in the back," Ryan declared, staring hard at the assembled people.

They nodded, looking at the fleeing woman with a mixture of avarice and raw envy.

Minutes passed before the running woman reached the trees and vanished into the thick foliage.

"Okay, everybody else go eat," Ryan directed with a curt wave.

Drooling with hunger, the starving people descended upon the dead animals, clawing at the hide and ripping off chunks of raw meat with their bare hands, stuffing the gobbets into their faces like wild animals.

Staying in a group, the companions headed for the second wag. Ryan took the lead, with Jak in the rear. The teenager's longblaster was primed and cradled in his arms in case of trouble. Unchained slaves were always grateful to the folks who freed them for a while, but often a few of them would turn on the very people who set them loose. Mildred had once said it was a form of transference. The former slaves felt guilty about not setting themselves free, and so they wanted to chill the folks who had as a kind of punishment. Of course, who they were punishing for what, Jak had no idea, and so simply chalked up the betrayal to stupidity and greed, the primary motivations in most human events.

Glancing skyward, J.B. shielded his face from the sun and frowned. "Damn, I miss my hat," he said. "I can replace the Uzi and explosives, but I'll never find another hat as fine as that." The man chuckled to show it was a joke, and everybody joined in, even though none of them believed the feeble lie. They understood how the loss of the glasses and the backup pair affected the man, and each of them swore to do whatever was necessary to help their friend.

Privately, the man burned with frustration over the loss of his sight. A chain was only as strong as the weakest link. Without the glasses, J.B. considered himself a liability to the group, reduced from a bull to an ox, and seriously thought about leaving them during the night. He wouldn't last long without them, but they would have a much better chance at survival without his deadweight slowing them down.

"Don't worry, old friend, we'll get our stuff back," Ryan said in a calm voice that sounded as if it came from beyond the grave. "We'll get every bastard thing back." Reaching up, he stroked the puckered flesh around the exposed hole of where his left eye had once been located. Jacking his blaster and boots only made sense, but stealing the eyepatch made the matter personal, a private debt to be paid in blood.

"And when we do, my friend, we shall deal most

harshly with the fools who sold us to the slavers and send them into hell!" Doc growled, his face twisted into a furious mask.

It was an unusual speech for the normally peaceful man, but the other companions fully understood. They had lost items before, but had always managed to get them back within a couple of hours. However, this time was different. Their possessions hadn't fallen off a cliff or been washed away in a flood, but jacked, taken from them while unconscious. Each of them felt violated and angry at themselves for falling into such an obvious trap.

Walking along, Mildred was lost in thought. The journal contained all of the secrets of the Deathlands—her story of being frozen in a cryogenic tube, how to fight a droid, villes to avoid, friendly barons. But most importantly, it told about the redoubts and the code to get inside, past the nukeproof doors! There was some small solace that she had written vital information in code, purely as a safety precaution. But it wasn't that tough of a code to break, and in the right hands, the secret of the redoubts could become common knowledge, and the companions would lose their greatest asset. Why in hell had she ever started the journal anyway? Once, it had seemed like a good idea, her legacy for the future to help others rebuild civilization. Now, it seemed like the most stupid idea in the history of the world, short of the invention of the nuclear bomb.

"Don't worry, Millie, we'll get your med bag back," J.B. said, misinterpreting her worried expression. The man patted her arm and grinned. "I'll bet that I'm just as nuking hot over them taking my fedora as you are about those medical supplies."

"Of course we will, John." She smiled back, her stomach a knot of fear.

Reaching the second wag, the companions checked over the team of horses first and were delighted to find the animals in good condition. Checking over the horses, Ryan found several with scarring along the outside of their mouths, showing that they had once been saddled and reined.

"If we recover the tack from the horses of those outriders we aced, we're back in business," Krysty said, patting the muscular neck of a chestnut gelding. The horse nickered in reply to the gentle touch and nuzzled her cheek with its hot, wet nose.

"Indeed, dear lady, if only we knew which direction to take," Doc rumbled, looking over the sylvan landscape to the forest on the horizon.

"Just follow trail of wags," Jak stated confidently, pointing at the ruts in the grass from the wooden wheels. "Somewhere along way, find where slavers meet other, then track them, and get stuff back."

"Doc and Jak, get those saddles," Ryan directed. "Krysty, search for our boots, Mildred stand guard, J.B. with me."

Leaving the others to their work, Ryan and J.B. walked over to the wooden cage in the back of the wag to scowl at the huddled people inside. Most of them had bloody noses, and one fellow was lying on the dirty straw knocked unconscious. Silently, the naked prisoners dully watched the armed men with a mixture of hope and fear.

"We're going to set you all free," Ryan announced coldly, looking them over. "But first, does anybody know who sold us to the slavers or where it happened?"

"Big Joe did the deal," an old man stated, grabbing the bars with both hands. "Don't know where he captured ya. Probably that damn waterfall." His eyes got dreamy. "After all that salt to see cool, blue water…"

"Where does Big Joe make camp?" Ryan said in a controlled voice. "What ville?"

But the old man merely shrugged in reply.

Resting the stock of his weapon on a hip, Ryan snorted in annoyance. At least they now had a name. That wasn't much, just barely a start. They would just have to go back to the waterfall and try to follow the tracks of Big Joe to pay him a surprise visit in the middle of the night.

"They find a lot of folks at the waterfall?" J.B. asked, lifting the iron key from the grass.

Most of the prisoners couldn't take their eyes off the object in his hand. Only the old man looked at him directly. "I hear the masters get folks there once or twice a moon. Stop by there regular."

Now, Ryan and J.B. exchanged glances. That raised some interesting possibilities. Find the waterfall, and eventually they would find the thieves.

"Set them loose," Ryan growled, cocking back the hammer of the flintlock.

Getting some rope from the front of the wag, J.B. knotted the length every couple of feet, then tied it firmly to the rear axle. Climbing on top of the cage, he undid the lock and flipped the hatch aside. "Come on out," J.B. commanded, throwing down the coil.

Grinning fiendishly, a skinny man knocked aside some of the other prisoners to grab the rope and scamper quickly to the top only to find J.B. still standing there, the pepperbox pointing directly at his face. "The old man goes first," he said in a dangerous tone.

Glowering, the man went back down the rope, and the old man slowly climbed to the roof, then down to the ground.

"Here's a knife and a bag of water," Ryan said, tossing the objects onto the ground. "Take anything else you want from the corpses, and help yourselves to the meat." He indicated the horses.

Nodding in understanding, the old man stumbled to a fat body to remove the shirt, shoes and a flintlock handblaster. The weight almost brought down his oversize pants, so the man tightened the rope belt, then headed directly for the other man who was tearing into the meaty flank of a palomino horse.

"Okay, you're next," J.B. ordered, pointing at a girl.

Sulking in the corner, the skinny man watched hatefully as the child did as commanded to join the wrinklie outside. In ragged order, the rest of the prisoners shuffled forward to take their turn, several of them obviously too weak to ever have made it without the addition of the knots.

Soon there was only the skinny man remaining, and a short woman with wild gray hair. Rocking back and forth on her heels, she crouched in the dirty hay, endlessly shaking her head.

"Come on, it's an easy climb," J.B. said, jiggling the rope.

"No," she muttered, looking away. "This is forbidden. We cannot leave without the permission of our masters."

"They're aced," Ryan said through the bars. "You're free."

"We must wait for the masters!" she screamed insanely, and then began to weep.

"The bastards broke her," J.B. muttered softly, tightening his grip on the pepperbox. Then he sighed, and looked at the skinny man standing in the corner. "Okay, your turn."

Rushing forward, he climbed the rope and crawled out the top to climb down to the ground. He jumped the last few feet and landed in the grass, with a wide grin. Then he turned and sprinted away, moving with surprising speed.

"What about her?" J.B. asked, shouldering the blaster.

"Forget her, and leave the hatch open," Ryan said gruffly. "Mebbe she'll come out when hungry enough. If not, it's as good a place to buy the farm as any."

Turning away to rejoin the companions, Ryan and J.B. paused as a short man with greasy hair warily approached.

"Excuse me, Baron?" a young man asked, bowing his head respectfully. "May I speak?"

"The name's Ryan," the Deathlands warrior muttered. "Say whatever you want."

"If you want a blaster," J.B. added, "then you better hurry and go get one. There's plenty about, but they're going fast."

"Oh, no, sir, I have no use for a weapon." The man smiled, displaying stained teeth. "But I was just wondering—" he lowered his voice to a whisper "—I was just wondering why you're letting everybody leave. I know a baron to the north who'll pay a lot of good brass for these animals, even in as poor a condition as they are, and—"

In a snarl, Ryan swung up his longblaster, but with the pepperbox already in his arms, J.B. fired first. The body went airborne for several yards and smacked into the wag with a juicy crunch. Sliding down the bars, the tattered corpse left behind a slimy contrail of life fluids until dropping limply into the grass.

"Anybody else think that is a good idea?" Ryan snarled, sweeping the crowd of people with his flintlock. But from their startled expressions, it was clear to the man that nobody here would ever make such a suggestion again.

In a clatter of hooves, Krysty and the other companions rode over to the men and reined their new mounts to a stop.

"Ready to go," the redhead said, tousling the mane of her mare. "We took everything useful." She smiled. "But never more than half."

"Fair enough," Ryan grunted, and climbed into the saddle on a black stallion.

"Wait! Leave us horses, too!" a man cried out, a half-eaten piece of smoked fish in his hand. He was wearing the pants of a slaver, the rope belt tied around his upper chest.

"Sorry, not enough to go around," Ryan replied

gruffly, sliding his flintlock into a worn leather gun boot. It fit perfectly, snug and secure.

"But we're in the middle of nowhere!" a woman wailed with tears in her eyes.

"Fireblast! We aced the slavers and set you free, then shared the jack and even left you some weapons," Ryan stated scornfully, adjusting the reins. "What else do you want us to do, wipe your ass?" In spite of his demeanor, the man felt sorry for the former slaves. They didn't have a chance in hell of reaching a ville alive. But this was a life-or-death situation, and before anything else, Ryan took care of his friends. These others would have to survive on their own.

Several of the former prisoners seemed to have something more to say on the matter, but the ready blasters of the companions kept them at bay until they rode off to a safe distance.

Starting the horses at an easy pace, Ryan led the companions around in a large circle until finding the original path of the three wags across the grasslands. Thankfully, the cages were very heavy, and the wooden wheels had pressed hard tracks into the grass and soft black loam.

Slowing in their scavenging of the contents of the wags, the half-dressed former prisoners watched the companions

"Stay alert for any glass ribbons," J.B. warned, his piebald gelding trotting along close to Mildred's roan mare. "Without our rad counters, it'll be mighty easy for us to ride into a rad pit, and then we're all wearing grass for a hat."

"Bad way buy farm," Jak drawled. The albino was holding the reins of a chestnut stallion with his good hand. His wide leather belt was stuffed with an assortment of knives, every one of them needing a proper sharpening.

"There is no good way, my young friend," Doc rumbled with a scowl, moving to the easy motions of his gelding. In spite of his bandaged chest, the old man rode a horse as if he had been born in a saddle. It hadn't always been so.

"How about...in bed, having sex, while watching your worst enemy have a heart attack and fall out the window?" Krysty asked, her animated hair flexing and moving around the woman like living flame.

"Into a rad pit, full of stickies," a squinting J.B. added, forcing a weary grin.

"Cannies," Jak corrected.

"With a tapeworm," Mildred finished with a flourish.

"Nice touch, madam," Doc said, managing a soft chuckle. "Well-done!"

Although bone-tired, Ryan almost smiled at that himself. Humor was sometimes the only thing that kept you going when times were tough. That, and raw hatred. Kicking his stallion into a full gallop, the one-eyed man started briskly along the dirt tracks toward the grassy horizon. He had no real idea where they were at the moment, or where they were going, but he knew their ultimate goal—find Big Joe, and that was more than enough for the moment.

Still inside the cage of the second wag, the old woman painfully climbed up the rope to the ceiling, only to close the hatch. Then she went back to her dirty pile of hay to wait for the return of the slavers or death. Whichever came first.

Chapter Six

With a low groan of tortured metal, the jet fighter began to sway on the top of the museum. Leaves sprinkled off the wings, and several bird's nests tumbled off the cowling.

Down on the ground, several of the coldhearts who liked to call themselves bonemen walked away from the front door of the predark museum and curiously glanced up, their expressions quickly changing into looks of horror.

"Nuking hell, it's…trying to take off!" a boneman gasped, touching his heart, lips and forehead in an ancient sign of protection from evil. "The skykiller is coming to life on its own!"

"Moron! It's breaking loose!" another boneman snarled, and ran inside the building to yank a cord. Instantly, a bell began to ring. "Everybody to the roof!" he bellowed into a speaking tube, the words echoing throughout the four-story building. "Bring ropes and nails! Everybody to the roof! The nuking plane is breaking free!"

Instantly, there came a snapping noise, almost sounding like distant blasterfire, and the jet fighter slid off the roof, sending out a flurry of sparks and loose debris as it scraped along the casement and plummeted straight down.

The bonemen at the front door had only enough time to scream before the multimillion-dollar aircraft slammed onto the pavement between them. The nose crumpled into a wad, and the cowling popped free, then the wings buckled, swatting both of the men into bloody pulp. Incredibly, the plane thunderously detonated, sending out a roiling fireball of flame and smoke, hot shrapnel zinging off the brickwork of the Boneyard and exploding in through the open front door like a shotgun blast. Four bonemen were torn to pieces, their bloody remains splattering against the marble stairwell of the predark museum.

"We're under attack!" a boneman screamed, firing a blaster blindly into the jungle around the building.

"Fire!" another man yelled from inside the smoky building. "The Boneyard is on fire!"

"Get water buckets!"

"Get grens!"

"Find Big Joe!"

As the tail section of jet unexpectedly exploded, the bonemen scattered like leaves in the wind, shouting and waving their arms, the rumbling detonation echoing across the crumbling metropolis like unchained thunder.

On the roof, the Pig Iron Gang peeked over the edge and grinned in delight.

"That worked well," Thal muttered in frank approval, tucking a spare pipe bomb back in his munitions bag.

"Think that'll keep them busy for a few minutes?" Rose asked, tucking a knife back into a sheath.

"Shitfire, they'll be running around like a mutie with

its head cut off for the rest of the bastard day," Charlie said with a smirk, adjusting his glasses.

"Look at 'em dance." Petrov grinned, showing all of his teeth.

A large man dressed all in black strode out of the museum, a rapid-fire in each fist, his bald head gleaming as if freshly shaved.

Instantly, Petrov jerked back to not be seen. "Now, let's go get those hogs," he whispered, crawling across the roof toward the skylight.

Using some oil from the munitions bag, Thal lubricated the hinges of the access hatch, and Petrov forced it upward, using the Steyr as a pry bar. Large red flakes of rust sprinkled off the corroded metal, and a bone-man stepped into view, first staring at the rust on the marble floor, then looking up.

"Hi," Petrov whispered, and stabbed the man in the throat with the sword hidden in the ebony walking stick.

As the man's eyes went wide in recognition, Rose pulled the trigger on the SIG-Sauer. The weapon gave a hard cough, and the head of the boneman jerked backward as a black hole appeared in the middle of his forehead. With a guttural sigh, the gurgling man eased to the floor, just as the Pig Iron Gang climbed down the ancient access ladder, neatly avoiding the rigged explosives attached to the third step.

Twitching feebly, the dying man tried to reach the blaster holstered at his hip, but Charlie kicked him in the face, then took the weapon, along with the spare ammo clips. Yes, exactly as Petrov had said, .38-caliber rounds, just what he now used. Perfect!

Risking a quick peek over the balcony, Petrov saw the people scurrying about on the ground floor, beating wet blankets on countless small fires, the air murky with thick smoke.

Tapping the man on the shoulder, Rose silently asked a question, and Petrov jerked a thumb to the right. Moving low and fast, the gang swept through the noisy building, passing numerous glass cases full of blasters, uniforms and such. It looked like a military storehouse to the gang, but Petrov had assured them not to waste any time trying to jack anything. The clothing was usable, but the weapons were dummies, the barrels blocked solid.

Back when Petrov was a kid running with the bonemen, it had been his job to scrape the barrels clean, using the parts of one blaster to fix another, slowly building an arsenal for Big Joe out of the mementos of the past. Then he had accidentally broken a mil weapon called a bazooka and been severely punished for the mistake. Petrov wouldn't talk about what happened, but the next night he escaped into the jungle and had been on his own ever since, stealing from the people he once called family.

Two more bonemen were ruthlessly dispatched before the gang reached the end of the corridor. Stopping at a glass case, Petrov used the panga to force the lock, then chose two slim books from amid the many inside.

"Fuel," the man whispered to the others, closing the door once more.

Grimly, they nodded in understanding.

Now, going to the elevator, Petrov thrust the sword between the double door and eased it down until there came a soft twang, as if the string on a guitar had been cut. With a grin, he sheathed the blade and pulled the unlocked doors apart. The shaft inside was dark and smelled of old dust.

Having been inside a predark elevator before, Charlie started to ask about the missing cables, when he remembered Petrov said that was what had been used to anchor the skykiller.

Flicking a butane lighter to life, Rose played the flame about until she found the steel ladder bolted to the interior wall. Without a word, she stepped onto the first rung and began to quickly climb downward. The rest of the gang followed, with Thal at the end. Carefully, he closed the doors, lashing them shut with twine, a predark gren securely knotted in place to hold down the arming lever, the safety ring already removed.

Reaching the basement, the gang checked over their weapons, then Petrov cut open the double doors and pushed them aside.

Sitting near a gun rack full of bolt-action longblasters was a boneman at a small table. An oil lantern gave off a soft glow, and the guard was noisily eating a plate of stew.

Taking a single step forward, Petrov froze as the guard quickly looked up, a hand going to the blaster on his hip. Then he beamed a greasy smile. "Pete!" the boneman said in delight.

"Goodbye, Frank," Petrov growled, and Rose fired twice, punching out the man's eyes, the 9-mm Parabellum rounds cracking the back of his head.

As the body tumbled from the chair, Petrov searched the boneman's pockets, but came up empty. Snarling in frustration, he moved onward, the rest of the gang only pausing for a heartbeat at the cabinet to grab some loose rounds on a shelf. Who knew if they were right for their weapons? But you just didn't pass up free ammo. The last in line again, Thal used another length of twine to rig a fast trip line across the floor at ankle level, one end attached to the gun cabinet, the other end to another gren, this one marked with a broad red stripe. He had no idea what the marking stood for, but hoped it was something good; high-explosive or poison gas maybe, not just smoke.

Several empty prison cells lined a wall. Only the two at opposite ends held a prisoner, a teenager who beamed at the gang in delight and a naked woman who stared at them in open hatred. Moving quickly, she tried to crawl underneath the bed that filled most of her cell. Petrov paid no attention to the slut. However, Rose paused to aim the SIG-Sauer and mercifully end the woman's years of imprisonment.

"Waste of brass." Charlie snorted, watching the body drop.

"Let's hear you say that after you've been ridden by fifteen men in an hour," Rose growled hatefully, her pretty face distorting briefly in an inhuman mask of hatred.

Wordlessly, Thal touched her on the shoulder, and Rose jerked away, only to relent and gently elbow the giant. Big enough to take whatever he wanted, Thal would never join her in bed unless asked first. In her dark world, that was as close to love as Rose would allow herself to imagine.

"That was mighty hard mercy," the teenager whispered. "But I guess there was no other way. Quick, now, get the keys for my door! You'll find them near the gun cabinet!"

"We're not here for you, little baron," Petrov drawled, walking past the cell.

"B-but I know you!" he stated with growing conviction. "The something gang…the Iron Boys…from that tavern, Haven…no, Heaven! You live in my ville!"

"Not anymore," Thal rumbled, walking away.

Reaching a steel gate, Petrov paused at the sight of a long corridor on the other side. There was a plain wooden door at the far end, and beyond that…freedom.

"Nuke it," Petrov commanded, sheathing the sword.

While Thal got busy with a pipe bomb and fuse, the rest of the gang moved away from the gate to go into an empty cell. Puzzled for only a moment, the teenager flipped over his bed, quickly taking refuge behind the hard mattress.

"Razor up, boys," Petrov said, swinging up the S&W M-4000 and working the pump. "Because, once this blows…"

There came a loud hissing, and Thal charged away from the gate to dive into the cell. A split second later, the world seemed to explode, the entire four-story building rocking as dust rained down from the ceiling and loose bricks tumbled out of the walls.

The roiling smoke of the blast still filled the air as the Pig Iron Gang stumbled out of the cell. Coughing from the acrid fumes, they shuffled to the ruined gate and kicked aside the mass of twisted metal to head for the wooden door. Dimly from the floors above, they could hear raised voices and a bell clanging.

"Here they come." Charlie laughed softly, hefting both of his blasters.

"Frag 'em!" Petrov shouted, using the scattergun to remove the lock. The wood and metal vanished under the assault of the 12-gauge cartridge, and the door slammed aside. Clutching a bloody arm, a boneman was crouching on the floor, his face covered with splinters as if he was some sort of a mutie porcupine.

"Hello, Kelly," Petrov whispered, pressing the barrel of the weapon against the man's stomach.

"Wh-who the f-frag are you?" Kelly asked, confused.

Enraged at the lack of recognition, Petrov shifted the aim of the weapon and shot the man between the legs. Shrieking in pain, Kelly hit the floor, clutching the ghastly wound that had once been his manhood.

Walking past the weeping man, Petrov turned and fired again into his buttocks. Thrown forward, blood erupted from the boneman's mouth, and he landed sprawling in the corridor, crimson gushing from both ends.

Thumbing in fresh cartridges, Petrov saw Rose look at him in sudden understanding. She started to speak, then shook her head and walked on, brushing aside a heavy tarpaulin that hung from the ceiling like a curtain. A garage came into view, the walls lined with spare parts and tools and various machines. A concrete ramp led upward to a set of wooden doors, and light came from several small alcohol lanterns hanging from the ceiling.

Quickly, the gang spread out, hunting for their targets. The garage was filled with wags, most of them in various stages of disassemble or repair, but off to the side were five motorcycles, the windshields slightly milky but intact, the tires black and firm.

"Jackpot!" Charlie grinned. Any one of these hogs would fetch the entire gang a year of room and board from any baron west of the Darks.

"Nothing with a sidecar!" Petrov directed sternly. "We've got some deep water to ford. Two-wheelers only!"

Just then, something detonated in the distance, closely followed by the screams of wounded men dying.

"Thal, open the exit!" Petrov bellowed, the time for secrecy long over. "Rose, stand guard! Charlie, start filling gas tanks!"

As the gang rushed to their tasks, Petrov went to a wall locker and used the stock of the scattergun to smash off the padlock. Inside was a collection of keys for the vehicles. Ignoring the fakes, Petrov pushed on a corner of the board, and it swung around to reveal the real keys. Big Joe was smart, and a master of the rigging traps, but he talked too much when drunk, and Petrov remembered everything he had ever heard.

"Payback's a bitch." Petrov chortled, taking the keys for the bikes and walking over to shove them into the ignitions.

A second detonation came from the other end of the corridor, and Rose sent a long spray from the Uzi into the expanding cloud of smoke. A man cried out, but more in surprise than anything else.

"How many of them are there, boy?" Big Joe demanded from inside the cloud. "Are they barbs? Muties?"

"Nuke you!" a youthful voice replied defiantly. "There's a thousand of them! All ten feet tall and armed with rapid-fires!"

Quickly, the gang took cover behind the wags.

"Tough kid," Charlie whispered in grudging admiration.

"Now I'm sorry we didn't set him loose," Rose snarled in agreement.

"Frag him," Petrov whispered, then loudly shouted, "Hey, Joe! Why don't you come on down and count us for yourself!" Then he unleashed three rounds from the scattergun, the spray ricocheting off the cinder-block walls of the corridor to no effect whatsoever, but sounding like predark artillery.

A hail of blasterfire replied from the other end of the passageway, the assortment of lead punching different-size holes into the sheet-metal bodies of the predark cars or ripping off chunks of the fiberglass fenders. Undamaged, Petrov and Rose answered back with hot lead as the other members of the gang feverishly tried to get their tasks done in time. A split second either way, and they'd be on the last train west.

In a splintery crash, the exit doors burst open, and Thal blinked at the sunlight streaming into the basement. Then he saw figures moving through the ruins and drew both of his blasters to instantly fire. The double discharge threw the big man backward from the brutal recoil, and he almost dropped both weapons. An arrow came out of the shadows across the street, and Thal used just the Colt, sending out five fast rounds.

A window shattered, leaves went flying and a bone-man stumbled into the middle of the street, his shoulder pumping lifeblood. Holstering the Colt, Thal used both hands to aim the LeMat and fire. The trigger merely clicked, then Thal remembered to cock the hammer first and try again. This time, smoke and flame lanced from the black-powder weapon, and the boneman flipped over backward from the triphammer arrival of the .44 miniball.

Hosing a long stream from the Uzi, Rose lost control of the chattering rapid-fire, the 9-mm rounds hitting nothing in particular. Dropping behind a derelict police car, the woman frantically reloaded, while Petrov sent off four thundering discharges from the S&W scat-tergun. As he knelt to reload, Rose stood. Switching to short bursts, she found the weapon much easier to control and began to hammer away at the people on the other side of the corridor. A flurry of boomerangs sailed down the corridor to smack into a stack of tires, and several arrows slammed into windows, the sheets of glass shattering into tiny green squares that rolled and bounced everywhere underfoot.

Ducking, Charlie almost got hit in the head while forcing open another unmarked canister. A lot of them were filled with a mixture of gasoline and sugar water, which would ace the engine of a hog in only a few minutes. Just another fragging trick of Big Joe's to stop a thief. However, Charlie was smart enough to taste the fluid inside each canister until finding the real juice, a combination of gasoline, diesel and shine that worked perfectly in the old engines.

Still standing in the open exit, Thal saw another

movement in the lush greenery, but did nothing until he saw a boot. Aiming carefully, he shot once, and a bone-man howled as his foot erupted into ragged meat and bone, the boot torn off to tumble down the street. As he fell, Thal fired the LeMat again, sending the body rolling back into the grass and weeds.

Trying to fool the others into thinking she was out of brass, Rose pulled out the panga and threw it at the bonemen, but the curved blade merely wobbled in flight and smacked into the floor, skittering out of sight. Shitfire, what a crappy knife! That one-eyed man had to have been a feeb.

Unexpectedly, the blade came flying back, but this time it was spinning sideways, moving parallel to the floor. Only a blur in the air, the panga skimmed over the police car, just missing Rose, and slammed into the wall. She gasped in astonishment at that and started to reach upward, when an arrow smacked into the wall just below the panga.

"Clever," Rose growled, quickly tugging the panga free, then pulling a spent clip from her pocket to throw it on the floor. At the clatter, three bonemen charged out of the smoke, grinning like fiends. Instantly, she cut loose with the Uzi and mowed them down, wasting precious brass until the bodies were barely recognizable as humans anymore.

"Done!" Charlie announced, screwing the cap back on the gas tank of a motorcycle. Tossing away the empty gas canister, the man then drew both of his blasters and banged away at the unseen attackers.

"Rock and roll!" Petrov shouted, lighting a stubby

candle and placing it strategically on the floor, just behind a heavy toolbox.

Going to the largest hog, Thal revved the knuckle-head engine alive and roared out of the basement, leaving behind a trail of blue smoke. Hopping onto another bike, Rose needed three tries to make the twin-V engine catch, then she twisted the throttle on the handlebars and charged out of the basement, driving at breakneck speed.

"They're jacking the hogs!" a boneman yelled.

Howling like banshees, a mob of the Boneyard boys charged into view. Petrov laughed insanely while triggering the scattergun. The range was too great for a chill, but the barrage of double-O buckshot drove the men back inside the main building, limping and bleeding.

"Whoever you nuke-suckers are, I'm gonna personally rip out your fragging hearts!" Big Joe yelled, stepping boldly into view, both of his Ingram machine pistols spitting fire. The streams of small-caliber rounds knocked paint off the walls and zinged about the garage, shattering more windows, throwing sparks off tools and punching holes in oil cans.

"Don't you know me anymore, Father?" Petrov screamed at the top of his lungs.

There came a moment of silence.

"Peter?" Big Joe asked in a strained whisper.

"Not anymore!" Petrov answered, kicking over a row of open gas canisters. Pinkish juice gushed out to spread fast toward the waiting candle.

Climbing onto a couple of motorcycles, Petrov and Charlie gunned the hogs alive and raced out of the basement at full throttle, thick black fumes pouring from the exhaust pipes. They collided on the exit ramp, almost knocking each other down, but the confines were too tight, and the men stayed in motion, reaching open ground outside to separate and head in different directions to confuse any trackers.

Charging into the garage, Big Joe and the bonemen looked about for any traps before heading after the thieves. They found the candle a split second before the fuel did, and a boneman dived forward to grab the wick and crush it dead in a fist.

Charging out of the exit ramp of the basement, Big Joe and the others opened fire with every weapon they had at the departing thieves, but the bikes were already out of range of the small-caliber blasters.

"Juice up the war wag!" Big Joe snarled, holstering a piece. He ran a hand along his neck and inspected his blood-smeared palm. The ricochet had only grazed his neck, nothing more. "I want it running in five minutes!"

"No prob, Chief," a boneman replied, dumping out the spent rounds from his .32 revolver and pocketing the brass to reload later.

Then the man blinked at the half stick of dynamite lying on the side of the smooth road.

Turning fast, the boneman started to yell a warning, when the entire world seemed to explode, and bodies went flying into the trees like burning rag dolls....

As THE AFTERNOON faded into evening, Ryan called a halt to their progress for the day. There were still some lingering aftereffects of whatever drug had been used to render them unconscious, and everybody needed some rest. The smoked fish and rolls had made decent sandwiches during the ride, but now it was time for a hot meal and some proper sleep.

Making camp in a glen, the companions fed and watered the horses from a small creek trickling through the weeds. Then they curried the animals clean, carefully checking for any wounds that might fester. But the horses were undamaged and nuzzled their new owners to show they were ready to keep going. After so many years of dragging the slave wags, the weight of a single rider meant nothing to the hardy animals. However, the companions had been pushed as far as they could go this long day and ached for some real sleep.

Pitching the canvas tent, the weary companions dug a pit to hide their campfire and cooked dinner—fish stew, as there was nothing else, aside from the grain for the horses. Afterward, the friends spent a few hours cleaning and tailoring their new clothes until sleep sounded a clarion call, and everybody piled into the tent to share the two thin blankets, all of them far too exhausted to even try standing guard. Hopefully, the horses would warn them of any intruders in the night.

The sun was high in the sky when the companions finally stumbled out of the tent, yawing and scratching. Breakfast was the same as dinner—stale bread and dried fish—but the food eased the ache in their bellies and was good enough for the present.

Washing as best as possible in the tiny creek, the companions got dressed and strapped on their new weapons. Ryan had a strip of torn cloth tied around his head in lieu of his former eyepatch, deerskin moccasins and a rope belt on his pants that supported a bullwhip and a machete. A battered leather bag was slung over a shoulder, containing plastic jars of black power, lead balls and wadding for his longblaster, plus two spare flints.

Unable to find a pair of pants that she could wear without tripping over the loose folds of cloth, Krysty was wearing one of the slavers' huge shirts as a make-shift dress, the material reaching midthigh. A canvas gun belt cinched around her trim waist supported two flintlock pistols and a small knife.

Amused by the Old West appearance of the woman, Mildred started to make a comment about Annie Oakley, but then decided reticence would be the wiser course, since she was wearing something similar, with the hem reaching to her shins. Mildred hadn't been able to find a pair of shoes that fit her feet, and so had made peasant boots, or whatever they had been called back in the Middle Ages. The boots were just thick folds of cloth wrapped around her feet and legs, lashed into place with leather straps. Between the boots and the shirt, not an inch of her showed below the neck.

Passing on a flintlock, Mildred was armed with a crossbow and a full quiver of arrows, along with a .22 zipgun. The numbing recoil of the black-powder pistols hurt her hands, and a physician without a delicate sense of touch would be worse than useless during surgery. She would have to depend upon accuracy, instead of stopping power.

In contrast, J.B. had managed to trim down some of the slavers' clothing to a reasonable fit, although the cloth was covered with stains that he didn't want to think about too hard. The pepperbox longblaster was rigged to hang across his chest with a sling made from the leather reins, and an unsheathed machete was tucked into a rope belt. J.B. considered them both excellent weapons for a man who couldn't see very clearly. In tight confines, he would be as deadly as ever.

The wiry man also had a loose sack slung over a shoulder. The inside of it reeked of smoked fish, but it now held a couple of pounds of black powder wrapped in cloth bundles, some spare wadding, five worn flints that needed to be resharpened, a plastic bottle half-full of shine, some rope cut to the various lengths and a single butane lighter. It was a feeble collection in comparison to the formidable armament the man had formerly carried in his munitions bag, but it was a start, and that was what counted.

Sporting another .75 musket, Jak was in a tunic made from a shirt, horsehide moccasins and rag leggings that reached his knees. His wide leather belt bristled with five assorted knives, none of them with a decent edge yet, and the hatchet, which had been honed to a razor edge during the long ride yesterday.

After some due consideration, Doc hadn't altered the clothing of the chilled slavers, instead concentrating on pounding out the various stains and smells with a rock and a little sprinkle of black powder. His shirt and pants were almost clean now, although ridiculously loose, the excess material fluttering in the breeze. The old man was overarmed with a bullwhip, crossbow, a machete and a .22 zipgun. To help manage the weight of the canvas gun belt, the man had added two leather straps that hung over his shoulders like suspenders.

"Not run fast carrying weight," Jak stated with a snort.

"True, but I am astride a horse at the moment, so I have no need to challenge Hermes," Doc retorted, checking the draw of his zipgun. "Besides, the best defense is a good offense!"

The homemade weapon was made from a block of soft wood, some copper pipe, a roofing nail and a mousetrap. It looked like junk, but there were notches in the handle. So either it did work, or else the previous owner was a blowhard.

Probably a little of both, Doc decided.

Breaking down the campsite, the companions packed everything away carefully, then buried the campfire. They rode around in circles for a few minutes to disguise their numbers, then continued along the fading trail of the wags. If there had been any rain, acid or otherwise, they would have been completely out of luck. But so far, the weather had held, the dark clouds overhead merely rumbling. Stubby grass was already starting to grow where older plants had been crushed under the weight of the wooden wheels, and Jak often had to stop and study the ground for minutes before figuring out which way the slavers had come from.

Animals were in the dwindling forest, and the companions hunted along the way, using the crossbows as much as possible so that Big Joe and his people wouldn't hear their approach. It also gave Mildred and Doc some much-needed practice of quickly reloading the cumbersome weapons. The bows were made from the leaf-springs of predark cars and required a lot of raw muscle to pull back into position.

By late afternoon, the pommels of every saddle were festooned with rabbits and squirrels. Jak had brought down a hawk in flight using his hatchet.

"Might good balance," the albino teen said, grinning as he extracted the blade from the fallen hawk.

An apple tree had yielded the last of the summer fruit, and Mildred had collected a good supply of wild onions and dandelion leaves.

"Find taters, I make stew tonight," Jak said, honing the edge of a knife across the top of a smooth stone he had found. The steel was slowly getting a decent edge.

"We don't have any bowls or spoons," Krysty reminded him, plucking the feathers off the hawk as they rode through the rolling countryside.

"I can carve us some of those," Doc said confidently, then grinned. "Just not enough for everybody in the span of a single day."

As evening fell, the companions stopped to make camp in a wooded glen alongside a small creek. There were plenty of bushes to hide their campfire and enough wildlife to tell them that no big muties infested the area.

Dinner that night was the roasted hawk with dandelion greens and onions simmering in the dripping fat. The apples were given to the horses to extend the dwindling supply of grain and grass. Properly gutted and skinned, the rabbits were set to smoke above the smoldering embers to preserve them for the following day, and the companions were forced to turn their attention away from the delicious smells coming from the slow-roasting meat.

Each of the companions stood guard through the night, J.B. being an exception due to his poor eyesight, watching the darkness for any indication of suspicious movement. But the world was hushed and still, as if for a brief time, it had forgotten about them completely.

Or more likely, it was merely the calm before the storm, Ryan thought in somber contemplation before fading into sleep.

An hour after huddling in conversation with Ryan, J.B. strode to where Mildred had hunkered down, only to discover that Mildred had moved both of their bedrolls off to the side, partially obscured from the rest of the companions by some flowering bushes.

"Evening, John," Mildred said with an inviting smile, as the man stepped out of the night.

"I thought you might be too tired tonight after everything we did today," J.B. said. As he approached, he saw that Mildred had one leg tantalizingly exposed to the hip, her full breasts only slightly covered by an arm supporting the rough horse blanket. Millie looked like a goddess, and the man struggled to find the right words to say so.

"Never that tired." She smiled, blushing from his frank appraisal. "How about you?"

"Millie, you are always just like a bullet," J.B. stated with conviction.

Puzzled, the woman arched a questioning eyebrow.

"You always get under my skin," he explained with a grin.

She laughed and, pretending to stretch, allowed the

blanket to slip from her arm. Her nipples instantly hardened at the touch of the cool night air, and J.B. inhaled at the glorious sight, then began to quickly remove his clothing, hanging it over the bushes to afford the couple the tiniest bit more of privacy.

As the man undressed, Mildred watched him with growing interest. The wiry man was covered with scars: the puckered circles of a bullet wound, the slash of a knife, acid burns and the freckling tones of shrapnel. She knew that he had lived a hard life before they met, and that history was burned into his flesh. Born a century apart, they were exact opposites, the healer and the killer, yet Mildred loved J.B. in a way she found difficult to express, or even to fully understand. But that was the mystery of life. Sometimes lightning hit, and a person was changed forever. There was no rhyme or reason, just the unalterable fact that when you found that special somebody the knowledge filled your mind and body until it seeped into your very soul.

"Dark night, I feel so damn naked," J.B. said, slipping under the blanket.

"Bullshit, you just miss that damn fedora." Mildred chuckled softly, running her hand across the top of his head.

"That, too," he admitted honestly, then leaned in to kiss the woman full on the lips, gently at first, savoring the delicious contact.

The couple parted and smiled, then kissed again, this time their mouths open to allow their tongues free range as their passion began to grow. Eager hands began to explore familiar flesh. Mildred raised her head to breathe in deeply, and J.B. kissed her along the throat, savoring the salty tang of her sweaty skin. Softly, he whispered her name, and she looked at him with an eager smile, her eyes full of promise. Mouths and hands roamed freely, tasting, touching, stroking in a banquet of intimacy.

The two lovers began a dance as old as man, and for a brief time peace was granted to the weary travelers, who had somehow found a kind of heaven deep in the heart of the savage Deathlands.

Chapter Seven

The next day, small patches of sand appeared in the grasslands, reminding Doc of Scotland, and Mildred of a golf course. The companions were glad they had smoked the rabbits as they found a lot less game—only a couple of scrawny prairie chickens and a gopher. The reason for the lack of wildlife was soon abundantly clear when wispy streaks of salty sand extended into the greenery like the bony fingers of a corpse. By afternoon, the temperature had risen considerably, and the companions were riding over a mixture of grass and hard-packed sand, both areas twinkling with chunks of rock salt.

"The edge of the Great Salt," Doc muttered, slowing his mount to an easy canter. "Behold, my friends, this is quite literally hell on Earth."

"Just a desert," Ryan muttered, adjusting the new leather patch covering his left eye again. The replacement patch was made from rabbit skin and was starting to curl along the edges. It kept making the man think there was an insect crawling on his face.

Reining her horse to a stop, Krysty slid out of the saddle and scooped up some of the smaller salt crystals. Taking her flintlock pistol, the woman pounded the salt in her hand, crunching it into much smaller particles, and offered it to Ryan.

"This'll help cure that leather," she said.

"Better than pissing on it," Ryan agreed, taking off the patch and rubbing the salt into the leather as hard as possible. Hopefully, the salt would finish the curing process.

The rabbit skin had been thoroughly scraped and cleaned, then treated with its own brains. It was odd that there seemed to be just enough brains in most animals to cure their own hides, including man. Doc thought that was the work of the Lord; Mildred thought it was merely ironic.

"Not more tracks," Jak said, leaning forward in the saddle. His horse snorted in pleasure as the teenager patted it on the neck.

"Don't need them anymore," J.B. said, shielding his face with a hand to study the cloudy sky. "Look there!" Just a few miles ahead of the companions were some vultures circling about in tight formation.

"Probably more folks asleep," Ryan said in agreement, leaning forward in the saddle. "Those birds are carrion eaters, just waiting for the meat to tenderize."

"You mean die," Doc corrected with a dour expression.

"Same thing to a vulture," Ryan said, kicking his horse into an easy gallop and pulling the longblaster out of the gun boot to cock back the hammer.

The companions heard the waterfall long before they saw it and spread out in a skirmish line to converge on the poisoned lake from different directions.

There were some bodies splayed on the ground, a man and a woman, his limp hand still touching the cool water. Both of the people were aced and covered with flies. Partially consumed, they both had most of their clothing torn away and long strips of skin removed from their still forms.

Hunching over the corpses was a feasting stickie. The humanoid mutie was using its sucker-covered hands to rip fresh pieces off the bodies and gobble them down, the grotesque face covered with blood and entrails.

Snarling a curse, Jak raised his longblaster, then stopped. Stickies often hunted in packs, and the red-blasted things were actually attracted to the sound of gunfire.

Holstering the blaster, the albino teen went for his throwing ax, when Mildred and Doc both sent arrows into the stickie. The bolts slammed into the mutie, driving it off the corpse to splash into the lake. Hooting in fright, the stickie tried to remove the arrows from its chest, when the hatchet arrived. With a meaty thwack, it split the forehead of the creature, pinkish brains splashing into the lake. Shuddering, the stickie knelt, went terribly still, then fell forward, the water becoming cloudy with spilled blood.

High overhead, the flock of vultures called out their annoyance at being denied a meal, and winged away in search of other carrion. For eaters of the dead, the Deathlands was always a bonanza of corpses.

Preparing for a rush by more stickies, the companions sat on their horses for a long time, weapons in hand, watching the shifting sands for any sign of more muties. But the dying hoots had either not been heard by others of its kind, or this stickie was a rogue and traveled by itself.

"Okay, we're alone," Ryan stated, easing down the

hammer on the flintlock so there wouldn't be unnecessary strain on the firing spring. "But from now on, we stand guard in pairs. Jak and me, J.B. and Mildred, Doc and Krysty."

"So that there is always a crossbow and a blaster," Doc said with a nod. "Most wise, my dear Ryan. Silence is golden, eh?"

"But a brass will save your ass," J.B. countered, resting the enormous pepperbox across his saddle.

"Well," Krysty said, "I don't see any signs of a horse or a wag. Looks like these folks walked out of the Great Salt the same as we did."

Scowling, Jak seemed as if he wanted to say something, but kept his peace. The albino teen thought the two people had to be feebs for both drinking at the same time from a strange waterhole. However, he recalled his own burning thirst when the companions stumbled out of the desert, and felt a little embarrassed at the outrage. Hunger made a person weak, but thirst drove you mad.

"And there, but for the grace of God, are us," Mildred muttered, lowering her crossbow to make the sign of the cross.

Closing her eyes, Krysty said a brief prayer to Gaia for the strangers.

"Mildred, how long have these folks been aced?" Ryan asked, thoughtfully cracking the knuckles on a hand.

"Hard to tell in this heat," she replied, studying the bodies. "Say…a couple of days. Certainly no more than five."

"More like four," Jak stated confidently.

"Then it's just about time for Big Joe to come gather

his new supplies," Krysty growled in understanding. "Okay, Doc and I can bury the stickie behind a sand dune. Jak, do your best to erase our tracks, but be sure to leave the footprints of those two."

"J.B. and Mildred, make the chilled look like they're still alive and just asleep," Ryan continued, hefting the longblaster. "I'll stand guard."

Wrapping the stickie in the waterproof canvas of the tent, Krysty and Doc got the mutie out of the lake, holding their breaths for no sane reason against the poisoned water. It just seemed like a wise precaution. Dragging the body off behind a dune, they found a small gully and rolled the stickie into the open ground. Recovering the arrows and hatchet, they used their bare hands to pile on rocks and loose sand.

"This foul abomination now becomes manna from heaven for the beetles and scorpions," Doc muttered, steadily hoisting stones. "But then, the conqueror worms make feasts of us all, eh, dear lady?"

"I just hope the bugs like their meat well salted," Krysty agreed, throwing handfuls of salty sand onto the bedraggled form.

"Mother Nature would be cruel indeed, if she granted the lowly dung beetle any kind of a taste bud."

"Amen to that!"

Splashing some shine on a rag, Mildred made crude masks for herself and J.B. to keep back the smell of the decomposing bodies, along with any possible infections. They packed the gaping wounds with handfuls of salt from the desert, then did the same to mouths and noses of the corpses before rearranging the clothing to hide the gaps. Denied their juicy meal, the flies soon left, buzzing loudly in annoyance.

Cutting a blanket into pieces, Jak wrapped two sections around his moccasins to disguise his tracks, then used the rest to sweep the desert clean of any trace of the stickie or the horses for a hundred paces. The teenager couldn't remove every print, but that should be enough for any cursory inspection.

Finished with the grisly task, J.B. got an empty waterskin from his horse and filled it near the base of the waterfall. "Never can tell when this could come in handy," the man said, corking the sloshing leather sack tight before returning it to a saddlebag.

"Just don't get it confused with the good water," Ryan said with a scowl. The man said nothing more, but his dislike of using poison was readily evident. Ryan would do whatever was necessary to stay alive, but if at all possible he preferred a straight fight to ambushing somebody from behind. It had nothing to do with machismo or chivalry or even some outdated code of knightly honor. The feelings went deeper than that. They were primordial, something that came from his very bones, that made attacking an enemy without a warning seem foul and cowardly. There were just some things a man couldn't do and still consider himself human.

"If we ever find the source, the stuff they put into the water might make an excellent anesthesia for surgery," Mildred said, removing her mask and stuffing it into a pocket. "But more than likely, the pure version of the compound would kill us faster than a drain-cleaner martini."

"That useful, too," Jak said with a grin.

Finished with the tableau around the waterfall and lake, the companions led their horses behind a nearby dune, with Jak wiping out the tracks. Setting up the tent, they covered it with sand as camouflage, then settled in to wait, watch and hope for the best. Unable to risk a campfire, dinner was cold rabbit with dandelion greens and onions. Dessert was half an apple each, primarily to kill the smell of the onions. If they had to do a nightcreep later, it wouldn't be smart for them to have breath detectable a yard away in the dark.

In gradual stages, the heat of the day faded with the setting of the sun, and the familiar cold of the desert closed around the companions, making them huddle closer together, thankful for the sand dune at their back. Slowly, a full moon rose into the velvety sky, a billion stars twinkling like jewels in the firmament. Mildred had lived in a time when city lights blocked the grandeur of the nighttime sky.

The following day, the companions went hunting in the dunes and returned with only a few lizards. Those were skinned and consumed raw. Hardly appetizing, but the meager food quelled the rumbling in their stomachs. However, the horses wanted more than their small ration of grain and apples, and loudly made their wishes known. With no other choice, the companions gave the animals the rest of the grain. If nothing happened this night, somebody would have to ride back to the forest in the morning to forage for fresh supplies.

The day faded into night, and the companions were huddled under the tent, Doc and Jak snoring softly, when a new sound could be dimly heard in the distance.

At first Ryan thought it was a coming rainstorm, then Krysty sat bolt upright and shook everybody awake.

Quickly, the companions grabbed their weapons and scrambled out of the tent to crawl around the dune just in time to see a pair of electric lights bouncing along the ground and coming this way, the mechanical growl slowly increasing in volume. Motorcycles!

Relaying messages with hand signals, Ryan had everybody stay low to the ground to reduce their silhouettes against the starry sky. Reaching for the Navy telescope, Ryan frowned and changed the action to scratching his hip. It was difficult to see very clearly, the halogen headlights of the bikes almost blindingly bright in the darkness. However, the moonlight reflected off the waterfall and lake, allowing the one-eyed man to vaguely see a cargo van traveling with them, its headlights turned off to keep it masked in shadows.

A body wag for sleepers, Ryan reasoned, his hands tightening on the flintlock. This had to be Big Joe.

Leaving the bikes running, the riders got off and walked toward the still forms on the shore of the lake. Each was carrying a wooden club and a net for capturing the sleepers alive in case they were starting to come around.

Kneeling, the riders started to turn over the bodies when they cried out in surprise.

"Nuking hell!" a man gasped. "This bitch is cold as snow. These fuckers have been aced for days!"

"Look at these wounds! Now, why would anybody pack the fragging bodies in salt to kill the smell?" the second man asked in a terse whisper, then his voice came back strong. "Nuke me running, this is a trap!"

Instantly, the headlights of the van blazed on, brightly illuminating a swatch of empty desert. "Move!" somebody yelled from inside the wag. "I got your six!"

But at the exact moment the two riders charged for their bikes, there came a couple of soft twangs from the direction of a sand dune and arrows slammed into them. Staggering from the impacts, the men tried to draw blasters, and two more arrows pierced their throats, the shafts fully coming out the other side to dive into the lake.

"Hot damn, it's *them* again!" a man cursed from the van, and the engine of the wag surged into life, the tires briefly spinning in the loose sand before finding traction. In a spray of salty particles, the wag shot away from the lake, knocking over one of the purring motorcycles in the driver's frantic haste to escape.

Standing tall, Jak flipped over the hatchet in his hand and threw it hard. Perfectly aimed, the wooden shaft slammed into the rear of the cargo van, making an enormous bang. Inside the wag, cursing people began firing blasters randomly, lances of flame stabbing into the darkness. Fishtailing the wag to dodge any additional arrows, the driver continued to accelerate until the wag vanished in the distance.

Scrambling out of hiding, the companions converged on the fallen men and the bikes. Going to the first rider, Ryan checked for any sign of life, but the man was still.

"Aced!" Ryan announced.

"Same here!" Krysty replied, kneeling alongside the second figure.

Quickly searching the body for any weapons, Ryan

found a police gun belt carrying a regulation S&W .38 revolver, the loops full of live brass, and incredibly, a large blade tucked into a makeshift sheath. It was the panga!

"These are our thieves!" Ryan announced, checking the warm body for anything else before taking the gun belt and knife.

There was something in a pocket that smelled like beef jerky, but in the poor light Ryan decided not to risk a taste. The man had gone this long in life without eating long pig, and Ryan planned to keep it that way.

"Nothing of ours on this one," Krysty muttered, slinging another police gun belt over a shoulder.

The blaster was huge, a .357 Magnum revolver. Drawing the blaster, she cracked the cylinder to check the brass. They were all reloads, but expertly done.

"I have a .357 Magnum blaster here, lover," Krysty said. "That's too big for me. What did you find?"

"Police .38 Special. Want to swap?"

"Please!"

Eagerly, the man and woman made the exchange and inspected their new weapons.

"These bikes are fine!" J.B. grunted, hoisting the fallen machine back on its wheels.

The sidecar clattered as it hit the ground. Warily, J.B. checked inside and a heavy curtain attached to some chains. To drag along behind to mask the tire tracks? Smart. However, there also was a fuel canister and a pair of stained leather gloves. Gloves to handle fuel? Sniffing hard, J.B. couldn't detect any aroma of gas, shine or even juice from the canister. Instead, there was a sweet smell, almost like moss freshly washed by a summer rain.

It was the poison! With a snarl, J.B. gingerly took one of the gloves and hauled the canister out of the sidecar and threw it away. Going to the second bike, the man again found a blanket and chains, along with a heavy canister in the sidecar. However, this container smelled right and proved to be filled with juice for the bikes.

Suddenly, they heard the sound of hoofbeats, and Jak came riding around the sand dune, closely followed by Doc and Mildred.

"Think they have enough of a head start?" Ryan asked, slinging the canvas belt across his chest like a bandolier, then buckling the gun belt around his waist. The weight of the .357 Magnum felt good. Then Ryan grunted at the realization that the coldheart had been left-handed. The holster was on the wrong damn side.

"More than enough distance," Jak stated, listening for any sound of the vehicle on the evening breeze. "No way hear us coming now."

"Indeed, Mr. Lauren, but can you follow their trail in the moonlight?" Doc asked, reining in his mount. The animal didn't like the smell of fresh blood and kept trying to shy away from the warm bodies.

Dismissing that with a snort, Jak shook the reins to trot forward, then slid off the saddle to recover his hatchet. Climbing back onto the stallion, the albino youth kicked his mount into a full gallop and started after the cargo van. Staying close, Doc and Mildred flanked Jak, while Ryan climbed on one of the bikes, and Krysty took the other. Unhappily, J.B. got into a sidecar, cradling the massive pepperbox.

Sliding the longblaster into a gun boot set alongside the front yoke, Ryan kicked the engine alive and tested the throttle and brakes a few times, then studied the dashboard and turned off the headlight before pushing back the kickstand and roaring away. Doing the same, Krysty stayed right alongside the man, and they drove into the night, leaving the moonlit waterfall far behind.

As Ryan bent low in the saddle, the tire tracks of the predark wag were as readily discernable to Jak as footprints on the beach. The van was riding low, the tires making deep depressions in the hard-packed sand, which meant that it was either hauling a lot of folks to a routine check of the trap, which seemed unlikely, or else it was armored, which was much more believable. However, that made the wag that much easier to follow. The first couple of miles were tricky, as the driver clearly knew what he was doing, driving through a shallow creek, then over some rocky soil, and even doubling back on himself once, but those were old tricks to the bayou hunter, and soon he could see the twin halogen headlights of the cargo van bouncing through the night. Then, the lights winked out. Jak grunted. Nice try, but it was far too late for that trick now.

Staying at a safe distance, Jak followed the trail of the wag into a muddy swamp that soon changed into a proper jungle with giant ferns everywhere, and trees festooned with vines and colorful flowers. Soon the tree branches closed overhead, blocking out most of the moonlight, and Jak began to have trouble seeing the ground. However, he was still able to catch sight of a crushed plant here, or some disturbed leaves there, and still follow the wag, although at a much slower rate.

In the darkness around the albino teen, things rustled through the leaves, an owl hooted from a low branch, a creature ran along the treetops and something small briefly screamed in mortal agony, then was abruptly silenced as whatever had aced the creature began to noisily feast.

"Easy, boy, easy," Jak spoke gently to the horse, rubbing its neck with his good arm and scratching behind its ears. The tense animal whinnied softly in response and relaxed a little, but it was clear the animal didn't want to be here.

Gradually, the ground became a solid carpet of roots, and Jak drew a knife and kept it ready in his hand. The last time he had seen a jungle like this the companions had encountered a puppetmaster, a horrid mutie that sank tiny roots into the living flesh of a person until they reached the brain. The plant took over the body and used the norm, mutie or even an animal as an unwilling slave until they starved to death, then the rotting corpse would be walked to someplace private to simply lie down and rot to become fertilizer for its hellish master. In his opinion, it was quite literally a fate worse than death. However, Jak knew that puppetmasters hated machines, so the area was probably clear. But the teen kept a good grip on the knife, planning to slit his own throat before becoming a puppet for a nuke-sucking hellflower.

Soon, the vines and roots began to thin, and irregular pieces of a cracked pavement began to appear, along

with the crumbling remains of some predark buildings
set amid the lush greenery. Relaxing slightly, Jak realized that this was the outskirts of a town, which meant
he was dangerously close to their base.

Slowing his mount, Jak waited for the other companions to join him before proceeding. There was safety
in numbers, especially when dealing with folks who
loved traps and poison. Chuffing softly in the gloom,
the three horses moved easily over the tangled roots,
but the two bikes had a hard time bouncing over the
constant obstructions. Hunkered down in the sidecar,
J.B. was hugging the pepperbox as if drawing strength
from the weapon, and looked just about ready to explode, or get sick, it could easily go either way.

Unexpectedly, the roots abruptly stopped and there
was a paved road ahead of the companions. Staying
under the canopy of the trees, they scrutinized the ruins
ahead. There were houses, offices, stores and factories,
a typical Midwest ville. Except that now everything
was heavily overgrown with ivy and weeds. What few
windows were still intact were gray from decades of
accumulated dirt. Most doors hung from a single hinge;
the rest of the doorways gaped open like hungry mouths
waiting for innocent explorers to wander inside. There
were no wags on any of the streets, the wrecks probably
harvested for spare parts. None of the buildings in sight
were over five stories tall, several of them obviously
sliced off at the height from violent wind shear.

"Gotta be a rad pit somewhere nearby, say fifty miles
at the most," J.B. warned, forcing himself not to glance
at the rad counter no longer on his lapel. "And it must
be a huge one."

Proceeding warily along the side of the road, the companions kept a sharp watch out for any traps, but the van hadn't made any detours along this stretch. It charged straight down the middle of the road until reaching a wide intersection, then it turned left so fast, it was traveling on only two tires for a short stretch.

"Move fast. Scared?" Jak asked with a frown.

"Not of us," Ryan noted bluntly, throttling down the engine. "But they were triple-scared of whoever the frag they thought attacked them at the waterfall."

"The enemy of my enemy," Doc rumbled in offering.

"Is still my fragging enemy," J.B. retorted, stepping out of the sidecar. The man stretched, his joints creaking and popping. "Okay, let's recce this place, find those sons of bitches and start some chilling!"

Easing down from her horse, Mildred was taken aback by the harsh tone in the man's voice, then realized that if somebody had stolen her hands, she would have moved heaven and earth to get them back. J.B. was clearly feeling very vulnerable. That was probably why he seemed somewhat distant to her in the tent the previous night. As a physician, she understood the basic psychology. A man needed to feel important somehow to the woman he was attracted to: physically strong, rich, smart, honest, funny, brave, whatever. If that was taken away, he could suddenly feel vulnerable and retreat within himself. An angry man had no real friends but solitude. She wanted to shake J.B. back to reality but knew it would do no good. The man had no reason to feel inferior. During the fight with the slavers, a nearly blind J.B. had whipped up a bomb out of odds and ends and blown a dozen of the bastards straight to hell. John Barrymore Dix wouldn't be rendered help-less if you ripped off his arms and legs. Pride swelled in Mildred at the thought, and she started to reach out a comforting hand to the man, but wisely stopped and changed the gesture to pat her horses. The male ego... sheesh!

Advancing slowly, the companions tried to stay in the shadows as protection from snipers. Turning a cor-ner, Ryan found himself looking up a scrupulously clean boulevard. The potholes had been patched, the windblown debris swept away and even the ivy had been neatly chopped off at the curb.

"This is a shatterzone," J.B. said softly.

Silently, Ryan nodded agreement. The road was a chill zone, an open patch of ground offering nothing for an invader to hide behind as cover. This was a trap for fools. Or was it a diversion to make a wise person avoid the road and keep to the sidewalk? Studying the concrete blocks ahead, Ryan noted that several of them were different colors, and one had a leaf jammed be-tween the edge of the concrete and the curb. *Mantraps.* One step on those and the fake concrete block would flip over on a pivot, and down you'd go, probably to get impaled on spikes.

"Get razor, people," Krysty said, her hair flexing and curling nervously. "That has to be their base."

Situated at the far end of the boulevard was a brick building situated on top of a small hill, the sides com-pletely solid, the windows blocked with multicolored bricks from other buildings. There had once been let-ters carved into the granite lintel above the bronze front door, but now it was masked by the ever-present ivy.

However, flanking the front door was a Roman cata-pult and Civil War siege cannon. Ryan almost smiled at that. This was some sort of a military museum! That would explain the origin of the flintlocks and pepper-boxes. Fulminating mercury percussion caps for car-tridges were a bitch to make these days, but any damn fool could hammer a chunk of flint into a triangle for a black-powder flintlock.

"Big Joe must have busted in to steal the exhibits to equip his crew with blasters," Mildred muttered in grudging admiration. "Using the past to arm the future. That's pretty smart."

"What that?" Jak asked with a scowl.

Some sort of machine had crashed and burned di-rectly before the building, and even in the bright moon-light, it was impossible to tell what the thing had once been.

Gesturing at Krysty, Ryan turned off his bike, and she did the same. A thick silence descended upon the companions, and there was only the panting of the horses and the rustle of the trees from the gentle breeze. Soft voices could be heard coming from the building, along with shouted orders, rattling chains and a dull boom.

"They're barricading themselves in for a fight," Ryan sagely guessed, rubbing his unshaven chin. "It's going to be triple-hard to get inside now."

"Not necessarily," J.B. said slowly, turning to study the street behind them. "Big Joe knows traps, but how much does he know about predark cities?"

Slowly, Ryan nodded. "Okay, start searching under

the roots. In a mountain town like this, there must be quite a lot of them around."

Retreating a couple of blocks, the companions parked the motorcycles in the lee of a crumbling movie theater where they couldn't possibly be seen from the museum. While J.B. removed the ignition keys, Jak, Mildred and Doc tethered their horses to the machines, then everybody began poking and prodding among the leafy vines covering the street until they were rewarded with a dull clang of metal. Cutting away the greenery, the companions exposed a rusty manhole cover.

Working together, Ryan and J.B. started to shift the heavy disk, and it squealed loudly in protest. Stopping instantly, they waited to make sure the coldhearts up on the hill hadn't heard the brief noise, then they lubricated the edge of the manhole with oil taken from the motorcycle engines, and it moved aside easily. There was only darkness underneath.

Quickly, torches were made from the posts of a picket fence, the ends wrapped in lengths of knotted rope and soaked in juice from the gas tanks. Scraping a spare flint across the curb, Ryan set a torch on fire and dropped it down the hole. Tumbling freely, it fell for several yards before hitting the bottom. There was nothing in sight below but brick walls. The companions grinned. It was a storm drain, not a sewer. Bingo.

Climbing into the manhole, Ryan landed in a crouch, his .357 Magnum handblaster at the ready. When nothing reacted to his presence, the one-eyed man reclaimed the torch and looked about. Designed to handle the runoff water of the melting winter snow, the drain was huge, easily ten feet wide and just as high. The walls were smooth masonry, a few of the bricks having fallen out over the decades to reveal the undamaged concrete underneath. Walking a little ways, Ryan saw that the drain extended out of sight in either direction, the glow of the torch fading away to absolute blackness. There weren't any signs that animals had ever been down here, and the air smelled clean, but stale, without any trace of seed pods, old bones or even rotting vegetation.

Softly whistling like a whip-poor-will, Ryan stood guard while the rest of the companions climbed down.

"I really hate to leave that open," Krysty said, studying the circle of starry sky through the opening. "But I can't figure out how to close it without at least one of us staying behind."

"There is no way," Ryan replied gruffly, starting along the drain, his blaster held at the ready, the torch held high to light his way.

Proceeding up the slope, the companions had to pause numerous times at unexpected intersections to guess which turns to take purely on gut instinct. But Ryan was operating on the theory that as long as they were heading uphill, that had to be the right direction.

Every sound the companions made echoed softly along the brick-lined passage, so conversation was kept to an absolute minimum. On a regular basis, they passed more manhole covers, along with slotted openings where the floodwater could pour into the drain, and occasionally they found some debris: a rusty shopping cart, a shoe and a car tire—the last vestiges of predark civilization preserved for posterity.

Reaching the base of a steep ramp, the companions tried to crawl up the drain on their hands and knees, but the drain was level again at the top. They dimly heard muted voices from above. Men shouting and cursing. They were very close.

Encountering another intersection, Ryan paused to add more juice to his flickering torch, then he studied the walls and ceiling. Trader once told him that many government buildings had direct access to storm drains for them to be used as emergency exits in times of civil unrest, which was old-speak for a riot, and for once, the man was glad of the paranoid thinking. Sometimes, the companions even found bomb shelters hidden beneath buildings, but Ryan didn't think that would be the case for a museum. What he was hoping for was a manhole cover, but one that locked airtight like the hatch on a submarine. This was an old trick that Trader had taught Ryan to gain entry into locked buildings with steel grates over the windows.

The other companions joined in the search, and soon Jak found another manhole cover. Passing his torch to Doc, Ryan cupped his hands, and J.B. put a moccasin into his palms to be hoisted upward. Listening carefully, he heard people talking and caught a whiff of something that smelled like smoked fish. Testing the cover with fingertip pressure, the man looked at the others and shook his head. Frowning, Ryan eased his friend back down and they continued the hunt.

Three more useless manhole covers were found, and Ryan was starting to think the plan wasn't going to work, when Doc grunted softly and pointed upward. Set into the bricks was a fiberglass door, without a lock or hinges.

"No way," J.B. whispered, rushing to the door. Running hands across the smooth material, a questing finger punched through a thin section, and the man grinned as he expertly peeled away the rest of the Mylar film covering a standard wheel-lock.

Experimentally, J.B. tested the lock, and it turned freely without any resistance. In a few moments there was a hard click, the fiberglass door swung away from the brick wall and out poured a small avalanche of white stones.

Forming a relay, the excited companions dug out the stack of stones, ferrying them neatly to a nearby pile, trying to make as little noise as possible. Soon, a small cubicle was revealed. Set into the concrete wall was a stainless-steel ladder leading directly to an airtight hatch with another wheel-lock, and an exposed hinge on the side.

Trying not to grin, J.B. checked the ladder for any traps, then climbed to the top and took an oily rag from a pocket to swab down the hinge and the spindle of the lock. Taking hold of the wheel, the man applied the tiniest bit of pressure clockwise to break any corrosion that might have built up over the decades, and let the engine oil seep in deeper. Then he gently turned the wheel counterclockwise. At first, nothing happened, then the wheel-lock began to move with a low grinding noise.

Instantly, the man stopped and listened intently, but there didn't seem to be a reaction to the noise. Fervently wishing that he had a compass to check for proximity sensors, J.B. swabbed more oil on the hinge and spindle, then took a deep breath and threw his full weight against the wheel. The locking mechanism resisted for only a split second, then it spun freely and disengaged with a dull thud. Shifting the hatch upward a crack, J.B. stole a glance through the narrow opening. At first, the torchlight from below didn't reveal much, but as his vision adjusted to the gloom, he could see the contents and arrangement of the small room. *Jackpot!*

Chapter Eight

Climbing through the opening, J.B. slowly stood and looked about the cramped area. It was difficult to see clearly. Something brushed against his face, and the man reached up to find a dangling string. Pulling on it gently, he heard a soft crack, and a greenish chemical light began to infuse the darkness, slowly brightening to full illumination.

There was a set of twelve bunks spanning a wall, each with a footlocker and privacy curtain. A chemical toilet sat in the corner, directly opposite a stack of glass water bottles that reached to the ceiling. An air-purification machine sat on top of a wooden table alongside a rad counter and a shortwave radio. There was a sealed cabinet right next to another door set into the concrete wall. He opened it to see a storage room, the shelves completely packed with hundreds of plastic-wrapped canned goods, clothing, tools, books, board games and medical supplies. At the far end was another door, sealed with another wheel-lock and lined with lead. J.B. could scarcely believe his eyes. There was no doubt about it, this was a bomb shelter, a predark bomb shelter! Fully stocked and apparently hidden right under Big Joe's nose.

Going to the hatch, J.B. smiled down at Ryan, his

tense features flickering in the firelight. "It's a fall-out shelter," he said, then turned to go directly for the cabinet.

Using a thumb, J.B. eased up a corner of the sticky tape edging the metal door, then carefully peeled it away in one long strip. As Ryan climbed into the shelter, J.B. opened the cabinet to reveal stacks of U.S. Army ammunition tins marked .38 and 30.06, plus a row of Browning Automatic Rifles, perfectly preserved under a thick brown coating of cosmoline jelly. That startled the man. Cosmoline? he thought. Who used that anymore? The military weapons stored at the redoubts were sealed inside Mylar bags.

Just for a moment, J.B. wondered if this was a fake, some sort of an exhibit for the museum, then he remembered the chemical light in the ceiling. No museum would waste the effort to install something the patrons would never see or even know about. No, this was the real thing, just an incredibly old bomb shelter.

Warily, Krysty popped up, blaster in hand. "Can we talk here?" she whispered.

"Lead-lined door," J.B. replied, jerking a thumb. "They couldn't hear us if we fired a bazooka."

"Excellent!"

"But keep it low, anyway," Ryan added in a growl.

Nodding, Krysty came out of the hatch, as Ryan went to a control panel on the wall and fiddled with some switches inside. There was an electrical snap, a brief whiff of ozone and fluorescent tubes in the ceiling strobed into sluggish life. Two of them immediately winked out again, but the rest stubbornly maintained a stark white illumination.

"Egad, this is a Civil Defense bomb shelter," Doc rumbled, rising to his feet. There was a CD chart on the wall detailing how to test the outside air for radiation. "That's from the Cold War era, correct? Circa 1950. I read about that during my captivity."

"Something like that," Ryan agreed, going to the gun cabinet and taking down an ammunition can. Breaking the seal, he let the inert gas hiss out, then popped the top. Inside were fifty pristine 30.06 long cartridges for a Browning.

"Think they're still good?" Mildred asked hopefully, a hand resting on the .22 zipgun in her holster.

"After a hundred and fifty years? Your guess is as good as mine," Ryan replied, putting the can back on a shelf. There was a drawer at the bottom of the cabinet. Opening it, Ryan found a dozen S&W .38 revolvers, the handblasters and gun belts packed solid in cosmoline, along with more U.S. Army cans of ammo.

"Blasters okay, once clean. Can reload brass," Jak stated, closing the hatch in the floor. With a spin of the wheel, he locked it tight. "Not gonna be lot of help chilling Big Joe."

"You got that right," Krysty muttered, lifting a bulky grenade from a box full on a wall shelf. She had seen one of these before. It was a World War II model, what her mother had once called a pineapple, because the outside was covered with squares full of shrapnel. The oblong military explosive was a lot bigger than a modern-day sphere, easily weighed twice as much, and Krysty wouldn't risk pulling the arming pin unless she was already aced and buried for a week. The chances of the antique grenade exploding in her hand ranged from good to goodbye.

Doing a fast recce of the shelter, Ryan saw that their stroke of good fortune had been reduced to merely finding a way into the fortified museum. Everything in the shelter was pretty much useless. The ancient cans of food had expired decades before skydark. The rice might be okay, as well as the jars of honey, but everything else he wouldn't feed to a mutie. The medical supplies would probably ace a patient by now, although Mildred could use the scalpels, forceps and such as replacements for her lost med bag. Thankfully, steel didn't age.

Unfortunately, the Browning rifles would take hours of painstaking work to clean, and even then there was no guarantee that the brass would still be good. The cabinet was packed with military ordnance, and there wasn't a damn thing they could risk using. The companions would have to stick with what they had brought along. On second thought, Ryan stuffed a pineapple gren into a pocket. Just in case.

Going to the storage room, Ryan went to the lead door and pressed his ear against the cool metal to try to hear any movement on the other side. Not a sound could be heard. Suddenly, the fluorescent lights winked out, casting the storage room in total darkness. Then Ryan saw everything come back into focus from the dim green light of the chemical glow stick. As ever, J.B. had his six.

Waiting for the other companions to get behind him, Ryan gently rotated the wheel-lock, then cocked back the hammer on his Magnum blaster and slowly opened the heavy door.

The next room was dark, the air thick with the taste of ancient dust. Stepping out of the light, Ryan could see this was a repair shop of some kind, probably for the museum exhibits. The worktables and shelves were covered with assorted bits and pieces, all carefully labeled in tiny boxes and marked with the year. Piles of excelsior stuffing were thrown about, empty packing cases were toppled over, coils of rope lay on the linoleum floor like petrified snakes. Stepping into the room, Ryan raised tiny clouds with every step, and he could see there were no other tracks in sight. If the thieves had ever been in this room, it was many years ago.

Two other doors were in sight, a double set chained closed and a plain wooden door. Ryan and J.B. headed that way, watching where they stepped to avoid tripping over anything. Passing a cluttered worktable, Mildred spotted a magnifying glass and happily tucked it into a pocket for J.B., while Doc pocketed a butane lighter, and Jak snared a bowie knife resting in a partially assembled deerskin sheath.

As Krysty closed the lead door to the bomb shelter, the room was cast into darkness, but the eyesight of the companions soon adjusted. They could clearly see a sliver of light coming from underneath the wooden door.

Dropping to the floor, Ryan peeked under the door and saw a pair of U.S. Army boots only a yard away. Then he caught the distinct aroma of Mary Jane. A guard was smoking on duty. Perfect. Standing again, Ryan motioned for the others to hide behind the packing cases, then he softly scratched at the door. When nothing happened, he tried again.

Muttering curses, the coldheart on the other side of the door tromped closer, fumbled with the handle for a second, then yanked it open. Grabbing the man by the throat, Ryan squeezed brutally hard while dragging him into the darkness and shutting the door. Caught by surprise, the coldheart tried to get loose for a second before going for the blaster on his hip. But it was too late; the holster was empty.

"Mine now," J.B. said softly, painfully shoving the two barrels of the sawed-off shotgun into the man's side.

Glaring hatred, the coldheart said nothing.

"Tell us what we want to know, and you can live," Ryan whispered, maintaining an iron hold. "Shout for help, and you're on the last train west. Savvy?"

Turning red in the face, the coldheart nodded agreement.

"How many sec men does Big Joe have?" Ryan demanded. "What kind of blasters do they carry? Are there any reinforcements? Dogs or trained muties, anything like that?"

The questions seemed to surprise the man, but before he could answer, the door unexpectedly opened again, and there stood another armed coldheart. Gasping at the sight of the companions with their prisoner, he went for his blaster. In a blur, Mildred raised her crossbow and fired. The arrow slammed the newcomer in the chest, going in so deep the point came out his back.

Gushing blood, the dying coldheart staggered away. Now, Doc fired, his arrow taking the man in the throat, sealing forever any chance of a cry for help. Still clawing for the wheelgun tucked into his belt, the coldheart shuddered, and the weapon thunderously discharged, blowing off his own foot.

As the dying man toppled over, Ryan snarled in rage, then ruthlessly broke the neck of the struggling prisoner just as the coldheart pulled a knife out of his sleeve. Tossing aside the limp corpse, Ryan drew his handblaster and walked into the light, grimly followed by the other companions.

Fireblast! Ryan thought. There went their only chance to make this a nightcreep, fast and silent. Now, they would have to clear out the building the hard way, a straight firefight against an unknown number of coldhearts armed with a nuke-load of different blasters.

The sound of running came from down a hallway. "What the fuck happened?" a coldheart asked, coming into view. He was carrying a Civil War musket, the bayonet almost the same length as the longblaster.

In response, Ryan shot the man in the face, the copper-jacketed .357 Magnum round punching a hole in his forehead to come out the back of his head in a grisly explosion of bones, brains and blood. As the coldheart fell, his longblaster fired, the .68 miniball slamming into the wall and cracking a cinder block into pieces.

Suddenly, a gong began to clang, and people started shouting from a host of different directions. Doors slammed shut, and there was a lot of running.

"They're here!" somebody shouted from the floor above. "Bar the door! Don't let that bastard inside again!"

"He is inside, ya feeb!" another man answered. "Protect Big Joe! Chill any outlanders ya see!"

"Bonemen!" somebody bellowed as a war cry.

"Once more into the fray, dear friends," Doc muttered, taking the smoking Colt and gun belt from the dead body. At first glance, the old man approved of the blaster. The Old West six-shooter was a single-action, just like the LeMat, except that it took regular ammo.

"Stuff it, ya old coot," Mildred replied, glancing at the musket, then turning away as J.B. took the ammunition pouch off the oozing corpse.

"You keep saying that, madam, but always neglect to tell me where it should be stuffed," Doc rumbled in his deep bass, slinging the gun belt over a shoulder. Cracking the cylinder, the man removed the spent round to shove in a live brass.

Opening her mouth to speak, Mildred decided better and concentrated on nocking an arrow into the crossbow.

Taking point, Ryan started down the hallway, keeping his blind side to the wall. There seemed to be a lot more commotion upstairs than he would have deemed likely, and the man guessed that the coldhearts were trying to make it sound as if there were greater numbers than they really had. Several more times he heard the word *bonemen*. That had to be what the coldhearts called themselves. Interesting.

The ceramic-tile hallway was lined with military posters from a place called Korea and ended at a suite of offices, the desks and filing cabinets removed to convert the rooms into barracks. Expecting to be attacked at any moment, the companions moved from cover to cover, their blasters ready. There were a dozen bunks with disheveled clothing scattered about and a lot of gun racks, all of them empty. But the barracks proved to be deserted. Nobody was hiding in the closets or anywhere else for that matter. Their suspicions of a trap steadily growing, the companions paused when they reached the marble flight of stairs that led to the ground floor. There was only silence and darkness at the top of the staircase.

"Mutie shit," Jak drawled. "This ambush."

"Then it's time to kick over the table," J.B. said meaningfully, hefting the bulging canvas ammo pouch in a palm.

Without comment, Doc offered the butane lighter to the man, but Ryan waved that aside and took out the unprimed pineapple gren and flipped it up the stairs. It hit the wall and rolled out of sight. Instantly, there came a flurry of activity, and several blasters spoke, blowing chunks off the wooden banister.

"What the… It's a dud!" A boneman laughed contemptuously.

"No, the idjits forgot to pull the fragging pin!" a man said in a gravelly voice.

"Then throw it back!" another boneman encouraged.

"Don't touch that!" a man yelled in warning, but his words were terminated by the powerful explosion, closely followed by shrieks of pain.

Boldly charging up the stairs, Ryan and the other companions stayed close to the walls and erupted into the lobby of the museum, their weapons firing into the roiling cloud of smoke. Debris and broken furniture were scattered on the terrazzo floor, along with several hunks of flesh. Wearing a variety of uniforms, several more bonemen were clutching wounds and blindly triggering their assorted weapons in a wild cacophony of destruction, ricochets zinging everywhere.

A screaming boneman was staggering about, his arms ending at the elbows, torrents of blood pumping from the severed arteries. Kneeling to take aim, Mildred put an arrow directly into his heart, then tossed away the crossbow to rush over and take his gun belt. The blaster was a bulky handcannon of blue steel that she was unfamiliar with, but the loops were full of live brass, and that was all that mattered right now.

Taking refuge behind a water-cooled machine gun missing an ammo belt, J.B. kept guard over the woman while she strapped on the gun belt, his 12-gauge sawed-off blowing a two-stage maelstrom of death at some bonemen behind a sandbag wall. The bags jumped from the arrival of the bent nails, sand pouring out like desiccated blood. The bonemen responded in a flurry of small-arms fire, the .22 blasters snapping away, while the .38 revolvers banged steadily.

Holstering the weapon, J.B. swung the pepperbox. Resting it on top of the machine gun, he braced for the recoil and fired. The roar of the black-powder weapon filled the lobby of the museum, the barrage of mini-balls catching two of the coldhearts on the rise. Torn to pieces, the men fell backward with most of their faces removed.

"Son of a gaudy slut!" a boneman snarled, popping up with a World War I–era Enfield longblaster.

But as he clumsily worked the bolt, Mildred hammered the man with .38 rounds from her blaster, the seventh discharge sounding unnaturally loud to the woman.

Closing the breech of the reloaded sawed-off, J.B. blinked in surprise as she ejected the spent shells and shoved in seven more. Mildred shrugged in reply, then together the man and woman moved onward, hunting for more targets.

Quickly reloading, Jak aimed and blew the arm off a boneman wearing military camouflage and carrying a flintlock longblaster. However, when the albino teen knelt to ram home a fresh load of powder and ball, the crippled man insanely charged, screaming obscenities and waving a cavalry saber. Sidestepping the rush, Jak slammed the longblaster into the stump of the mutilated arm, the explosion of pain knocking the boneman unconscious. Ducking behind a medieval suit of gilded French armor, Jak reloaded the bloody longblaster, then took the saber from the coldheart, along with a U.S. Navy flare gun.

Placing her shots, Krysty aced a big boneman with a Nazi swastika tattooed on his bald head who was clumsily trying to work a crank-operated Gatling gun. Then she inhaled sharply as something went through her hair. Instantly, Krysty braced for the terrible onslaught of pain, but her animated filaments were undamaged, merely tousled. Mentally thanking Gaia, the woman answered with a single shot from her Police Special. The glass reservoir of the alcohol lantern hanging from the wall shattered, and liquid fire rained down upon a boneman fumbling with a gren launcher as he hid behind a bust of George Washington.

Shrieking in pain, the man cast away the big bore blaster and stood to wildly slap at the flames with his bare hands, which only spread the crackling blaze to his loose sleeves. In seconds, he was a human torch, impotently flapping his fiery arms. As Krysty took aim to end his misery, the boneman unexpectedly disappeared in a thunderclap as the 40-mm shell in the launcher ignited from the heat. Steaming goblets of flesh and bone smacked into the posters on the walls.

Firing at darting figures on the second-floor balcony, Ryan aced a boneman wearing a rain poncho, and the man tumbled over the railing to land on the terrazzo floor with a sickening crunch. A split second later an AK-47 assault rifle crashed alongside the mangled corpse, the weapon bursting into pieces, springs and loose brass flying in every direction. Then another rapid-fire chattered from the balcony, the 7.62-mm rounds digging gouges across the flooring as the gunner tried to track Ryan. As he fired back, Jak appeared to send a sizzling magnesium flare into the balcony. The lambent glare filled the entire landing and temporarily blinded the snipers. Bitterly cursing, their shots went out of control, chilling a boneman on the ground floor and smacking the plumed helmet off the French suit of armor.

A sandbag nest had been built in the middle of the lobby, a brass Napoleon cannon supported by a wheeled carriage aimed directly at the front door. Several wounded bonemen were attempting to rotate the heavy cannon to point toward the companions. At the ominous sight, Doc stopped triggering single rounds from his blaster and held down the trigger to fan the hammer with his palm and fire the remaining four rounds incredibly fast. Two of the bonemen were hit, but not seriously. The deadly Napoleon cannon was shifted into position and the fuse lit.

"Incoming!" Doc yelled, scrambling for distance.

Separating fast, the companions dived to the sides just as the cannon thundered smoke and flame. The air loudly hissed from the passage of a hundred miniballs, and an entire section of the lobby was swept clean of bodies, weapons and furniture. However, this close to the Confederate Army artillery, the powerful concussion slapped into the companions like a punch in the back, and they fell in a stunned daze.

His ears ringing, a disorientated J.B. unleashed both barrels of the shotgun at nothing in particular. Moving with practiced ease, a boneman started ramming a damp rag down the hot barrel of the Napoleon as a necessary prelude before reloading. Momentarily unable to find his dropped flintlock, Jak threw the bowie knife. Gurgling horribly, the boneman dropped the mop as steel sprouted from his throat, crimson life pushing out the sides. As the others rushed to his aid, Krysty shot one of them, Ryan got another and Mildred the last.

Stumbling over, J.B. cut open the ammo belt of a boneman and placed a .68 miniball on the touchhole of the cannon. Grabbing a cannonball from a small pyramid, he hammered the soft lead round into the hole until it was flat.

"Not firing this again today," he said loudly, clear liquid trickling from a badly bruised ear.

Taking a moment to rest and reload, the companions now started for the stairs to the second floor. Instantly, a sniper behind a marble pillar opened up with a Kalashnikov, but the rapid-fire promptly jammed, and the companions replied in a volley of fire that hammered the man into the shadows, his body spurting blood from a score of holes.

Sprinting ahead of the other companions, Ryan barely reached the next level before a Molotov cocktail came sailing down from the third floor. He fired twice, and the bottle exploded into a harmless fireball that continued on to the ruins of the lobby. Cleared of anything flammable by the Napoleon cannon, the blaze simply pooled on the terrazzo floor and soon died out.

Raising another Molotov, the boneman lit the rag around the neck, and Doc fired, missing the man's head by an inch and chipping off the marble from the column alongside. The boneman grinned in triumph, then froze motionless as the hatchet thudded into his belly. With a low groan, he slowly knelt and toppled over sideways, the lit Molotov gently slipping from his twitching fingers to roll away and harmlessly clunk against the wall and sputter out. Charging forward, Jak recovered the hatchet and took a handblaster from the fancy shoulder holster on the warm corpse.

Sweeping fast through the second floor, the companions saw that this level was mostly a kitchen and laundry. Barrels of soapy water stood about with underwear soaking, washed clothing drying on rope tied between the marble pillars. Dried vegetables hung in thick clusters from the ceiling to protect them from rodents, and slabs of meat lay inside glass display cases on thick beds of white salt. Burbling merrily, a heavily patched still stood in a corner, the coil of copper tubing steadily oozing a thick liquid into a waiting plastic bucket. Nearby were wicker baskets of dry wood, cases of empty glass bottles and a bathtub piled with some weird kind of potato or possibly turnips. Across the balcony, a colossal iron stove was visibly radiating heat, an aluminum pot of something boiling on top, the tantalizing aroma brutally reminding the companions that their last meal had been raw lizard.

Moving past rows of redwood picnic tables, the companions saw a lot of toppled-over chairs next to steaming plates filled with hot stew and trays of lumpy corn bread.

"Musta caught in the middle of meal," Jak whispered, his blaster sweeping the kitchen for targets.

"Their last meal," Doc retorted, snatching a square of corn bread and taking a huge bite before passing it on to the teen. Jak stuffed the rest in his mouth, and the men continued their hunt, quickly chewing and swallowing. Oddly, there were some plates of food on the floor.

Finished with the recce, the companions started for the third floor, when Ryan raised a fist. Instantly, everybody stopped moving. Dropping to his stomach, the one-eyed man slid forward to inspect a piece of nearly invisible fishing line stretched taut across the bottom of the stairs. It was attached to the safety ring of a gren, the arming lever of the square canister on the floor nearby.

Drawing a small knife, Ryan cut the trip wire and reattached the arming lever when the familiar rattle of a rapid-fire sounded from above, the rounds smacking into the banister just above his head and throwing off a corona of splinters. Rolling away fast, Ryan reached the safety of the wall, while the rest of the companions gave cover fire.

"Nice try," Ryan growled, releasing the lever once more and yanking out the pin.

Rushing to the edge of the balcony, he hit the banister hard and whipped the primed charge upward. The rapid-fire spoke again, the boneman sweeping the stream of lead toward Ryan. The canister erupted into a staggering fireball that filled the central passageway. The writhing plasma washed over the wooden banister to flow like lava across the third floor.

As the companions raced up the marble stairs, three bonemen screamed and began to run about, waving their arms, their clothing and hair ablaze. Snatching a rapid-fire off the floor, Mildred sprayed the men with death until the weapon cycled empty. Not seeing a spare magazine lying anywhere, she dropped the weapon and leveled her handblaster to keep going.

Checking a dark alcove, J.B. found it was full of pornography, the walls lavishly covered with posters depicting the most amazing things. Chuckling, the man turned to leave, when there came a soft scuffle of boots from behind a tapestry, followed by a hard metallic click. Knowing that sound well, J.B. triggered both barrels of the sawed-off. The small rocks and buckshot rebounded from the heavy ballistic cloth, but the bent nails punched through, and several men grunted in pain.

"Shoot the curtains!" J.B. yelled, stepping out of the way, as he cracked the breech to eject the spent cartridges.

Instantly, the companions riddled the curtains with blasterfire, making it flutter as if caught in a strong wind.

Closing the breech with a snap of his wrist, J.B. fired both barrels again from the side, blowing the curtains open and riddling the man behind. For a moment, there was so much smoke from the discharges that nobody could see, then the fumes dissipated and there were four more bonemen aced on the floor. The bodies were propped around a weird blaster mounted on a tripod, and it took J.B. a few moments to realize it was an Atchisson. The autoshotgun used 12-gauge cartridges like a rapid-fire did brass! One burst of that, and the companions would have been reduced to a hamburger.

Kicking the bodies out of his way, J.B. turned the autoshotgun toward the wall before clicking on the safety and then yanking out the huge aluminum drum of cartridges. There were too many cartridges to stuff into his pockets, but the man took what he could and left the rest of the partially filled drum on a wooden table covered with candles and alcohol lanterns.

That was when J.B. noticed the chairs placed near the window, the alphabet painted along the ceiling and the multiple shelves of books. A reading room? That was quite literally the last thing the man had ever expected to find inside this military fortress. Then again, somebody obviously knew weapons, and how to convert the black powder of the slavers into the much more powerful gunpowder to use inside the rapid-fires.

"That's gotta be Big Joe," J.B. said aloud, reloading the sawed-off with sure hands. Unless the chief boneman was chilled downstairs, they had yet to meet the man, and that was surely going to be a bloody confrontation.

Going back to the others, J.B. told them of the discovery, along with his suspicions. Moving a little more warily, the companions finished the sweep of that level, finding no more traps or snipers.

"Upstairs?" Krysty asked, closing the cylinder of her blaster.

"Gotta be," Ryan growled, reloading his weapon with his last four rounds.

Checking for traps every step along the way, the companions proceeded to the top level of the building. The area was strangely still; the only sign of recent activity was a doorway marked Exit that had been bricked shut, the concrete still fresh enough to smell.

"Has our elusive Pimpernel bricked himself inside a stairwell to deter our pursuit?" Doc postulated, hefting the assault rifle. "Or have these bonemen offered him a final drink from the dreaded cask of Amontillado?"

"Stop mixing your literary references," Mildred whispered, gesturing with her blaster toward a set of double doors. One of them was ajar, and lantern light could be seen coming from inside, the glow dancing on the smooth floor.

Ready for anything, Ryan took the lead. Stopping alongside the open door, he peeked around the hinges to see inside before boldly walking into the room. The place was large, the ceiling covered with a sculpted relief, the walls lined with Doric marble columns. The floor was dark marble, no terrazzo this time, and there were a lot of shiny brass fixtures everywhere. The effect was a kind of quiet dignity, but what it was doing inside a military museum, not even Mildred could hazard a guess. However, these days it was clearly being used as a combination private suite and audience hall, the bedroom and throne room for Big Joe, king of the bonemen.

Off to the side was a curtained alcove containing a four-poster, overflowing bookcases, liquor cabinet, gun rack and even a bathtub, of all things. However, at the far end of the hall was a raised dais with a huge man sitting in an elaborately carved wooden chair. Big Joe was a giant. His muscular body had probably once been almost too big to fit into the ornate throne. But now a pair of empty boots sat on the floor in front of the throne. Both of his legs were gone from the knees down, the stumps swaddled in bloody cloth held in place by leather belts. His left arm was also missing, as were both of his eyes, the unshaved face deeply scored with fire damage. However, his intact right hand was gripping an Ingram machine pistol pointed straight at the open door.

"My ears are fine," Big Joe rumbled, moving the rapid-fire back and forth like a metronome. "So, stop fucking around, Peter, and come on in. Let's finish this, once and forever."

"We're not him," Ryan said, staying behind a Doric column.

At that, the man jerked up his head. "Say…that again," he softly demanded.

"Nobody here is called Peter," Ryan stated. "Is that the name of the coldheart who took your legs?"

"Coldheart…" Big Joe repeated as if he'd never heard the word before, his dour expression morphing into a belly laugh. "Nuke, yes, he took my legs, eyes and arm! Tossed a stick of dynamite over his shoulder while speeding away on my best hog! Blew twenty of my bonemen to hell that day. By the lost gods, we never had such a beating before!" He paused. "Fragging bastard even stole some of my books. Probably for fuel. He always was smart."

"Fuel?" J.B. asked confused.

Dismissing that with a shrug, Big Joe raised his head, tears in his blind eyes. "My son!" he stated. "My boy did that to us, with three of his fragging friends! Three, and one of them so small you could tuck her into a pocket like a spare brass. The Pig Iron Gang, they call themselves."

"Everybody loses a fight now and then," J.B. stated. "Anybody says different is a liar."

"True enough," Big Joe muttered. "That's true enough." Then his voice came back strong. "So who the nuking hell are you folks? Sec men from the ville?"

Ryan wanted to ask which ville, but that would have revealed too much. There had to be a settlement nearby. "I'm an escaped slave. My friends and I ran into your trick waterfall on the edge of the Great Salt."

Big Joe shrugged. "I've gotten lots of folks from there. That moss in the water works great. Makes folks sleep for days."

"There were six of us," Ryan persisted. "I only have one eye, and there was a woman with red hair, a tall guy, a short guy, a teenager with white skin and a short woman with dark skin. That mean anything?"

"Oh, those! Yeah, I remember you folks. Nice tits on the redhead, great ass on the raven."

"Raven?" Mildred bridled, then realized the man meant her black hair color and not her skin. Just about the only good things to come out of the nuclear holocaust was the abolishment of racism. These days, there were only norms and muties, nothing else mattered.

The blind man grinned in memory. "Oh, she was a looker, nice and curvy, just my type." He chuckled. "Almost rode the girl myself, but that lowers the price too much. Biz comes first, then me!" He roared with laughter, a slightly hysterical edge creeping into his voice. Slowly, the man calmed, his breathing ragged and uneven. "But that was a woman's voice I just heard. Angry bitch, too. That you, little raven?"

"Yes," Mildred hissed, blushing furiously.

"Wow, you're hot for blood, ain't ya?" Big Joe chuckled. "Can't say that I blame you much. Being escaped slaves and such." His fist tightened on the checkered grip of the rapid-fire, and the companions shifted positions, their own weapons raised and ready.

With a sigh, Big Joe relaxed his grip. "Well, if you came back for revenge, it sure as nuking hell sounded like you got it," he rumbled. "I heard the fight downstairs. You folks beat my whole damn crew. There ain't nobody left alive but me." Then the man growled, "But you never could have done it if my son hadn't pounded us flat only last week! He opened the gate, so to speak."

"That could be," Ryan said diplomatically. "But we're not here for revenge. Let's talk some biz."

The blind man scowled. "What are you yammering about?"

"When we were captured," Ryan said, trying not to grit his teeth over the word, "we were carrying packs, blasters and some tech. Give it back, and we let you live."

"Blasters?" Big Joe grunted, waving his weapon. "Shitfire, One-eye, take what you want. Take it all. We lost, the Boneyard belongs to you folks now."

"There was a canvas bag with lettering on it," Mildred hastily added, trying to keep her tone soothing. "That was a medical bag."

"No shit, yaw'll had a predark med bag?" The man whistled, the stump of his missing arm twitching slightly. "Son of a bitch, a man could retire for life with one of those. But nope, never saw it. My son must have gotten there first. He often looted the traps for stuff before we gathered in the prisoners. Come to think of it, weren't no clothes there, neither. Shoulda aced him years ago for that, but he was kin, and…well, you know how it is…" His voice trailed off, almost as if he was going to sleep.

"Your son is Peter, the leader of the Pig Iron Gang," Doc said in a carefully measured tone, the one he used to encourage reluctant students to speak before the class.

"Yeah, goes by Petrov now," Big Joe added. "Mother was a Soviet, probably something there, I dunno…" The man shrugged, tiny splotches of fresh blood welling up from his many wounds.

Impatiently, the companions waited a few minutes,

but it was soon obvious the man wasn't going to add anything more.

"Look, if we get back my med bag I can repair your eyes," Mildred lied outrageously. "I can transplant some from your aced men. Easy as shifting brass from one blaster to another."

"That…can be done?" Big Joe whispered, a fleeting touch of hope in the words.

"Absolutely. I'm a skilled healer," Mildred said, feeling sick to her stomach over the lie.

"Just tell us where to find your son," Ryan added, clumsily holstering his blaster to let the other man hear. "He lives, you live, everybody wins. That's good biz. Deal?"

Inhaling deeply, Big Joe raised his head to blindly face the universe, then nodded as if coming to a long-delayed decision.

"No deal, outlanders," he growled with a smile, then turned the Ingram around to squeeze the trigger. The chattering rapid-fire danced as the stream of hot lead tore into the shirt of the wounded man, blowing open his chest and internal organs. As the body slumped, the smoking blaster dropped from his hand to clatter onto the cold marble floor.

"Shit," Jak drawled. "Now what do?"

Holstering his blaster properly, Ryan brushed back his hair. "Okay, first we recce this place to make sure it's empty," he said gruffly. "Next, we loot this place to the walls."

"Then we find that ville Big Joe mentioned and start hunting for the Pig Iron Gang," J.B. added, recovering the Ingram from the floor and working the slide to eject a jammed round. "After that…it's chilling time."

Chapter Nine

Starting at the top of the museum, it took the companions several hours to check every room, closet and alcove to make sure the top four levels of the museum were clear of any more bonemen.

"Okay, last level," J.B. said, pushing open the door to the basement with the stubby barrel of his new Ingram MAC-10 machine pistol. The sawed-off scattergun was holstered at his hip, and a fringed leather bag hung at his side, pleasantly heavy with road flares, spare ammo clips, packs of black powder, a coil of fuse and some assorted odds and ends.

"Looks like the bonemen saw some hard fighting down here," Ryan muttered, working the bolt on the Marlin longblaster. The predark hunting rifle had been locked inside Big Joe's gun safe, along with some reloading equipment, a military Starlite scope with no batteries and six full boxes of brass. His handblaster was strapped around his waist, and an ammo pouch across the back was packed with spare rounds for the titanic Marlin. Personally, Ryan would have preferred the much more reliable Browning autoblaster down in the bomb shelter, but this would do for now. A rock in your hand was better than a rapid-fire at the bottom of a well, as the Trader liked to say.

"Big Joe's people weren't very good shots," Krysty

said skeptically, hefting an AK-47 rapid-fire. There was a lot of loose brass scattered about the floor, and the walls were pockmarked with hits. Several of the holes still contained the embedded lead.

Her new rapid-fire had no stock, which made it nicely compact for indoor combat, and there was a bayonet attached to the end of the barrel. The woman had a pocket full of spare clips for the weapon, and the Colt .38 handblaster was holstered at the front of her gun belt for easy access.

"Too much time laying traps and not enough on the gun range," Mildred agreed, thumbing back the hammer on her oddball Taurus blaster. "But the other group were pretty damn good, better than most sec men we encounter." A WWI ammo belt was strapped around her waist, the canvas pouch heavy with spare rounds for the Taurus manstopper, and a canvas bag hung at her side, a replacement for her lost med bag. At the moment it only held some strips of clean cloth, a jar of sulfur, a small knife and a plastic bottle of shine, but it was a start.

There had been plenty of replacement boots for all of the companions to take, but she wisely decided to keep the moccasins until the boots of the corpses could be thoroughly cleaned first. Whatever good qualities the bonemen had, hygiene wasn't one of them.

"Not practice shooting, get shot," Jak declared as if that was a self-evident fact. The 9-mm weapon he'd used earlier was tucked into a fancy shoulder holster, along with two spare clips. But tight in his fist, the teenager sported a S&W .44 Magnum blaster. He had found the weapon hidden under a pillow on Big Joe's bed and

claimed it immediately, along with a gun belt and holster. The leather loops were full of spare rounds from
the massive handcannon, and his hatchet was hung at
the side from a leather thong.

"Practice makes perfect," Doc rumbled, keeping
a finger on the trigger of the M-16/M-203 assault-
rifle grenade-launcher combo. The weapon had been
another gift from Big Joe, along with a wide leather
belt lined with canvas ammo pouches, very similar
to his old gun belt for the LeMat. Now, the old man
almost clanked from the wealth of spare magazines for
the M-16 rapid-fire, and the six 40-mm shells for the
M-203 gren launcher attached under the main barrel.
The man had been sorely tempted to take the Atchisson autoshotgun from the curtained alcove, but the
nearsighted J.B. needed a weapon that delivered a wide
spray, so the scholar had graciously accepted the combo
in compensation.

Moving through the battlezone, J.B. saw a lot of
spent brass lying along the baseboards and under the
tables where it had been kicked out of the way to not
trip running men. Bending, J.B. lifted a brass casing
and recognized it was one of his reloads for the Uzi.
"This was them, that Pig Iron Gang," he growled, pocketing the shell for no reason.

"Can't wait to meet them," Ryan growled, using the
barrel of the Marlin to push open a closet door. There
was nothing inside but cleaning supplies, mops and
buckets.

At the far end of the room were the tattered remains
of a wooden door. Stepping carefully through the debris
and spent brass on the floor, Krysty listened hard for

any movements on the other side of the doorway and clearly heard somebody muttering curses.

Waggling her fingers for the others to stay close, Krysty took the point through the doorway, quickly stepping to the side so that the rest of the companions would have a clear field of fire if there was any trouble. Several lanterns hung from the ceiling, but only one was still burning, the wick down to the barest nubbin. Jail cells lined the left wall in the room, only one of them containing a prisoner. A teenager with a scraggly beard stood with an arm outside the iron bars, a bent piece of metal jammed inside the lock of his cell door. On the floor nearby was a rapid-fire with a bent barrel, the weapon completely disassembled.

"Who the frag are you, Red?" the youth asked, never ceasing in his attempts to trick open the lock.

"I could ask the same of you," Krysty replied, lowering the Kalashnikov. "And seeing how I'm the one holding a blaster..."

"Cranston," he muttered, fumbling with the makeshift lockpick. "Dunbar Cranston." He stopped working and stepped back as the rest of the companions entered the room. "Shitfire, is this a rescue party or an execution squad?"

"That depends upon why you're in there," Ryan answered gruffly, looking around the cell. There was a bed with a mattress and blanket, a bucket with a lid for nightsoil and even a lantern and a couple of books. Obviously, this wasn't a punishment cell, which left only one option.

"I'm a hostage," the teenager growled. "As long as I'm still alive, my mother won't attack this place."

"Who she, boss of slavers?" Jak asked, going to the ruin of the iron gate and looking down the long corridor. There were still dried bloodstains on the floor, and the walls were chewed by ricochets, both coming and going.

"My mother is no slaver!" the teen snarled, grabbing the bar with both hands. "She is the Baron Althea Cranston of Delta ville, and I am her eldest son, Dunbar Cranston, the future baron!"

"Ryan," the one-eyed man replied, jerking a thumb toward himself, then introduced the rest of the companions.

"Salutations," Doc rumbled, bowing slightly.

"Yeah? Don't know if it is yet," Dunbar said, studying the people carefully. "I heard a lot of blasters talking before. You taking over the Boneyard?"

"Nope, blew to hell," Jak replied, then he glanced at Krysty. The woman nodded, and together they walked down the corridor along opposite sides of the walls.

"Does...does that mean Big Joe is aced?" Dunbar asked, hope brightening his young face.

"Yes, quite aced," Doc rumbled, then flashed a grin.

In spite of everything, the teen briefly smiled back. "Okay, then, let's talk biz," Dunbar said eagerly. "Get me out of this nuking cell and back to Delta ville alive, and you'll need ten horses to carry the reward my mother will pay. Blasters, brass..." Awkwardly, the teen paused. "But you already have plenty of those. Okay, tell me what you want. Horses, wags, anything but slaves and it's yours. Just ask!"

"We already have anything your ville can offer,"

Ryan said, resting the Marlin on a shoulder and kneeling to look at the teen directly. "But we can use some information."

"What do you want to know?" Dunbar asked cagily. "I'm not telling you anything about the defenses at Delta. Ain't no knife sharp enough to make me squeal on my ville!"

"Good to know," J.B. agreed, going to the door. Kneeling, he yanked out the bent spring from the broken Kalashnikov, then inspected the lock. "Dark night, this was hit with a ricochet! There's no nuking way I can pick this lock."

"Then use plas-ex," Dunbar commanded urgently, a touch of fear in his eyes. "Don't leave me here to starve. I really am the son of the baron."

Pretending to think over the matter, Ryan reached out to take hold of the door and tried to shake it. The metal didn't move in the slightest. "Know anything about the folks who hit this place before us?"

"You mean Petrov?" Dunbar asked in surprise. "They came through a couple of days ago, shot the place up, aced a bunch of Big Joe's bonemen and jacked some hogs." He paused. "You savvy hogs? Those are machines, kind of like a wag, but they only have two wheels—"

"Motorcycles, yes." Ryan waved that aside. "Do you know where they were going?"

Dunbar was startled that a coldheart would know the old word. Clearly, these people weren't just boots with blasters. "Yes, I know where they're going," the teen said, looking meaningfully at the locked door.

Just then, Krysty and Jak returned.

"All clear," Krysty reported. "There's nobody else around."

"Found van in garage," Jak added, holstering the S&W Magnum. "Plenty tools and juice."

Still watching the prisoner, Ryan merely grunted at the news.

"Anything inside?" Mildred asked, tightening her grip on the Taurus.

"Nothing we can't dump to replace with blasters and brass," Krysty replied with a hard grin.

"Excellent!" Doc beamed in delight. "This cornucopia of ordnance will be of the greatest assistance in helping us to convince the thieves to return our property."

"Then dig hole and have climb inside," Jak added grimly.

"Absolutely, my dear lad!"

"First, we gotta find them," J.B. said, slowly standing and dusting off his pants. "Now, what did Petrov and his crew look like again?"

Expecting this question, Dunbar answered promptly. "Petrov is tall, wears a long coat, blue boots with a bird design and fingerless gloves. He was carrying a bolt-action longblaster, a scattergun and a black stick with a sword hidden inside."

Easing off the arming bolt of the rapid-fire, Doc inhaled sharply at that, but said nothing.

"There was a woman, triple-small, wearing a camouflage jacket with feathers and bits of metal debris all over it, and carrying a rapid-fire. Never heard her name," Dunbar continued. "The third man had a beard, and—you're not going to believe this, but I'm telling the truth—pieces of glass on a wire frame wrapped around his head. He was packing two blasters, both wheelguns, but one was broke because it had no hammer."

Ryan and J.B. gave no reaction to the description. Slinging the rapid-fire across her back, Krysty forced herself to stay calm at the description, but her long hair flexed and curled, betraying her excitement.

"Now, the last guy was bald and bigger than a wendigo," the teen continued. "They call him Tall, or something like that, and he carried a couple of big bore handblasters and had a patched canvas bag with a faded word on the side."

"Okay, stand back," Ryan commanded, swinging up the Marlin and taking aim. "Better yet, get under the bed."

Quickly, the teen did so, and Ryan fired. The entire room shook from the thunderous discharge of the longblaster, and the iron door actually seemed to bend for a second under the triphammer impact of the big Magnum round, then the lock exploded into pieces and the door flew aside to slam against the bars in a ringing crash.

Rising back into view, Dunbar walked out of the cell and spit into the palm of his hand. Resting the Marlin on a shoulder, Ryan did the same and they shook.

"I'd like a blaster, if you don't mind. Heard Big Joe had some mutie dogs."

"No problem there," Ryan replied, releasing his grip to pull his handblaster and point it at the teen. "That is, once Baron Cranston confirms who you are."

Startled for only a second, Dunbar broke into laughter,

then walked back into the cell and sat down. "Let me know when you're ready to leave." The teen chuckled, picked up a book and started to read.

BRAKING THEIR motorcycles to a halt on top of a hill, the Pig Iron Gang turned off their engines to conserve fuel, then looked down into a lush, green valley.

Most of the landscape below was filled with Tickle Belly Lake, the ridiculous name coming from an expanse of naturally carbonated water, which most people had never seen or even heard about before. Incredibly, animals and muties detested the fizzy stuff and avoided the entire valley as if it was a glowing rad crater, which just made the bubbling waters ever more attractive to thirsty people. The rest of the landscape was thickly covered with gigantic mutie pines trees, some of them with trunks thicker than a person could spread his or her arms, and even on the hill the gang caught the woodsy smell of pine sap and green nettles.

Curving along the shore of the noisy lake was Redstone ville, the high walls made entirely of wood, the exterior bristling with sharp nail points. The buildings inside the wall were in excellent condition, the former mobile homes now permanently anchored with a dense cover of adobe bricks.

Parked just outside the ville was a massive war wag, the armored chassis bristling with rapid-fires. Steel shutters covered the windows and tires, and the spiked roof was frothy with coils of concertina wire, the razor-sharp lengths glistening in the afternoon sun. But much more importantly a tall pole jutted from the top of the war machine, the flag fluttering from the top bearing the very simple design of a circle with a diagonal line cutting through it, the symbol of a non-combatant, a trader.

There were some folding tables and chairs alongside the war wag, and the armed occupants of the formidable transport were doing business with the ragged locals, buying and selling whatever was available: food, black powder, old boots, new leather and the like. Plus, a lot of small items carved out of the local pinewood: rifle stocks, knife handles, belt buckles, hair combs, bowls, spoons, drinking mugs and anything else the locals thought would bring a fair price from travelers coming to drink from the effervescent waters of Tickle Belly Lake.

"And there he is, right on schedule," Petrov said, smiling in frank relief, his arms resting on the handlebars.

"Good thing, too," Charlie stated. "Baron Ronson would never sell us shine again, not after the last time."

"There was nothing wrong with those tampons!" Rose snapped defiantly. "They're perfect for deep bullet wounds."

"True, but I hear she was just a little pissed that we had used most of them already," Thal said with a hard grin.

Rose snorted. "Well, we had to test the merchandise, didn't we?"

"Not all of it, no."

"Hey, buy your own underwear, as the ancients used to say."

"The phrase was 'buyer beware,' and that's why we're only dealing with the trader and not the ville,"

Petrov stated, opening his full canteen to empty it onto
a bush. Screwing the cap back on, he slung it over a
shoulder, then kicked the big twin-V8 engine alive.
"Now, cut the talk and start smiling. Remember, we're
just here for fuel, nothing else matters."

Riding down the bumpy hill, the gang was thankful
when they finally reached smooth grassland. Rolling
along a dirt ground that meandered through the titanic
pine trees, Petrov and the others slowed their speed
when the trader's campsite came into view. Instantly,
the rapid-fires sticking out of the armored hull shifted
directions to track the advance of the four riders. Playing it smooth, the gang rode to the edge of the lake and
filled their canteens again with the fizzy water, being
sure to drink some of the stuff on the spot just like
every other outlander who tramped through the mountain valley.

"Damn bubbles go right up your nose," Thal
growled, trying not to smile at the weird sensation.

"Hence the goofy-ass name of the lake." Rose
laughed, pouring some into a palm to rub the back of
her neck. Her hand jerked at the touch of the hidden
razor blades in the feathers along the collar, and the
woman did her best not to curse out loud. There were
a dozen tiny cuts on her fingers from them already.
Someday, she would love to meet up with that albino
mutie again and rub the razors across his groin in
thanks for his secret gift.

Driving slowly back to the war wag, Petrov and the
others parked their bikes facing the machine to show
they weren't getting ready for a fast escape. The ancient

recipe for rabbit stew came unbidden to his mind: step one—catch a rabbit.

Climbing off the motorcycles, the gang tried to ignore the .50-caliber machine guns following them every step of the way. At first, Petrov began to bridle under the unwanted attention, then the man reasoned it was only prudent. The gang was very heavily armed, and nobody sane, not even a trader, allowed this much artillery to get within shooting range without taking some basic precautions. Attempting to be casual, Petrov glanced upward and saw that the missile pod on the roof was now pointing directly at the bikes. Fair enough. That's exactly what he would have done in their place.

Feeling awkward, the gang joined the queue of ville people and sec men shuffling toward the war wag. At the head of the line were several large tables piled high with assorted items, wood boxes, wicker baskets, canvas bags and lots of glass bottles. Several people were sitting behind the tables, counting items, making a list or working scales. Only one person sat in front of the table, a burly-looking woman with blond hair and a long scar across one cheek. Her clothes were clean, her boots shining with polish, and she carried a small autoblaster in a shoulder holster, plus a massive handblaster on her hip and a bandolier of shells across her chest. Petrov knew that the display of blasters wasn't to frighten the ville people, but to let them know she was a successful trader. Petrov approved. That was smart. Nobody ever wanted to do biz with a pauper.

Standing behind the trader were the real muscle, a couple of crewmen, each cradling a sleek rapid-fire that gleamed with fresh oil, the wooden stocks carefully exposed to show the neat rows of notches in the wood.

"Mutie shit," Rose whispered out of the corner of her mouth.

"Subtlety," Thal corrected softly.

"So, we have a deal, then?" the trader asked, lighting a cig with one hand, the other resting strategically on her gun belt.

Eagerly, the woman nodded and headed over to a wicker basket full of fresh bread, the hot loaves still steaming slightly. A crewman took the basket, and a woman passed over a pair of U.S. Army combat boots.

As the grinning woman walked away, marveling over her new possessions, the trader waved the next person in line closer.

"Morning, son. The name is Rissa, you buying or selling?" she asked around the cig. The words came out in a single breath, as if she said them a thousand times a day.

"I'm Jimmy, and I'm selling," the boy replied, tugging on the reins of an old mule. The animal was almost a swayback from the load of bulging cloth sacks piled on its back.

"What have you got there?" Rissa asked, studying the boy more than the trade goods. The kid was wearing a buckskin shirt and fur pants, clearly homemade and properly tanned. Still in his teens, the boy's face was gaunt from hard work, not starvation. If he was selling food, it was good stuff, and not some mutie plant that'd ace you after two bites.

"Mountain taters," Jimmy stated defiantly, almost as

if it was a challenge. "Hand dug, no rotters or muties. One hundred and nineteen."

"And you hauled 'em all the way down here? Well done, boy," Rissa said, glancing at the mountains on the horizon. Actually, she wasn't very impressed. The trip couldn't have taken more than two days, but part of her job was to establish good relations with the people in this valley. Profit wasn't always the goal of a trade. A friendly ville where a trader could keep her crew warm and safe during a hard winter was often worth more than a ton of brass.

"Whatcha gimme?" Jimmy asked in an explosion of breath.

"You sure it's a hundred and nineteen taters?"

"I kin count," the boy snarled. "And do sums."

"Can you now?" Rissa said, exhaling a long stream of smoke. "Then tell me, how much is four times six?"

"Twenty four," the boy replied instantly.

The guards nodded their heads at the correct answer, and the other people in the line murmured among themselves, clearly impressed.

Rose looked at Charlie and the man shrugged.

"Fair enough." Rissa smiled. "Okay, a hundred and nineteen good taters will get you…a used pair of boots, a plastic poncho that'll hold off the acid rain, a compass and two forks, knives and spoons."

"Make it the boots, a steel knife, the blaster, the poncho and four forks, knives and spoons."

"Boots, knife, blaster, no poncho and three forks, knives and spoons."

"I want that poncho."

"Well, now," Rissa said, taking the cig out of her

mouth to tap off the ash. "You drive a hard bargain, James. But okay. Deal?"

"Deal!"

"Pay the man," the trader directed the crew behind the table.

As the goods were exchanged, Rissa waited politely as a young woman shuffled closer, holding a bundle in her arms. The trader started to repeat her usual spiel when the bundle started crying.

"Please, my baby is sick," the young woman said. "I went to the healer in the ville, and he tried leeches, but—"

"Leeches?" Rissa roared, looking furiously at the nearby ville. Turning, she bellowed at the war wag, *"Daniel, customer!"*

Immediately, there came the sound of running, and a concealed hatch in the chassis slammed open. "What's the problem?" a short man demanded, looking around quickly. He was wearing a long vest covered with tiny pockets that bulged with packets, bottles, twine, knives and other tools of his trade. His shirt was open at the collar, exposing a tattoo on his chest of a red cross and two snakes, the symbols of a healer.

"It's my baby," the woman began again.

Climbing down, the man strode over quickly. "Let me see," Daniel interrupted, folding back the blanket to inspect the crying infant. "Hmm, yes, just a nasty ear infection. Nothing to worry about. I have some meds that'll fix her in a day. Come on inside."

"Yes, of course, the payment first," the mother whispered, loosening the strings holding her tattered dress shut.

"Whoa! None of that now," the trader growled, holding up a palm. "My folks don't charge for healing a child."

That flustered the young mother completely. "But…I mean…that's how the ville healer…"

"Does he now?" Rissa muttered, her eyes narrowing. "Well, I'll go have a little chat with him about that later." *During the night, in the dark, when there are no sec men around to stop me before he loses some teeth,* the trader thought.

Turning toward the mother, her face softened. "Had a baby myself once. Lost her to the black cough. Now, get on inside."

"No," the young woman repeated, hugging the child closer. "I can't. Not for nothing. It's not right."

"Fine." Rissa sighed. "If you can cook, Shirley will be glad of some help in the kitchen. If not, there are always lots of pots and pans to scrub. Deal?"

"Yes, Trader!" she cried in relief, and followed Daniel through the doorway and down a metal corridor.

"Next!" Rissa said, watching them disappear inside the vehicle.

"We need juice for our bikes," Petrov said as a greeting.

Turning slowly, Rissa studied the man. "Juice, eh?" she repeated slowly. "We have some to spare. What do you have for trade?"

Reaching into the munitions bag, Petrov extracted a cloth bundle and laid it on the table. Folding back the cloth, Rissa gasped at the sight of a leather-bound volume, Collier Encyclopedia, volume RE-STO.

"It includes detailed pictures of how to make a steam engine," Petrov said, flipping open the book to that page.

Astonished, Rissa almost dropped the cig as she stared at the full-color illustration. Then Petrov slammed the volume shut again. "A peek is all you get for free," he said.

"Well, I place a high price on books," Rissa said honestly. "You got any more?"

"Nope," Petrov lied. "This is it." The other was going to buy them into the next ville, where they would steal the next load of juice. After that, they would reach the Darks and some real forests. If Petrov never again found sand in his food or clothing, he would die a happy man.

"Pity," Rissa muttered, trying to hide her disappointment. Her gut instincts told her not to trust this man, but…a book! An entire book! That was worth risking a little gas for any fragging day. "Okay, that will fill all of your tanks. Real gas, too, not coal-oil mixed with shine. You savvy mileage?"

"Sure."

"Good. Well, my gas will double what any shine mix gives you in those hogs."

"Not enough," Petrov said, crossing his arms. "Fill the tanks, and twenty extra gallons."

"For one book? No deal."

"Ten gallons."

"No."

"All right, I have a second book," Petrov growled, placing the other volume on the table.

"Thought you might," Rissa said drily, lifting the book for a brief inspection.

Holy crap, it was a dictionary! Rissa thought. She had only heard about those before!

"Hmm, this one isn't from an encyclopedia," Rissa said, trying to act casual. "And no pictures, huh? Well, a book is a book. Okay, full tanks, fifty extra gallons and two quarts of oil."

"Three quarts. Deal?"

"Deal," Rissa said with a nod. "Pay the man."

The exchange was made, and a couple of crewmen came out lugging ten-gallon canisters that sloshed with every step.

While the fuel tanks of the bike were filled, Rissa had the two books escorted into the war wag under armed guard and securely locked in her private safe. A scribe could start copying the books tomorrow, but tonight she would read them herself as a special treat.

"I wonder where they got them, Chief," a crewman asked softly, watching the outlanders check over their bikes. "Then again, where did they get any of that stuff? Bikes, a rad counter, rapid-fires…" He frowned. "Think they jacked a trader?"

"Maybe," Rissa said, tugging thoughtfully on an ear. "I haven't heard of anybody we know who recently went missing, but these things do happen."

The crewman grunted in agreement, then asked, "What are those things the guy with the beard is wearing? I've never seen anything like that before."

"They're called glasses," Rissa said, and the word unexpectedly triggered a flood of memories from a while back when she had been working for another trader called Roberto. A bunch of outlanders had saved his life, and one of them had glasses very similar to what this man was wearing.

Suddenly, the woman felt galvanized, as if hit by lightning. Shitfire, these folks had the exact same style bolt-action longblaster, SIG handblaster, Uzi rapid-fire, hammerless wheelgun, fedora, camouflage jacket with feathers and bits of metal, munitions bag, bearskin coat...

That raised the ugly question of how they got all of these things. One or two items might have been used to pay off a debt, but not fragging everything! Especially the glasses. If Rissa remembered correctly, the gunsmith who traveled with Ryan had been damn near blind without those. Which means these outlanders either aced Ryan and his people, or else found them chilled and looted the bodies. Ryan meant nothing to Rissa, but he did to Roberto, and that was good enough.

Dismissing the rest of the lineup with a wave, Rissa waited until the disappointed ville people were heading back to the front gate of the ville, before calling over one of the guards.

"Triple red, close the door," Rissa said, scratching her belly to move a hand closer to her blaster.

The crewman blinked in confusion for only a moment, then nodded and strolled away to climb into the war wag, pull the heavy door shut and lock it securely.

At the loud clang, the Pig Iron Gang looked up, but never stopped their work.

"Damn, you're right," Rose said, checking the oil in

her bike. "That bitch is watching us like a stingwing does a fresh chill."

"Told ya," Charlie whispered. "I think she recognizes these hogs as belonging to Big Joe and wants them for herself."

"What should we do, Chief?" Thal asked, screwing on the cap to the gas tank.

"Gimme a tick," Petrov muttered, kneeling to pretend that he was checking the tension on the chain.

As her crew began packing away the trade goods, Rissa started ambling over to the coldhearts. "Nice bikes," Rissa said with a smile. "Where did you find them?"

Snarling in response, Petrov turned with a gren in his hands, the arming lever tumbling away. "Run!" he yelled, pulling the pin and throwing the explosive charge at the woman.

As Rissa dived out of the way, a brace of rapid-fires chattered into life from the front of the war wag, the streams of high-velocity lead chewing a double line of destruction across the ground and heading straight for the motorcycles, a strange musical chime sounded. Instantly, there was a blinding flash of light and a powerful wind buffeted the gang, almost knocking them over.

A split second later, the wind died away, and Petrov looked about in confusion. What the hell kind of gren was that? Explosions pushed things away, not pulled them closer! Then the man noticed that the war wag was gone. Or rather, most of it had vanished; only the front grille and a single tire remained on the ground alongside a wide depression in the soil. The hole was a perfect circle, the sides mirror bright, and at the bottom was a small lump that resembled a chunk of old lava. There was no other sign of the armored transport, or any of the crew, aside from a hand tottering on the rim of the crater.

"What the frag just happened?" Charlie demanded, adjusting his glasses with one hand, the other brandishing the Czech ZKR. "Where did everybody go?" In the distance, the ville people were pelting madly toward the ville gate. On the wall, the sec men were waving them to run faster. Somewhere, an alarm bell started to clang.

"Nuked if I know," Thal said, walking to the edge of the depression and picking up the hand. The flesh was still warm, the fingers twitching slightly. Tossing the grisly object over a shoulder, Thal kicked some loose nettles into the depression just to see what would happen. They scattered across the hole like green snowflakes to sprinkle down across the odd lump of material situated exactly in the middle of the half sphere.

"I think that lump is them," Thal said hesitantly. "The war wag and the crew."

"What?" Charlie scoffed. "Impossible!"

"Then you tell us what the hell just happened," Rose said, looking around the area, the Uzi tight in her grip. "There was a flash of light, and a fifty-ton wag vanishes, just like that."

"Mebbe we fell asleep," Charlie muttered uncertainly, turning as if half expecting to see the war wag charging through the forest. "Or mebbe we—"

"An implo gren," Petrov interrupted, his face alive

with excitement. "Blind NORAD, that must have been a mutie-loving implo gren!"

"But those aren't real," Thal muttered hesitantly. "There's no such thing as a…an implosion." He stumbled over the tech word.

"Until this moment, I always thought so, too, but now…" Petrov left the sentence hanging. Slowly, the man holstered the SIG-Sauer. He could see the footprints in the grass leading to the edge of the depression, and then they stopped. Wildly, he wondered if the lump at the bottom of the hole was all that remained of the war wag and its crew. Dimly, he recalled his father talking about implo grens and how they created a microsecond gravity vortex. That was tech talk for a reverse explosion, an implosion. Apparently, there had been an exhibit of the grens in the museum, weapons of the future, that sort of thing. Only now it seemed that they were very much real. The man felt giddy at the idea, almost drunk. This had to have been what it was like to nuke a city. Power. The raw power of a god held tight in the palm of your hand.

"Got any more?" Rose asked excitedly, licking her lips. "We could take over a ville and make ourselves barons with only a couple of those things! Or trade it for a war wag."

"Nope, that seems to have been the only one," Petrov told her, carefully checking inside the munitions bag.

"I know where we can get more," Charlie said, tugging thoughtfully on his beard. "Those folks we jacked gotta know where they got it. There could be more. Lots more!"

"Mutie shit." Petrov snorted. "If there were any more, don't you think they'd be carrying them?"

"And those slavers must be on the other side of the Missy Sip by now," Rose added, slinging the Uzi.

"But—"

"Which changes nothing," Petrov stated, climbing onto the hog and kicking the bike into life. "We stick to the plan. Ride to Deepwater, jack more fuel, then set up base in the ruins outside of Modine."

"After that, we lay out traps for travelers and start selling prisoners to the East Coast slavers," Rose finished, starting her own bike. "Then it's the easy life for the rest of our lives!"

"We have the blasters, the hogs and the moss," Thal said, patting a bag on his chugging hog. "Those are real, my friend. Let your desire to become a baron pass. Mortal man may dream of flight, but feet alone carry him to the stars!" Twisting the throttle, he felt the engine sputter for a few moments, then it settled down into a powerful purr. It seemed that the lady trader had dealt with them fair and square. The fuel was working smoother than the bore of a new blaster.

Sullenly, Charlie nodded his agreement. But as he rode away with the others, his gaze kept drifting back toward the western mountains, his private thoughts on a distant ville and a certain female baron kneeling at his feet, stripped to the waist and begging for her life....

Chapter Ten

In the garage, the companions found a van parked in the middle of the garage, surrounded by a score of civilian wags in various states of repair or disassembly—it was hard to tell. A ramp led to a wooden door that was in pitiful condition. It looked as if somebody had blasted their way out of the garage and the bonemen had clumsily tried to nail the broken planks back together.

"How did these people ever manage to repair military weapons?" Krysty asked scornfully.

"Big Joe must have done all of the gunsmithing," Ryan replied. "A good way to stay in power is to make yourself absolutely vital."

She scowled. "But if he got chilled without passing on that knowledge, his men would be helpless."

"I guess he didn't care." The man shrugged.

The cargo van proved to be too small to carry the entire inventory of the Boneyard, so the companions concentrated on taking the best of the brass, along with several dozen blasters and a crate of assorted rapid-fires. The spare tires were strapped to the outside of the wag, along with some leather skins of clean water and a bag of the dried moss. Mildred had great plans for the material, that was, if she could dilute it down to a more usable potency.

Unfortunately, the medical supplies in the bomb

shelter were so old they were completely useless, and it seemed that the bonemen relied upon raw shine for most of their medicinal needs. Mildred was sorely disappointed, but understood the thinking behind the decision. For people who held human life in such low esteem, preserving it wouldn't be a high priority, not even their own.

"Pity about the Napoleon." Doc sighed, mopping the back of his neck with a cloth. "But without any roads, the carriage would break in pieces after the first mile or so."

"Cannonballs," Jak added with meaning, the single word saying volumes.

Once the vehicles were fully fueled, double-checked and ready to go, Ryan and Krysty climbed onto the Harleys and kicked the bikes alive. The sidecars were packed with barrels of spare brass and the hand-operated Gatling Gun. That alone should buy them anything needed at the ville. Or help them get out again, in case Dunbar was lying.

Climbing into the saddles of a couple of horses, Jak and Doc checked the ropes tethering the other animals to follow along behind. The packhorses were piled high with boxes of trade goods, kegs of black powder, tools, bundles of books and extra cans of fuel. There were also a couple of bags of smoked fish taken from the kitchen of the Boneyard, the exact same kind of fish carried by the slavers.

Getting behind the wheel of the van, Mildred started the engine and let it idle for a few minutes to warm while J.B. finished jury-rigging the rad counter from the bomb shelter to the cig lighter in the dashboard.

"You sure that's going to work?" the physician asked just a moment before the dials brightened and the speaker began to softly click.

"You say something, babe?" he asked, getting into the passenger seat.

"Not a thing, John," she replied, trying not to grin.

"Is that really a rad counter?" Dunbar asked from the rear of the van.

"A rad counter? Bet your ass," J.B. replied, cradling the Atchisson. As the gunner for the van, the man needed something with range, and the devastating power of the Atchisson offered that in spades.

Driving the hogs up the ramp, Ryan and Krysty waited outside for the other companions to join them before circling around the boulevard and then heading due north, toward a banyan tree with a hangman's noose dangling off a high branch.

"It's a pity that Big Joe didn't own a compass," Mildred said, the cargo van shaking as it rolled over the carpeting of roots.

"We'll get mine back soon enough," J.B. growled, squinting at the thick canopy of tress for any suspicious movements. For the time being, his plan was to shoot first and ask questions later. Spend the brass and save your ass. Wise words from the Trader, indeed.

"What's a compass?" Dunbar asked curiously, holding on to a ceiling stanchion.

As the man and woman attempted to explain about the invisible magnetic field surrounding the planet, the convoy left the jungle behind and was soon deep in a proper forest of pine trees, oak and dogwood. The predark ruins were soon left behind.

WITH DUNBAR GIVING directions, Mildred drove the
cargo van out of the ruins and soon the companions
were crossing a rolling field of miniature wheat, the
tufted shafts only reaching a yard high.

"Perfect for minimuffins and doughnut holes," Mildred said, chuckling.

"What was that?" J.B. asked, tilting his head.

"Nothing." She sighed, shifting gears. "Forget I said
anything."

"Now, be careful out here," Dunbar said, leaning
forward on the crate. "There's something in this area
that chills folks. It looks like rad poisoning, hair and
teeth falling out, shitting blood and the likes, only there
aren't any glowing rad craters around here."

Just then, the rad counter started to wildly click. Immediately, Mildred steered to the left and the clicking
soon dropped back to normal levels, only a click or two
every minute.

"Must have been an airblast," J.B. said, reaching up
to adjust his missing glasses for the hundredth time.
Angrily, the man shoved his hand into a pocket. "There
would be no crater that you could see… No, wait, look
there!" Then he pointed at a heavily corroded pile of
metal dominating the middle of the wheat field. There
were no plants of any kind growing near the rusting
machinery, which made it that much easier to see the
general outline of what had once been a sleek war
machine.

"There's your rad pit," J.B. said confidently. "A submarine. A crashed predark sub."

"In the middle of Utah?" Mildred asked, glancing
sideways to arch an eyebrow.

The man shrugged. "Seen it before with a bridge, so why not a sub? It must have been thrown into the air by an underwater nuke, mebbe one of the big jobs that busted apart California. Eventually, the sub landed here, and the reactor core split open from the impact."

"But it doesn't glow," Dunbar said accusingly, as if trying to trap them in a lie.

"The low-level stuff doesn't, not enough for you to see, anyway," J.B. said. "But the reactor slugs will still ace your ass if you stop there for a nap, or even to get out of the rain."

"Just a few minutes, and you're a corpse looking for a grave," Mildred added grimly, steering around a tree stump that appeared out of the waving wheat as unexpectedly as an iceberg in the middle of the ocean.

"So, never touch metal that has no plants growing nearby," the teenager said, watching the crumpled wad of machinery disappear behind. "Once again, I am in your debt. I wish my ville could offer something that you needed. New clothing, perhaps? Although, I freely admit we don't have enough to even dent what I owe you."

"Well, I'd love a hot bath." Mildred sighed. Ever since their impromptu sojourn through the storm drain, there had been a noticeable reek coming from her ratty moccasins, and even stuffing in some fresh kudzu leaves hadn't really helped kill the smell.

"A hot bath," Dunbar said slowly, as if he had never heard the two words combined before. Then he smiled. "If that is your wish, consider it done!"

"Just tell us where to find Petrov and we're even," J.B. growled, hunching lower in the seat.

Slowly, the day progressed, and Dunbar sent the companions zigzagging across the landscape to avoid quicksand, an underground warren of muties or some oak trees supposedly infested with flapjacks.

"Aside from the wheat field, you really know this valley," Mildred said, braking slightly to avoid a billboard sticking crazily out of the ground, its vaunted message long gone to the cruel winds of implacable time.

"Over the past three years, I have walked home many times in my dreams," Dunbar replied wistfully. Then he pointed straight ahead. "There it is, the Whitewater River!"

Looking about, Mildred couldn't find what the teen was talking about. Then there came a flash of blue among the trees, and suddenly she was driving along a wide river. Countless limestone boulders rose from the wild foaming currents, and both of the muddy banks were thick with reeds.

"I can see why you folks don't use boats," J.B. stated. "That river would smash anything into kindling."

"Good fishing, though," Dunbar said proudly. "Trout, catfish and hardly any muties."

In a sputtering roar, Ryan drove up alongside the van. "There's farmland just over the next rise," he shouted through the window. "That belong to Delta?"

"Means we're close!" Dunbar yelled back. "Better slow down or they'll think we're a raiding party and come out blasting!"

Sagely, Ryan nodded in agreement, then angled away on the bike to tell the other companions.

Reducing the speed of the van, Mildred breathed

a sigh of relief as it became much easier to steer the rattling wag along the rough dirt road. There were so many potholes, rocks and rain-wash gullies that she had been worried about the center-support bearing for the drive shaft. It had clearly been repaired numerous times over the years, and if it broke, they would lose the drive shaft completely. With no possible way to fix the van, they would be forced to set it on fire and destroy the stockpile of blasters to keep them from falling into the hands of coldhearts, or worse, more slavers. The companions had chilled a lot of the bastards, but slavers were like cockroaches; there were always a few more of them hiding just out of sight in the dark.

In less than a mile, the companions were driving past waving fields of corn and barley, wooden stockades set among the rows of plants raised off the ground to protect the farmers from the night hunters. But as the farms dropped behind the convoy, the rich loam slowly thinned into bare ground, and small patches of salt could be seen scattered among the rocks.

"Dark night, we're heading back into the nuking desert," J.B. muttered, trying to see into the distance.

"Nope, there she is, Delta ville!" Dunbar cried out, his face flushed with excitement.

Located at the junction of two rivers, the ville stood on a slab of bedrock that extended slightly over the river, offering a natural dock. Dozens of fishing nets hung into the rushing water, and a cluster of wooden racks stood nearby, the day's catch drying in the sun and salty breeze.

Reaching an easy eight feet high, the ville wall was made entirely of irregularly shaped fieldstones, the concrete fill sparking with jagged chunks of broken glass embedded to deter climbers. The front gate was made of heavy wooden beams banded together with heavy chains and studded with sharp iron spikes. The sandy ground around Delta had been leveled for nearly a thousand paces, every rock removed and pothole filled, so that there was no place for an enemy to hide. A score of sec men walked along the top of the wall, a few of them working the bolts on their longblasters, while others were running about shouting. One big man was beating a large circle of metal with a blacksmith hammer.

Heading directly for the front gate, Mildred eased to a stop about a hundred yards away, just out of crossbow range, then waited for the rest of the companions to gather around before turning off the engine. Softly, they could hear the alarm bell clanging and a lot of raised voices.

"I hope they still recognize you," Ryan said, resting his arms on the handlebars of the motorcycle. "Three years is a long time."

"They'll know me," Dunbar stated confidently. "But I better get out and walk from here. The sooner they see me, the less chance of some newbie getting nervous, putting a rocket into this wag and blowing us all to hell."

Suddenly, a squad of sec men appeared on the wall armed with what appeared to be a homemade bazooka.

"That work?" Jak asked with a scowl, the reins to his horse tight in a fist. The other horses shifted their hoofs into the sandy earth, snorting their displeasure over the lack of green grass.

"Does it work? Sure. How else do you think we kept Big Joe away?" Dunbar replied, sliding off the crate.

Stepping from the van, Dunbar smiled at the ville like a starving man would a banquet. "Home," he whispered softly, the word almost lost in the gentle murmur of the wind.

Just then, a wooden beam swung up from the top of the ville wall and a rope ladder was unfurled. A lone sec man climbed down the knotted length and strode over to the companions. The man was wearing a tan uniform and snakeskin boots, beautiful and tough. He wore a gun belt without a holster, the loops full of brass going all the way around, and a longblaster was strapped across his back, a double-barrel scattergun. It was perfect for chilling folks up close, but useless for attacking the wall.

Turning off the bike, Ryan almost smiled. This was clearly a seasoned sec man, tougher than a boiled boot and smoother than winter ice.

"Greetings," the sec man said, stopping a few yards away. "That's quite a little convoy you folks got."

"It got us here," Ryan said with a shrug. "This Delta?"

"The one and only…" His voice faded away as the sec man saw the teenager. He blinked a few times and grinned widely. "My lord!" the sec man cried in delight. "We never thought to see you again!"

"It is good to be home, Sergeant Fenton," Dunbar said with a curt nod. "You seem well. How is the ville, any problems?"

The abrupt shift in the teenager's demeanor didn't go unnoticed by the companions. Dunbar was friendly enough talking to them, but he addressed the sec man with the voice of authority.

"Nothing of importance, sir," the sergeant said, rubbing the back of his neck, fingers less than an inch away from the scattergun. "And who are these good folks, sir? Fellow escaped prisoners?"

"Just some outlanders passing through," Ryan said, crossing his arms, a hand touching the checkered grip of his handblaster. "We tangled with Big Joe and brought Dunbar here for a reward."

"That so, my lord?" Fenton asked, looking hard at the teenager.

"The spring was too wet this year for a good crop of corn," Dunbar said formally.

With that, the sergeant visibly relaxed and turned to wave at the other sec men on the wall. "Spring corn!" he yelled through cupped hands, and the guards lowered their weapons.

Surprised, the companions exchanged glances. Coded phrases? Triple-smart. Whoever ruled the ville clearly knew what they were doing.

Turning, Fenton started back to the ville. "So, how did you folks escape from the Boneyard?" he asked, slowing his pace to match that of the others. "The place burn down, or did you sneak a wad of that fragging moss into his shine?"

"We attack, ace everybody," Jak said simply, his hands crossed on the pommel of the saddle.

"Right...you use a nuke, or just stare 'em to death?" Fenton chuckled.

In reply, Jak merely shrugged, feeling no great need to convince the other man of the truth.

"No, that's what actually happened," Dunbar stated forcibly. "They took out Big Joe and his whole crew." He started to mention the cargo of blasters and brass, but at a glance from Doc, the teenager changed his mind. The weapons belonged to these folks now, fair and square, and thus were really not the business of his ville. If his mother wanted some, she would have to barter for them just like anybody else.

"Well, nuke me running! Big Joe is on the last train?" Fenton laughed. "Shitfire, what are you, part wendigo?"

"Are those creatures real, sir?" Doc rumbled. "Or just a local myth you use to scare Big Joe and the slavers?"

"Ask them," the sergeant muttered, jerking a thumb toward a large patch of sand lined with hundreds of low mounds of dark earth.

Shocked at the proximity of a graveyard to the ville, Mildred started to ask why the graves were across the river, but then realized the common sense of the matter. It wasn't sanitary to bury decomposing corpses inside the wall near the fresh water supply, and if interred too far away, the local animals would only dig up the bodies for food. In the Deathlands, sometimes even the dead needed protection.

As the sergeant and Dunbar stopped before the massive gate, Mildred braked the van to a halt right alongside, the rest of the companions clustering behind. Just in case of trouble, the first thing the locals would encounter would be J.B. and the Atchisson. The ammo drum was only half-full, but the autoblaster could discharge all fifteen of the remaining shotgun cartridges in only a few seconds. Anybody left standing after that thundering maelstrom of hot lead would be easy pickings.

Softly, there came the sound of a gasoline engine from inside the ville, and slowly the imposing barrier rumbled aside to reveal tracks set deep into the bedrock. A dozen sec men were waiting for them, armed with blasters and crossbows.

"At ease, ya gleebs!" the sergeant gruffly commanded. "These outlanders have aced Big Joe and brought back Lord Dunbar alive and well!"

"Son of a bitch, it is Dunbar!" a sec woman gasped, lowering her scattergun. "Three cheers for the outlanders!"

As Dunbar strode into the ville, the guards quickly holstered their weapons and began to wildly cheer. Driving along after the teenager and sergeant, Mildred tried to keep a safe distance from them without falling too far behind. Once before the companions had been hailed as the conquering heroes at a ville, and the next day they were imprisoned in a torture chamber run by an insane eunuch who specialized in skinning people alive.

"We spot any fat bastards holding pliers, and I'm taking him out purely as a precaution," J.B. said.

"Most wise," Doc agreed, trying not to scratch under his shirt. The bandages around his chest had been washed daily, but lacking Mildred's usual collection of ointments and tinctures, the wound was slow to heal and itched like crazy.

Behind the companions, the gasoline engine started again, and the heavy portal cycled back into place.

Burly sec men used sledgehammers to drive home massive steel bolts and firmly lock the gate closed.

"If we want out of here fast, that's going to be a problem," Krysty murmured over the sputtering engine of the motorcycle.

"More for them than us," Ryan replied, forcing himself not to glance at the sheet of patched canvas covering the Gatling gun nestled in the sidecar.

It was an ordinary enough ville, the huts, shacks, homes and buildings constructed of anything available, a wild mix of adobe bricks, wooden planks, cinder blocks and occasionally even some aluminum siding. There were very few glass windows, but a lot of wooden shutters, and every roof was covered by sheet metal or plastic sheeting to keep out the acid rain. The entire ville seemed old and worn, but everything was clean, which was a pleasant change from most of the villes the companions visited.

The alarm bell had stopped clanging, and the air was redolent with the aromas of wood smoke, baking bread, uncured leather, boiling laundry, tobacco and horse dung—the smells of civilization. The street itself was smooth bedrock, the dense granite only slightly scuffed from generations of shuffling feet.

Through the gaps between the larger structures, Ryan kept getting glimpses of a squat stone building in the distance. He recognized the structure as a former National Guard Armory and naturally assumed that was the home of the local baron. After skydark, a lot of villes had formed around the fortified buildings as they were designed to keep out rioting mobs and came fully stocked with food, medicine, wags, fuel and most important of all, military blasters. The supplies would be used up by now, but the buildings remained.

Within minutes, word spread through the ville, and soon a jubilant crowd lined the street. Some of the people were only half-dressed, as if rudely woken from sleep. Wearing a bloody apron, a large man was brandishing a hatchet and the dismembered leg of a pig. Resembling a ghost, a small woman was covered with flour, a small child hiding behind her skirts. A wrinklie was smoking a corncob pipe, and a sec man stood with a razor in his hand, half of his face covered with foamy soap. In the sea of happy faces were young and old, healthy and sick, sec men and ville people, but everybody whooped at the sight of Dunbar as if he had risen from the grave, the only person in history to ever hop off the last train west.

"Never before have we been so royally welcomed," Doc muttered, feeling like a triumphant caesar returning from his victory in Ethiopia.

"Smiles not make 'em friends," Jak replied, nudging his horse with his knees to keep it moving. The animal didn't seem to like the noise and attention, and the teen was beginning to agree. He could feel something wrong in the ville; not a trap exactly—it was more like the calm acceptance of an unpleasant fact. Unwanted, but inevitable. Slipping a hand inside his deerskin jacket, the teen loosened his blaster in his shoulder holster.

Moving along the main street, Dunbar, the companions, cargo van, bikes and horses made a nice little parade, with a constant cry of "spring corn" heralding their advance. However, Ryan began to notice a few somber faces among the passing crowd. It was mostly the older people. They didn't seem angry, but sad, and many of them turned away to avoid looking at Dunbar as the teen strode past.

Situated on a corner was a large tavern, the second-floor balcony lined with gaudy sluts, one hand held demurely over their cleavage, the other steadily waving. But once the parade was past, the women sagged as if aging years in a moment and scuffled back inside to close the doors and bring down the shutters.

"Nice ville, eh, Alberta?" Ryan asked.

"Sure thing, Adam," Krysty replied calmly, letting him know that she had also picked up on the bad vibes. But it wasn't necessary. Her hair was slowly moving into tight curls as preparation for battle.

Reaching the center of the ville, Dunbar paused as the crowd parted to reveal a boy just into his teens. He was wearing a uniform very similar to the sec men, but of much better quality and scrupulously clean. The boy wore a blaster on his hip and was surrounded by a cadre of armed sec men, their faces as immobile as the bedrock under the ville. At the sight of them, Ryan and Krysty eased to a stop and turned off their engines. A few seconds later, the van arrived and Mildred did the same.

"Brother!" Dunbar cried, and started to rush forward, when the sec men closed protectively around the boy. "What are you doing? What's wrong?"

"Please keep your distance, sir," Fenton advised, holding up a restraining hand. "Things have changed since you were taken prisoner."

"Don't be a feeb!" Dunbar snarled. "I am the older

brother, I will be baron someday! Edgar, don't you recognize me anymore?"

"Sir?" the sergeant asked, his voice strained.

"Let him pass," the boy ordered, and the guards reluctantly parted.

Starting to walk forward, Dunbar stopped and looked upon his younger brother anew. He had never heard such command in his voice before, and Eddie was much taller than the teen recalled, more muscular. There were cuts on his face as if Eddie…Edgar was shaving these days, and that wild mane of long hair that not even their mother could get the stubborn boy to trim was now only a military buzz.

"It is good to see you again, brother," Edgar stated, placing both hands behind his back. "But after living with the bonemen for three years, my guards are naturally a little uneasy about having you rush toward me followed by a group of armed outlanders."

A low murmur swept through the crowd at that, and the companions forced themselves to not reach for a blaster. Six against fifty were bad odds, even with their new weapons. Besides, something important was happening, but they didn't know what it was yet or who to support. But there was a definite feel of blood in the air, the calm before the storm.

"Outlanders? Edgar, these are the people who rescued me and aced Big Joe!" Dunbar snapped, getting a sinking feeling in his stomach. "Brother, where…where is the baron?"

"Our mother died two winters ago from the black cough," Edgar said in a gentle tone, then the iron returned to his demeanor. "Two winters! You were gone, and the ville needed somebody to be in charge, so I assumed command."

Still straddling the motorcycle, Ryan didn't move or make a sound at the pronouncement. But Krysty mentally fought to keep her hair under control. This was why some of the ville people had looked so tense! Two brothers, one throne, it was a classic formula for disaster.

Unfortunately, standing in the open like this, there was very little that Krysty and the others could do at the moment. She and Doc each had a rapid-fire, but tucked into the gun boot of her bike and his horse, the weapons might as well be on the moon for all the good they offered. If the blood hit the fan, everything would depend upon J.B. and the Atchisson.

Sitting behind the wheel of the van, Mildred did something with her hands out of sight below the window, and J.B. gently thumbed off the safety of the deadly autoblaster.

"Two winters…?" Dunbar whispered, looking toward the royal castle. "Is she buried outside the wall?"

"Safely burned, like every baron before her. The ashes thrown to the solstice winds."

"Thank heavens for that," Dunbar said in relief.

"No, thank me!" Edgar snarled, advancing close to look up at his brother. His voice was thin, but held the iron ring of authority. "It was done on my command. I am the baron here, not you. Make no mistake about that!"

"But I am the elder brother," Dunbar declared, a hand going to his hip where a blaster should have been holstered. His fingers touched only cloth, and frustration fueled his rage. "I am the elder brother!"

"Is that a challenge for the throne?" Edgar asked softly.

Was it? Suddenly, Dunbar realized what a challenge would mean: it might split the ville apart, create yet another civil war like the one that had claimed his father and left his mother to rule the ville alone. He had always been assigned the role of heir to the throne, but did the teenager even want the authority? That simple question had never been asked before. His mind swirled with conflicting emotions, and Dunbar struggled to find a moment of clarity somewhere between truth and duty.

"There is no challenge. I obey my liege lord in all things," Dunbar said in the ritual oath of allegiance, kneeling before his brother and bowing his head. "Through fire and blood, I stand on the wall and serve the Rock. All hail Baron Edgar Cranston!"

A palpable silence filled the ville, and even the desert breeze seemed to stand still. Nothing moved, and nobody spoke. Their muscles tightening, the companions braced for combat.

Then the uniformed boy stepped forward to rest a hand on his brother's shoulder. "Rise, Lord Dunbar, chief sec man of Delta ville!" the baron commanded.

Just for a split second, the companions thought a bomb had exploded when the mixed crowd of sec men and ville people roared their approval. The noise was deafening, and several minutes passed before anybody could even hope of being heard.

"Thank you, my lord!" Dunbar replied, standing to give an awkward salute. It was his first.

"Sorry about the demotion back to sergeant," Baron Cranston said, making a conciliatory gesture. "But my brother is of royal blood."

"Not a problem, Baron," Fenton said with a rueful smile. "I kind of guessed that would happen when I saw the young lord alive at the front gate."

"You were the chief? But you said nothing when I called you sergeant," Dunbar said accusingly.

"Yeah, hadn't heard that in years." The man chuckled, hitching up his gun belt. "Damn near made me drop the brass about everything. But it only seemed proper that the bad news about the baron should come from kin." He shrugged. "So I lied."

"Balls on the wall are brass in a blaster," Dunbar said, quoting his father. "Baron, do I have your permission to make this man a lieutenant and my second in command?" He grinned. "I will need his help. After being gone for so many years, I don't even know where the sec men hide their secret stash of predark shine anymore."

That caused a ripple of smiles from the guards, and their postures became more relaxed. In the van, Mildred rested her hands on the steering wheel again, and J.B. subtly moved his thumb.

"It's under the last bunk on the second floor of the barracks," Baron Cranston said blandly. "Good stuff. I've had some when nobody was around."

The armed sec men gawked at the frank admission, then broke into nervous laughter.

"Yes, we know, sir. I've been watering it for years

until you were older," Fenton added. "Didn't want to stunt your growth. Some of that stuff would knock the nuts off a tank."

"As I very well recall," the baron muttered, touching a scar on his forehead, a souvenir from his first bottle of the ancient shine called brandy. "Very well, Sec Chief Dunbar, your request is granted."

"Thank you, Baron!"

"Damn, an officer at last," Fenton said, rubbing the back of his neck. "Thank you, my liege."

"Up a stripe, down a stripe," a sec woman said from amid the ranks.

"Oh, shut up, Lucille," Fenton ordered, but not very harshly. The woman grinned in reply, but went still. She would congratulate the man properly later on in their bed.

"I'll want an untouched bottle of that brandy for our dinner tonight to celebrate the return of my brother," the baron stated. "But for now, Chief, tell me about these people." The boy turned to face the companions. "Was there a revolt among the bonemen, or are these sec men from another ville?" The group had the look of coldhearts, or mercies, at the very least, and from the number of blasters on display, they were very good at the work.

Briefly, Dunbar described the events of the previous day. The crowd was delighted at first over the chilling of Big Joe, but their faces grew dark when the new sec chief told about the circumstances of Ryan and the others.

"That's mutie shit," a sec man growled. "Petrov and his gang would never deal with slavers."

"Didn't say they did," Ryan corrected. "They jacked our blasters at the waterfall, then left us for Big Joe to sell."

"You see 'em jack the iron?" someone demanded hotly.

Clearly annoyed, Krysty frowned. "We were unconscious."

"Then how do you know they did?" a sec woman asked defiantly.

"Big Joe said they did," Ryan replied calmly. Raised to be a baron, the man knew that a crowd had a mind of its own, and once it started moving, there was no way to stop it short of bloodshed, with the companions smack in the middle. If six versus fifty were bad odds for a fight, then six against a thousand was nuking suicide.

"Only a feeb believes a coldheart," a woman muttered, and a sec man spat on the ground.

"More likely Petrov stole those blasters from Big Joe, and these folks just want them for themselves!" a gaudy slut added, both hands on her hips. "I'm seeing lots of iron, but who says there's any brass in it, eh? That's what these bastards are after. Brass!"

"Don't give them any, Baron!" a man shouted from the rear of the murmuring crowd.

Knowing the cargo van was jammed full of spare rounds, Dunbar rallied. "I was there and saw Petrov and the others hit Big Joe. They never tried to set me free."

"Mebbe they didn't know who you were," a fisherman offered, scratching under his hat. "It has been years, sir."

"They knew," Sec Chief Dunbar stated. "I told them."

"They coldhearts, that fact," Jak stated gruffly.

"Well, they never jacked anybody in this ville!" a sec woman declared. "Shitfire, they helped defend Delta when those muties attacked last spring!"

"When the healer was sick, Rose delivered our first baby," a woman added, sounding oddly proud of the fact.

"And that big Thal fellow helped me patch my roof when the acid rains came early," a wrinklie added, angrily waving a cane. "Won't take nothing in payment but some dinner!"

"Petrov knifed that outlander who raped the basket-weaver!"

"Their credit is good at my bar!" McGinty shouted, the big barkeep staring with open hatred at the companions.

"Fucking outlander scum!" someone yelled, advancing a step. An angry mob of a dozen more people was close behind. One of them pulled a knife, another raised a hatchet, then a blaster.

Instantly, the companions swung up their weapons and aimed, fingers tight on the triggers, waiting for the first wave to charge. Inside the van, J.B. leveled the Atchisson, and Mildred worked the arming bolt on the Ingram MAC-10.

Quickly, the sec men closed ranks around the baron.

"Fenton!" Baron Cranston yelled, his thin voice cutting through the general chorus of angry growls and cursing.

Drawing his sawed-off blaster, Fenton fired both barrels into the sky. As the double booms echoed across the ville square, the crowd stopped moving, the heated rush neutralized as fast as it had started.

"Sec Chief Dunbar, the next person who threatens these outlanders goes to the wall post!" the baron yelled furiously. "Fifty lashes, man, woman or child!"

"But Baron..." a wrinklie started, lowering his homemade zipgun.

"My sec chief gave his word to these people they would have safe passage!" the boy snarled, radiating an adult fury. "And his word is law! My law!"

Lowering their weapons, the crowd shifted uneasily under the stare of the young baron. The companions didn't speak or move; the sec men did nothing. Then Dunbar reached out a hand, and Fenton slapped the re-loaded sawed-off into his waiting palm.

"Go home. We'll sort this all out tomorrow," Dunbar commanded gently, opening the breech to check the condition of the 12-gauge cartridges. With a jerk of the wrist, he snapped the blaster shut. "Or do you really want to spend the rest of the night cleaning your own guts off the street?"

"McGinty!" Fenton yelled. "The baron wants to buy the entire ville a drink to celebrate the return of his brother! You got enough shine?"

"Shine and beer," the barkeep amended, tucking a blaster back under his stained apron.

"Good enough." The lieutenant grinned amiably. "Everybody, drinks for free tonight!"

"All hail Sec Chief Dunbar!" Lucille shouted from the ranks.

Mumbling assent, the confused crowd began to thin,

everybody heading in different directions, none of them toward Heaven.

"Yeah, I thought the offer of free shine would make them too embarrassed to go to the tavern," Fenton stated, allowing himself to exhale. "Nobody will be getting drunk tonight and doing something stupe. The carrot and the stick, my grandy used to call it."

"My thanks for the loan," Dunbar stated, extending the blaster.

"Keep it, sir," Fenton said, unbuckling his gun belt and passing it over. "A sec chief can't walk around naked."

"Again, my thanks."

"As for you folks," Baron Cranston began, addressing the companions. "Have dinner with me at the castle. Nobody will bother your wags and horses there. You can leave in the morning."

"First thing in the morning," Fenton corrected.

"Be even better if we leave now," Ryan said, sliding the Marlin back into the gun boot of the motorcycle.

"Out of sight, out of mind, sir," Doc added, doing the same with the M-16 rapid-fire.

"Agreed," the baron said. "I know my people, and this isn't over yet. Fenton, take a squad and bring these folks food and water, enough for thirty days."

"And fuel for the wags," Dunbar added, looking at his brother.

"All they can carry," the baron confirmed.

"At once, Baron," the lieutenant replied with a salute. "Okay, you, you and you! Thanks for volunteering!" Breaking into a run, the man hurried off with the other sec men close behind.

"Now, brother, do you actually have something for these folks," the baron asked softly, "or was it just a trick to get out of the cell?"

"Head east," Dunbar stated, adjusting the new gun belt. "I heard Petrov talk about crossing deep water. That sounds like he's heading for Horseshoe Canyon and the ruins outside Modine. Big Joe once mentioned that would be a good place to start over again, if they ever got chased out of this area."

"Modine," Ryan repeated aloud. "Never heard of the place. Any chance of a map?"

"Nope, never needed one before since nobody sane ever goes there," Dunbar explained succinctly. He started to add something else, but then changed his mind. "Just head for the dawn, and if you run into a swamp full of stickies, you've gone too far south."

Scowling, J.B. said nothing, a hand flat on his hip where he normally had the munitions bag and his collection of predark maps. Horseshoe Canyon, why did that sound so familiar?

"What's to the north?" Krysty asked, watching the return of the sec men, their arms full of fuel canisters and lumpy canvas sacks.

"North is barb country," the baron stated with a frown. "Best stay away from them. The crazy bastards hate tech, even blasters, and they'd go triple-ballistic over those hogs."

"If no blasters, how chill?" Jak asked, furrowing his brow.

"Spears, and they're nuking accurate," Dunbar stated. "Our father told stories of them throwing the spears into the empty air. Seconds later, a griz bear ambles out of the forest to get impaled through the eyes by the falling spears."

"Very impressive," Mildred said, setting aside the MAC-10 to pull the handle under the dashboard and open the hatch covering the gas cap.

"We can handle barbs," J.B. asserted, patting the Atchisson cradled in his arms.

"Mebbe you can, but I'd rather circle around a pile of broken glass than prove how tough I am by running through the middle."

"A most sensible attitude, my dear baron," Doc rumbled. "On our journey to Modine, we shall be stealth personified! Ghosts in the night!"

"Damn well better be," Baron Cranston declared. "Or else the next time we meet, some hairy-ass barb will be wearing you as a vest."

THE DEAF WOMAN called Post stood very still on the second-floor balcony of the gaudy house, repeating the conversation several times to memorize it, before vanishing from sight.

Chapter Eleven

Night had fallen by the time the rest of the supplies arrived. The sky was heavy with black clouds that blocked out the stars and moon, only the occasional break allowing a flickering beam of moonlight to lance down and briefly touch the ville before it vanished again, gone with the wind.

The young baron and his personal guards had gone back to the castle hours earlier, leaving the new sec chief to arrange for what reward the ville could offer. Bottles of shine, fuel, oil, shower curtains altered into rain ponchos, decent boots, grain for the horses, baskets of bread, beef jerky and the omnipresent dried fish. The baskets and bags were put in the back of the cargo van, Ryan and J.B. taking them from the ville sec men to place on top of the stacks of hidden blasters.

Standing guard, Doc and Jak had stayed in the saddles of their horses, the additional height giving them a commanding view of the ville square and side streets. In spite of the earlier grumblings, there were no ville people in sight. Every window shutter was closed, the streets almost as dark as the rumbling clouds overhead. It was painfully obvious that a storm was coming soon.

"Sorry about that hot bath," Dunbar said, topping off

the fuel tank of a motorcycle. He spilled a little on the exhaust pipe, but made no attempt to wipe it off.

"It was Mildred who wanted one," Krysty answered, reaching for a cleaning rag.

With the Ingram slung over a shoulder, the physician had the hood open on the cargo van and was checking the oil level on the dipstick. Standing in front of the halogen headlights, her giant shadow was thrown across the square, reaching all the way to the wall.

"Ah, yes, good times," Dunbar said as if not hearing her response. Finishing off the canister, the teenager put the cap back on the fuel tank, then passed the empty canister to a waiting sec man.

"Nuking hell, I'm gonna miss you," Dunbar gushed, and stepped forward to fiercely hug the woman.

Startled by the unexpected display of feelings, Krysty patted the teen on the back in a friendly manner and started to push him away, when the teen whispered into her ear, "Remember the waterfall!"

Instantly alert, Krysty now went to hug the teenager ever closer, but Dunbar released his hold and turned to walk away, heading toward the barracks.

"Good journey!" he shouted over a shoulder with a cavalier wave and then vanished into the gloom between a tavern and the stable.

"What the hell was that about?" Ryan asked softly, pretending to check the straps on the canvas sheet covering the Gatling gun.

"We're in a trap," Krysty replied tersely, keeping her expression neutral. Trying not to be obvious, she dabbed a finger into the spilled shine, then scratched her nose to take a sniff. There was definitely alcohol present, but nowhere near enough the concentration needed to properly run the big twin-V8 of the Harley.

"Water?" Ryan guessed, studying her face.

She laughed and stroked his unshaved cheek as if the man had just made a lewd suggestion. Shrugging in mock acceptance, Ryan turned away to climb onto his own bike. Watered-down fuel. Fireblast! It couldn't be the baron. The boy had given the companions safe passage out of the ville. If Cranston broke his word, nobody would ever trust him again, and that would be the beginning of the end. This had to be the sec men taking matters into their own hands.

"Where next, lover?" Krysty asked, kicking the bike alive. The engine sputtered, but continued to operate. However, she knew that once the diluted fuel reached the engine, the bike would instantly become a millstone, deadweight that would anchor them to one location. Lambs for the slaughter.

"Front gate," Ryan answered, getting his own bike into operation. Straddling the machine, he walked it over to the cargo van and grabbed Mildred around the waist to pull her close. Confused, she resisted for a second, then her eyes went wide and the physician laughed gaily, tousling his long black hair before pushing him playfully away.

"Not here!" Mildred laughed, giving a wink. "Wait until we make camp!"

Stopping her bike between Doc and Jak, Krysty was annoyed to discover there were some people lounging inside a dark alley nearby. With no time to waste, Krysty grabbed Doc by the shirt and hauled the astonished man over to plant a passionate kiss on his mouth.

As his long hair fell forward to mask their faces, Krysty then nuzzled his ear. After a moment, Doc returned the favor, then patted her affectionately on top of the head.

"Of course, my dear!" He chortled, sitting back into the saddle. "Both of us at the same time, if you so wish! The more the merrier!"

As a grinning Krysty drove away, a very puzzled Jak asked a silent question. Smiling broadly, Doc rubbed his neck to surreptitiously run a thumb across his throat. Narrowing his pale eyes at the sight, Jak said nothing while loosening the Browning longblaster tucked into the gun boot.

Patiently sitting inside the van, J.B. waited until Mildred climbed behind the steering wheel and closed the door. "Trap?" he whispered, hefting the Atchisson.

"Diluted fuel," Mildred muttered in response, starting the engine. She tried not to scowl at the fuel gauge as the needle climbed to the top.

"Yeah, thought it didn't smell right," J.B. answered, trying not to move his lips. "Only one can went into our tank. When nobody was looking, I switched the others and used the stuff from the Boneyard."

"So the van is okay?"

"Should be," he said, sliding something across the floor with a boot. "Unless they used sugar water. Then we're nuked big-time."

"Only one way to find out." Mildred sighed, shifting into gear and driving slowly forward. Flashing a look down, she saw an AK-47 rapid-fire resting between the seats. "I love you," she said with a nervous laugh.

"Same here, babe," J.B. whispered, thumbing the

selector switch on the Atchisson from single shot to full-auto. Showtime.

With Ryan and Krysty taking the lead, the companions started along the empty bedrock road. Not a soul was in sight, not even a drunk or a sec man on patrol. Even the buildings along the street were unnaturally dark, with no stoves cooking dinner, lanterns or even candles burning. Just darkness. The ville seemed empty it was so quiet, the only noise coming from the tires on the street and the steady clip-clop of the horse hooves.

A block later, Ryan's bike sputtered, closely followed by Krysty's. Killing the engines, the man and woman let the bikes coast along for another block to gain some distance, then braked to a halt. Nothing stirred in the darkness around the companions. The only source of light came from the headlights of the van and bikes, and those were slowly starting to dim as the ancient batteries quickly drained.

Climbing off the bikes, Ryan and Krysty turned them around to point the fading beams back toward the ville square. In the distance, murky figures shifted out of view.

"Get ready," Ryan said, working the bolt on the Marlin. "Here they come."

As if on cue, something sighed in the air above them, moving across the stormy clouds as fast as arrows. With nothing in the vicinity to use as cover, Ryan and Krysty scrambled under the van, while Doc and Jak jumped off their horses to crouch underneath. The animals whinnied in surprise, then screamed in pain as the flurry of crossbow arrows rained down in the street.

The wooden shafts exploded against the hard bedrock, slamming into the roof of the van and piercing deep into the horses.

Rearing high, the bleeding animals pawed their hooves at the unseen enemy, their muscular bodies feathered with arrows. As more shafts plummeted downward, Doc and Jak dashed away from the dying animals to throw themselves flat against the side of a brick building. Once again, the bedrock street exploded into a spray of splinters, the sheet-metal roof of the van crunched from the hard arrival of a dozen more shafts.

Behind the wheel, Mildred cursed as she struggled to release an arm pinned to her seat, while an unharmed J.B. shrieked at the top of his lungs and dropped an empty Garland longblaster out the window to clatter on the street.

There came the sound of running boots from a nearby alley. Already under the wag, Ryan and Krysty opened fire with their blasters, the hail of hot lead invoking real screams of pain. Several people toppled over and a lantern crashed, a spreading pool of shine whooshing into flames and revealing a dozen more men carrying crossbows, wooden clubs and zipguns. Even as Ryan chilled two of them, he cursed at the sight. Ville people, not sec men! The damn fools. The odds of getting out of the ville alive just shifted dramatically against them.

In the bluish light of the burning shine, Doc and Jak felt horribly exposed and separated so they wouldn't offer a group target for snipers. Finally getting her wounded arm free, Mildred slapped the switch on the dashboard to kill the headlights.

Just then, an alarm began to softly clang in the distance.

"Muties at the south gate!" somebody yelled. "Sec men to the south gate! The ville is under attack by muties!"

Reloading her blaster, Krysty looked at Ryan and he nodded. They had been heading for the north gate. The ville people were drawing off the sec men to leave them alone with the companions. This wasn't an attack by an unruly mob, but a coordinated strike directed by somebody with combat experience. Time to do something unexpected.

"The bastards got Adam!" Ryan bellowed, letting the other companions know that he was lying. "Head for the castle! Chill the baron!"

"Consider him aced!" Doc boomed in his deep bass, then shuffled his boots going nowhere.

Rolling out from under the van, Ryan stood to focus the crosshairs of the telescopic scope of the Marlin on the castle, and fire. A window on the second floor noisily shattered, a shaft of bright light stabbing out into the night.

"Everybody to the castle!" a woman shouted. "Protect the baron!"

"Fuck that," a man yelled. "Chill the coldhearts!"

Tracking the masculine voice, Jak fired fast three times and was rewarded with a strangled gasp of pain. In return, another flurry of arrows arched down from the sky, but they descended along the path leading back to the ville square, obviously trying to bring down the would-be assassins.

Gently working the door, Ryan waved the others inside with his smoking blaster. Krysty scrambled in first, closely followed by Doc and then Jak, the albino teen carrying a bulging saddlebag over a shoulder.

A door slammed open in the building across the street, and several large men rushed toward the idling van. Waiting until they got into visual range, J.B. swung up the Atchisson and fired a triburst. The triple discharge filled the night with flame and buckshot. Riddled with holes, the men staggered backward, blood gushing from a dozen wounds.

Shifting into gear, Mildred let the van roll along at its own pace, slowly building speed, until they traveled at a decent clip. Swinging the MAC-10 into action, the physician cleared away some men dragging a cardboard box out of a log cabin. As they fled, the box dropped to the ground with the tinkling crash of breaking glass.

She grunted. Smart. That would have blown the van tires and left the companions riding on rims straight into hell. As more men appeared, she triggered another burst, sending them scurrying for cover, then the MAC-10 jammed. With only one hand free, the woman tossed the useless rapid-fire into the back of the van.

More arrows appeared from above, missing the zigzagging van, and the companions raked the rooftops with their blasters. The rapid-fires lit up the night with their stuttering muzzle-flashes. Brick chips went flying, glass shattered, a man screamed and a body slammed on the bedrock in a wet crunch, two more corpses arriving only seconds later.

"Floor it, Millie!" J.B. growled, triggering the auto-shotgun into an alley. In the fiery discharge, he briefly saw two men crouching with axes in their hands before the spray of double-O buckshot ripped away their lives.

Slamming down the gas pedal, Mildred shifted into high gear and tore off down the street, veering from side to side to try to avoid any incoming lead.

Taking positions at the windows, the companions smashed out the glass to keep it from exploding into their faces, then they settled down to start shooting at anything that moved. It was too dark to properly see their enemies, but that had been their choice, not the companions'. An arrow hit the van, and Doc sent off a brief burst from the M-16. Then something streaked from an open window in a ramshackle hut, and a boomerang slammed into the front windshield and shattered it.

Snatching the spare AK-47 from the floor, J.B. fired the weapon into the darkness ahead of the speeding van. A horse cried out in pain, a dog howled and several people cursed.

"Lights!" Ryan snarled, swinging up the Marlin.

Clumsily, Mildred pulled the switch, and the street ahead of them exploded into view, revealing a pair of ville men throwing handfuls of something from a saddlebag onto the street.

"Nails!" J.B. cursed, triggering both barrels, but the range was too great. Unharmed, the men ducked behind the dead horse to return fire with zipguns.

Even as Mildred braked the van, a headlight shattered, and Ryan cut loose with the Marlin. The powerful discharge of the Magnum round plowed down the street like sonic boom. Pulling back the rubber band to fire another .22 brass, a man jumped backward to land sprawling on the bedrock with most of his face removed.

Snarling a curse, a woman dashed behind a water barrel, her shaking hands fumbling to shove another round into the homemade blaster.

Working the bolt, Ryan stroked the trigger. The water barrel exploded into wet planks, and the woman limply hit the brick wall across the street, a handful of tiny .22 cartridges tumbling from her twitching hand.

Moving fast, Jak and Krysty scrambled from the van. Ripping off their shirts, they brushed aside the carpeting of nails and broken pieces of glass. A shadow moved on a rooftop, and Doc stitched it with his rapid-fire. A window shutter eased slowly open, and J.B. violently slammed it closed with a blast from the Atchisson. However, the weapon was starting to feel light. He was almost out of shells.

Just then, there was a clatter of hoofs. Charging around a corner, a sec man appeared, riding a horse and brandishing a rapid-fire.

Swinging the massive longblaster around, Ryan shot the horse, and the rider went flying to hit the street with a sickening crunch. He tumbled along for several yards, his bones audibly breaking.

"That was a blaster from our bikes!" Krysty snarled, knotting the torn shirt under her breasts before climbing back into the van. "If the sec men are coming to aid the ville people, we're outmanned and outgunned."

"Not yet," Ryan whispered tersely, aiming and firing.

The longblaster boomed, and the alarm bell instantly stopped ringing.

"Mildred, charge the front gate!" the one-eyed man commanded. "Doc, blow us an exit. Everybody else, hammer the top of the wall! Keep those sec men too bastard busy to try and stop us!"

Throwing the van into gear, Mildred stomped on the pedal, and the wag surged forward. Giving a wide berth to the dead horse, the woman then stayed in the middle of the street to give Doc a stable firing platform. They would have only one chance, and if it failed, they wouldn't leave this place alive.

"Don't miss, Theo!" Mildred shouted, both hands clenched on the steering wheel. Slowly, the speedometer climbed ever higher, the huts and shacks passing in a blur.

"Cover your eyes!" Doc replied, wiggling forward between the two front seats and raising his rapid-fire.

As Mildred and J.B. shielded their faces, Doc looked away himself before spraying the windshield with the 5.56-mm rounds. The safety glass resisted for only a split second, then shattered into a million pieces. As the tiny squares fell away, the old man took careful aim, preparing to fire the M-203 gren launcher.

Up ahead, ville people and sec men were doing something at the sandbag nest. Beyond that was the front gate of the ville.

Ignoring the people, Doc concentrated on the gate. It was an imposing barrier of railroad ties, bound with iron straps and thick steel chains. Off to the side was the predark generator rigged to a system of pulleys to haul the ponderous mass aside.

Even as Doc registered the fact, he saw a sec man slash the ropes attached to the pulleys with a machete. Grinning in triumph, the sec man sprinted away, his other hand clutching the spark plugs for the gasoline engine.

As the cargo van hurtled toward the gate, the companions raked the men at the sandbag nest with their assorted weapons, spending brass like it grew on trees. The sec men and ville men tumbled away in bloody ruination, their Molotovs crashing down beside them to set the wounded and the dying on fire.

Pressing his legs against the front seats, Doc tried to sway in rhythm with the vehicle as he took careful aim and fired. But as the 40-mm gren launcher gave a hollow thump, the man instantly knew that the shell was a reload. If the bonemen had replaced the wad of C-4 plastic explosives in the warhead with black powder, the shell wouldn't have anywhere near enough power to—

Slamming onto the upper hinge of the gate, the U.S. Army shell detonated like the wrath of God, spraying out chunks of broken iron. With a high-pitched screech of twisting metal, the shuddering door began to tilt, the remaining hinge completely unable to handle the colossal weight alone. It snapped, and in slow majesty, the gate toppled over to slam onto the bedrock outside the ville, the crash sounding like a nuclear explosion.

"Hold on!" Mildred shouted, bracing for the impact.

At full speed, the armored van rammed into the quivering gate, careening off the wooden beams and shoving them slightly forward. Loudly grinding, the gate rotated and the van erupted into the night.

"Armored outside, not inside." Jak laughed, releasing his death grip on the side door.

Charging into the darkness, Mildred squinted to try to see where the slab of bedrock stopped and the river began. Unable to do so, the physician took a wild guess and turned sharply to the right, her heart beating wildly.

As cold water sprayed over the cargo van, Mildred quickly turned farther away from the white-water torrent.

"Now what?" she shouted over the rushing wind.

"Follow this for a while," Ryan yelled back. "That'll kill our scent in case the sec men have any hunting dogs!"

"And then?" Mildred asked, trying not to look at the engine temperature gauge. It was fast moving into the danger zone, and the oil pressure was dropping.

"Then we wait for them to come to us," J.B. told her, thumbing a spare round into the hot Atchisson.

With a crackle, the headlight winked out, and the companions raced onward in near total darkness, guided only by the sounds of the river.

Chapter Twelve

"Come now, get those nuking bags into position if you want to live through the night!" Dunbar bellowed.

Moving in a steady hand-over-hand, a huge crowd of ville people were relaying the sandbags from the firebase to the gaping hole in the ville wall. The makeshift barrier was already four feet high, but only halfway across the opening.

A dozen armed sec men stood on the wall carrying longblasters and crossbows, while a score more clustered around the fallen gate, looking out into the night for any movement. An owl hooted in a tree, and a sec man fired from the hip. A stingwing flew by overhead, and in the far distance, a wendigo roared. Everybody tightened their grips on their blasters, and the people on the ground moved a little closer to the wall.

"Mother always said we needed a third hinge," the baron muttered, hugging the heavy bearskin robe draped over his shoulders. Standing off to the side, the boy stayed out of the way while the adults rushed about on grim tasks. "It would appear she was right, as usual, brother."

"That doesn't help much at the moment!" Dunbar snarled, trying not to look at the blood splattered on the inside of the wall. Some of it was still damp, and a boot lay nearby with a foot still inside.

"Nothing could help much, except the heads of the outlanders stacked in a nice pile for me to piss on," the baron agreed with a hateful sneer. "Have the blacksmith start heating up the forge. We repair those hinges tonight. I want the gate hauled back in place by dawn!"

"Brother, is that even possible?" Dunbar asked in a whisper.

"We have enough horses and tack. Besides, I decree that it is not impossible," the baron commanded, just for a moment sounding exactly like their father. "Now, tell me the bad news, brother. How many people did we lose tonight?"

"At least twenty," Dunbar answered, his face dark with shadows. "But we're still finding them inside houses, and on the rooftops." He grunted. "Must have been one nuke storm of a fight."

It seemed incredible that so many people could have been aced in such a short time. "Did we get any of them?"

"Unknown, Baron, but my guess would be no. I heard them fight Big Joe, and they're pure chilling machines."

"And you willingly brought them into my ville," the baron said softly, a warm breeze from the desert ruffling his loose uniform.

That caught Dunbar off guard, but before he could reply a group of panting sec men arrived carrying a canvas bundle. Placing it reverently on the street, they folded back the cloth to expose the disassembled Gatling gun found in one of the abandoned sidecars. The seven barrels gleamed with oil, and the sight of the colossal rapid-fire eased some of the fear in the faces of the ville people and the sec men.

"Check for traps and blocked barrels!" Dunbar ordered. "What kind of brass does she take?"

"Thirty-eight, sir!" a sec man replied.

"Don't have much of that caliber in the armory," the baron said unhappily, pulling his blaster and dumping out the .38 brass into a palm. "Better start scavenging for what we can find."

"No need, Baron. There was a container of brass with it in the sidecar!" a sec woman answered, placing a plastic box on the ground with a hard thump.

A container of brass. The baron had never heard of such wealth before. "Better check to make sure it's live and not packed with dirt," he commanded.

"Or plas-ex," Dunbar warned. "You there, Shamus! Take a couple of random shells apart to check inside."

Pulling a knife, the sec man checked the brass on the spot, his hands moving carefully in the bluish light of the alcohol lanterns. Impatiently, everybody waited for the results.

"They're live, Chief!" he called out happily, inspecting the dark gray gunpowder in his palm.

Smiling broadly, Dunbar let out the breath he had been holding. "Excellent! Get the thing put back together, and then we'll run a couple of test shots before trying it at full speed."

"But the waste of brass..." A man gasped in horror.

"We have to know the Gatling works before we can depend upon it to protect the ville," the baron replied in a clear, loud voice for everyone to hear over their assorted work. "Gotta walk before you can run, eh?"

A couple of the wrinklies merely grunted at the oblivious platitude, but everybody else slowly nodded in agreement. Wise, indeed, was their baron.

"Okay, brother, now tell me the bad news." The baron sighed, thumbing the rounds back into his blaster. "I know my people well. How many of the sec men jumped ship to chase after the outlanders?"

"A dozen, sir, on their own horses," Dunbar quickly added in their defense. "But they took a nuke load of brass and blasters from those saddlebags."

"Chill them with their own brass. I like the irony," the baron said. "And since I don't see Lieutenant Fenton anywhere…"

"Yes, sir, he's leading the hunting party."

"I wish them well," the baron said. "And so should you."

"Sir?" Dunbar asked curiously.

"Because if they're not back by dawn, then I'm sending you after the coldhearts alone," the baron said in a strained voice. "And this time, dear brother, you're not coming back inside without their heads in a basket."

SPEEDING ALONG the edge of the river, the rattling cargo van moved under the canopy of the apple orchard just as the dashboard indicators turned bright red.

"That's it, we're dead," Mildred stated, as the overheating engine sputtered and went silent. Throwing the transmission into Neutral, the woman steered the wag into a small clearing and braked to a halt.

"Good work," Ryan said, studying the lay of the forest. "Didn't think it would get us this far after that bastard crash."

"Millie's one of the best drivers I've ever met," J.B. boasted, resting the Atchisson on the cracked vinyl of the dashboard. "How's the arm?"

"Been better," Mildred admitted, gingerly probing the bloody cloth covering the wound.

Wordlessly, Krysty passed up the new med bag, and the physician scowled at the meager collection of items, then got to work. Exposing the wound, she cleaned the area thoroughly with shine before wrapping it with a strip of clean cloth. She grunted as the bandage tightened, then sighed as the trickle of blood stopped flowing.

"Well, we're Spam in a can if we stay inside this thing," Ryan dourly noted. "Everybody grab spare brass and take cover in the trees. J.B., see if there's anything you can do to get us mobile again. Jak, start choosing what blasters and brass to keep, then toss the rest outside. It's too crowded in here to fight properly, and lightening this wag will make the fuel go further."

"Dropping blasters like ballast." The teenager snorted. "Never thought see day."

"Needs drive as the devil must," Doc replied cryptically, then there was a wet smack and the van shook slightly.

Turning to look out her window, Mildred found herself staring directly into the open mouth of a sucking flapjack, the translucent mutie wiggling and writhing across the iron bars covering the broken window as it struggled to reach the woman.

Recoiling in disgust, Mildred felt somebody grab her by the collar and haul her roughly to the floor. She hit in a sprawl and looked up to see a semitransparent pseudopod coming through the air vent to probe the blood smeared on the vinyl seat. Son of a bitch!

As Mildred fumbled for her blaster, Doc released her collar and triggered a short burst from his rapid-fire. The muzzle-flash seemed to fill the van, and the flapjack was thrown off the protective grid.

Rushing outside, J.B. squinted in the darkness, then fired the Atchisson. The roar of the shotgun shook the trees, and the mutie wriggling on the ground died horribly. Oddly, the trees kept rustling, and another blob dropped onto a pile of leaves.

"Nest!" Jak snarled, pulling both blasters

"Light 'em up!" Ryan shouted, blazing away with his blaster.

A mutie thumped onto the roof of the van, landing amid the cluster of arrows still there. With a snarl, J.B. fired and blew the thing into pieces, a gelatinous rain flying back into the apple trees.

Her hair waving and flexing, Krysty shot a blob on a tree stump, then another flapjack landed on her barrel. The creature instantly began to sizzle from the hot metal and jumped off again. Krysty put a short burst into the horrible thing, then stomped on the remains with a boot.

Two muties smacked into the earth alongside Doc, and he shot one, then kicked the other. It hit a tree trunk and stayed there, undamaged and pulsating. Pulling the trigger on his rapid-fire, Doc cursed when the weapon jammed. Launching itself into the air, the mutie flew toward the man, and Jak sent it to hell with his blasters.

Tingling with adrenaline, the companions listened

for any more movement in the leaves, but the apple trees seemed deserted. On a hunch, Krysty swept the treetops with a long burst from her rapid-fire, and two more flapjacks smacked onto the ground. One of them a pulpy oozing mess, the other transparent mutie very much alive. Wriggling along, it scooted under the van.

"Nice try," J.B. snarled, shoving the sawed-off into the darkness and cutting loose with both barrels. The double discharge illuminated the undercarriage in hellish relief. However, the nimble flapjack escaped unharmed out the other side, only to encounter Doc and his machete. The sharp blade cut the creature neatly in two, and both pieces started moving toward the man. Scrambling to get clear, Doc tripped over an exposed root and fell into the loose leaves. Instantly, Mildred appeared with the AK-47 to hammer the inhuman mutie, blowing its halves apart at point-blank range.

"My sincere thanks," Doc rumbled, getting back on his feet. "It would seem that the dark goddess Luna does not favor me with her good graces this night."

"Had to pay you back for yanking me out of the driver's seat," Mildred replied.

"Sorry if I was too rough, madam."

"Ha! Under similar circumstances, feel free to throw me on my ass anytime."

"Wouldn't that make J.B. jealous?" Doc asked, trying not to smile.

"Crazy old coot." Mildred snorted, then playfully punched the man on the arm.

Levering a fresh round into his longblaster, Ryan looked about the clearing until finding the distant lights of Delta ville. There was a great deal of activity near the front gate, but nobody seemed to be coming after them.

"Mutie shit," Jak drawled, his hair ruffling in the breeze. "They come."

"Agreed," Ryan said, taking a position near a tree and settling down amid the tangle of exposed roots. Now he had an excellent view of the countryside, from the river to the farmlands past the ville. "They'll use horses to be quiet, at least ten sec men, mebbe a few more, just to help one another feel brave."

"Well, we did shoot up their ville," Krysty reminded him. "The fools. All we wanted was to leave in peace! Now we've lost almost everything! The bikes, the Gatling, our horses…"

"Still got some brass and our asses," Ryan retorted, placing the Marlin to the side and drawing his handblaster. Cracking open the cylinder, he started taking out the spent brass to reload. "Mebbe even wheels if J.B. can patch the engine."

The hood of the wag was raised, and J.B. was bent at the waist, fiddling with the machinery. A low, steady stream of metallic bangs and profanity could be heard.

"Sounds promising," Doc noted.

"No, it's dead," J.B. said, stepping back to wipe his hands clean on a rag. "The hoses burst when the radiator overheated. Without a spare, or a roll of duck tape, there's nothing I can do."

"Duct tape," Mildred corrected, feeling very vulnerable in the dark night in spite of the rapid-fire in her hands. High overhead, the storm clouds rumbled softly, and lightning flashed in the distance. "Okay, what do we do, try to cross the river?"

"That would be tantamount to suicide, madam," Doc stated, working the arming bolt of his rapid-fire to clear the jam from the ejector port. The bent shell casing finally came free to spin away in the darkness.

"Not seen worse," Jak agreed, glancing in the direction of the turbulent waterway. The albino teen couldn't see it through the trees and bushes, but the power of the river could be felt as a low vibration through his boots.

"Which leaves us with only one choice," Ryan stated, closing the blaster and tucking it back into the holster. "J.B., have you got any string?"

"Way ahead of you, old buddy," the man replied, unraveling a ball of twine recovered from the Boneyard. "I'd been planning on soaking this in black powder and shine to make some fuse, but now..."

"Wind chimes?"

"Bet your ass."

"Get razor, people, they're coming," Krysty whispered.

Moving fast, everybody went to the van and began stuffing extra brass into their pockets.

"ARE YOU SURE?" Fenton asked, cocking back the hammer on his Webley .44 blaster, a gift from Petrov.

"Of course," the sec woman replied, kneeling low in the grass. Closing her eyes, Hermonie tried to hear past the river and the wind, listening to the night with her whole body. "The outlanders drove into the apple orchard, and now they're doing repairs."

"Then we got them," Youngerford growled, the hair of the sec man stiff and matted with the blood of a friend. The outlander and his crew had aced a sec man, several of them in fact, and for that alone they should go to the wall post for a full moon. Sec Chief Dunbar wanted them alive, the baron wanted them chilled, but as the old saying went, what happens outside the ville wall stays there. As long as they brought back the bodies, nobody would seriously question how the out-landers got aced. His personal goal was to dig out the other eye of the big bastard Ryan and make his bitch eat it. Then she'd eat some other things of a more personal nature.

"We still better stay razor. These gleebs are trickier than a gaudy slut on wolfweed," Wild Bill growled, both hands resting on the buckle of his gun belt. His face and hands betrayed his real age, but he still walked with the swagger of a newbie, and nobody questioned the speed of his blaster. A dozen coldhearts and even more muties were in the dirt with no idea of how they got there aside from facing Wild Bill and then seeing a brief flash of fiery light.

Standing in a pool of shadow underneath a raised farmhouse, the rest of the sec men muttered their som-ber agreement. Their horses were exhausted, their hides shiny with sweat from the long, hard ride from the dis-tant south gate.

"Orders, sir?" Bellany asked. The kid was a newbie, as green as a spring rain, but there were already two notches in the handle of his Colt .44 blaster. The weapon was a gift from the baron himself in appre-ciation for the deft handling of a coldheart who had been raiding the outer farms for years. Bellany had lain inside a bin of taters for a week before the thief finally returned, and soon afterward the boy returned to the

ville with several teeth missing, blood on his knife and
a new pair of boots.

"All right, Dale, Leroy, guard the horses. The rest of
us will do this as a nightcreep," Fenton ordered, drawing a knife and his blaster. "Wild Bill and Youngerford,
take the left, Hermonie and Bellany, the right. I'll take
the slot with everybody else."

Tethering their horses to the thick wooden poles supporting the tiny farmhouse, the sec men divided into
groups and began moving low and fast through the tall
grass, their weapons hunting for targets.

The apple orchard was hundreds of yards away, but
Fenton could still vaguely hear somebody working on
the wag, the metallic sounds almost lost in the noise of
the river.

Trying not to step on any twigs or branches to reveal
their presence, the three groups of sec men eased ever
closer to the copse of trees. A sec woman inhaled
sharply at the discovery of a chunk of flapjack lying
on the ground, then another did the same. Clearly, the
outlanders had discovered what a nuking bad idea it
was to park under any tree along the river.

Crouching in the weeds near the wizened corpse of
a griz bear, Fenton studied the rustling trees for a long
time before finally deciding to take a chance. Easing
forward, the lieutenant felt his skin crawl while he
passed under the branches, but if there had been any
of the muties in the vicinity, they would have already
attacked. The name of the things was more than merely
what they resembled, but also how smart they were.
Fenton thought a flapjack was dumber than a barb, and
that was really saying something.

Pausing in the darkness, Fenton saw a battered wag standing in the center of a small clearing, and he strained to hear any voices or footsteps. But there was only the metallic clangs coming from under the raised hood and the soft ticking of the cooling engine. Wary of a trap, the man circled the vehicle, then stopped in surprise at the sight of nobody at the front of the wag. Instead, there were only some wrenches tied to pieces of string and hung from the hood. Moved by the wind, the tools softly clanged off one another, making it sound exactly like somebody doing repairs… Blind NORAD, this was a suck play!

"Nobody touch the wag!" Fenton yelled.

Instantly, everybody moved away from the vehicle, and Hermonie cursed as she felt a brief tug on her leg, then heard a string snap. "Run!" she screamed even as the blaster tied to the string discharged inside the van. There was a microsecond pause before the stores of black powder ignited, filling the interior with roiling flames. Then the stores of ammunition detonated into a thundering fireball that tore the wag apart, blew the leaves off the trees and sent the tattered bodies of the sec men hurtling away in a grisly carnage.

A hundred yards away, the five horses tethered under the farmhouse unhappily shuffled their hooves and snorted at the smell of blood from the two sec men lying on the ground nearby. On the horizon, the companions rode the other six horses into the eastern hills and soon galloped out of sight.

Chapter Thirteen

As dawn broke, the Pig Iron Gang was comfortably camped underneath a predark bridge located just outside Horseshoe Canyon. It was raining, cool, clear water, the deluge coming down hard onto the ancient bridge and oddly sounding like meat sizzling on a grill.

On guard duty, Thal was the only person awake, the rest still snoring in their bedrolls. Which was only natural, since they'd tangled with a wendigo yesterday and only barely managed to escape by chilling a wild boar and quickly stuffing the corpse with river moss. Since a wendigo would eat nearly anything, it happily consumed the entire boar before continuing the chase of the gang. Then while crossing a river, the mutie suddenly slowed and fell asleep, the currents washing it quickly away. Delighted the ploy worked, the gang reclaimed their hogs and raced away from the area as fast as possible. When it awoke, the wendigo would be insane with rage, but that was somebody else's problem to solve.

The crackling of the campfire was low and steady, perfectly matching the patter of the rain cascading over both sides of the bridge. Fishing had been good for the gang, and several fat trout were hanging from the iron rod near the flames, slowly jerking the meat for the long journey to Modine.

Sitting on a rock, Thal was going through the contents of the med bag. Most of the items he could understand, such as the curved needles for stitching shut wounds, tampons for deep bullet wounds, bottles of clean water, shine and such. But some of the things made no sense, like the strange curved scissors, or the skinny pliers that locked into position. Weird stuff, but Thal assumed it all served the same purpose—putting folks back together after a fight.

Exploring the lining for any hidden caches of drugs, the big man got excited when his fingers found a disguised zipper on the bottom. But pulling it aside, Thal discovered only a book. Bah, who could read anymore? That didn't put brass in a blaster. It was only by chance that he had been taught to read by an old trader who had hired him as sec for a journey through the Darks. Thal was an avid learner. He'd been getting sick of opening cans of predark cleaning supplies, hoping it was food.

Flipping through the pages of the book, Thal grunted in annoyance, his frown deepening with every passing second.

Rising from his bedroll, Charlie joined his friend at the fire. He poured a cup of warm coffee sub and took a sip, sloshing it about in his mouth to wash away the taste of sleep.

"Something wrong?" Charlie asked, sipping some more of the dark brew. "You have the look of a dog with a mutie trapped just out of biting range."

"Close," Thal replied, offering the journal. "I found

this tucked away at the bottom of the med bag inside a secret compartment."

A book? Why would anybody hide one of those? Unless the pages were exceptionally soft and the owner didn't want to share the lav paper with anybody else. "Curious. This isn't even written in English," Charlie muttered, setting the tin cup aside to accept the book. A fat ember in the fire banged just then, but the men completely ignored such a minor interruption.

"Yet the letters and numbers are," Thal countered, his brow furrowing. "Do you think it might be in code?"

"I've heard that other languages sometimes use the same alphabet that we do, just in other ways," Charlie said, engrossed in the mystery. "So that would be the same as a code, I guess." Turning a page, his interest piqued at the sight of a hand-drawn map. He wasn't sure, but it seemed like some kind of a bomb shelter, except that it was huge, five stories, with elevators, stairs and all sorts of odd things.

"What's for breakfast?" Rose asked around a yawn, shuffling over to the men.

"Fish and coffee, same as last night," Thal replied, smiling. "Sleep well?"

"Always do when it rains." Rose grinned, pouring herself a cup of the coffee sub. "What's that, lav paper?"

"Not sure yet," Charlie countered, tucking away the volume to peruse later. "Might be something useful, but probably not."

"Well, can I have a couple of sheets?"

"Try these instead." Thal laughed, reaching into a pocket to pull out a battered paperback. "Nice and soft."

Nodding her thanks, the woman wandered over to the section of the underpass blocked off by their bikes for a modicum of privacy, then squatted out of sight.

Still in his bedroll, Petrov turned over and began snoring louder than before.

"Think this might have anything to do with all of these fancy blasters and the implo gren?" Thal asked hopefully, rubbing his unshaved face.

"Could be," Charlie guessed. "But first we gotta break this code, or whatever it is."

With a laugh, Thal stretched and rose. "My turn in the sack," he announced. "At least that little book will give us something interesting to do in the rain aside from eat, sleep, play cards and fuck."

"That it will," Charlie replied.

A FEW DAYS LATER the companions were crossing a sylvan valley, rich in a wild profusion of flowers, a perfumed rainbow of nature's majesty. There were hundreds of tiny creeks and ponds in the area, the ground was soft, almost marshy.

The polluted clouds were thin overhead, and brief snatches of sunlight actually made it through to tenderly stroke the world. The grass was a deep emerald-green, and the trees were heavy with fruit. A swarm of butterflies was feasting upon the corpse of a wolf. Nearby stood a giant sunflower with a bite mark on the stalk.

Stepping out of some of the thick bushes, a bull moose looked about the greenery. Bending, he started to lap at the small pond, when there came a distant crack, very similar to the snapping of a branch heavy with winter snow. The moose snapped back its head, blood spraying from its throat. The longblaster sounded again, and this time the animal dropped to the ground.

Instantly, the cougar hiding in the bushes leaped on the dying moose and began savaging the corpse with its claws, snarling wildly as if claiming the kill for itself. But once more the longblaster sounded, and the cougar tumbled sideways. It hit the grass in a scramble and streaked away to vanish in the dense greenery.

"Fireblast! It got away," Ryan growled, lowering the Marlin. "The moose is fine, but always did love cougar. Not as much as bear, but still good eating."

"And I'll wager they say the same about us." Krysty chuckled.

"Same here," Jak said from the back of his horse.

Riding to the fallen moose, Ryan and Jak did the butchery, while the rest of the companions stood guard. Sprinkling the hunks of raw meat with some salt as a preservative, they tightly wrapped the steaks in pieces of the hide, then packed them away into the saddlebags.

"Ah, steak for dinner." Doc smiled. "I was beginning to despair of mulligan stew." The random mixture of rabbit, gopher, woodchuck, owl and anything else the companions could ace was filling, but generally rather bland, and there was no other word for owl meat but *wretched*.

"Now how do you know that phrase?" Mildred asked. "Mulligan stew comes from long after your time, during the Great Depression."

"Mayhap it does, madam, but I learned it from you," Doc answered with a smile.

Suddenly, the horses began to snort and shuffle their hooves, the six trying to sound like a hundred.

"Something in wind they not like," Jak said, drawing his blaster.

"I don't hear any hooting, so it isn't stickies," J.B. muttered, squinting into the forest as he worked the arming bolt on the MAC-10. Beyond a few yards, the world was a blur to the man, and his frustration over the matter was growing daily. He had prepared for such a contingency by making a couple of crude explosive charges from what he had managed to carry away from the van. But J.B. was rapidly getting to the point where he was going to start becoming a liability to the others rather than an asset.

"The smell of blood is attracting another predator," Krysty guessed, freeing her rapid-fire from its gun boot. "Probably just another cougar."

"No sense wasting brass when we're on horseback," Ryan decided, kicking his heels into the stallion and breaking into a full gallop.

But as the companions rode away, a section of the forest broke away from the trees and bushes to quickly follow after them. Streaking across the ground, the fur of the creature changed into an emerald-green, dotted with Shasta daisies. Only the eyes stayed the same, shiny black orbs fastened upon the hated two-legs with grim intent.

Leaving the valley behind, the companions galloped onto a section of a predark road, the concrete stained and cracked, but still in relatively decent condition. The clopping of the horse hooves on the soft earth changed into a clatter, and something roared behind them.

Turning in the saddle, Ryan scowled to see nothing unusual in sight. Then the man blinked, and his vision focused on a patch of concrete moving low and fast toward them—a patch of roadwork with two large black eyes.

"Mutie!" Ryan shouted in warning, clawing for a blaster.

The companions cut loose with their weapons, hitting the disguised creature several times. Yellow blood erupted from the hits, but almost instantly, the small wounds healed, like a mouth shutting.

"Gaia, it's a biowep!" Krysty yelled, switching her rapid-fire to full-auto. Going for the eyes, the woman put a prolonged burst of 7.62-mm rounds into the creature, but half of the rounds went wild as her horse bucked in fear, almost throwing her from the saddle.

With a bellow, the wendigo circled the armed companions, pausing for only a second to allow a writhing nest of tentacles loose from its humped back.

"Son of a bitch!" J.B. snarled, cutting loose with the MAC-10. The chattering hail of 9-mm rounds sent a score of the tentacles to the ground, where they flopped about madly like live snakes in a frying pan. Firing single rounds into the mutie, the Armorer started to reach for the Molotov in his munitions bag, but stayed his hand. There was only one, so he had to make it count.

Bellowing in pain, the wendigo tried to reach the oldest two-legs, but Doc put a burst of 5.56-mm rounds from his rapid-fire directly into the creature, then slashed at the tentacles with his machete, cutting off more of the flesh. Jak threw his hatchet, but the blade merely rebounded from the tough hide of the slavering mutie.

Constantly changing color, the wendigo circled the pack of two-legs, clawing for the riders or trying to bite the horses.

Raising the M-16/M-203 combo, Doc aimed the gren launcher but couldn't get a bead on the nimble creature. Damnation, it was almost as if the thing understood what a blaster was. J.B. had been unable to make a new warhead and so changed the gren launcher into a shotgun. Black powder, of course, as that much regular gunpowder would have blown the weapon apart.

Testing to see how smart the mutie was, Ryan dropped a handful of spent shells onto the road, the brass tingling musically as he pretended to fumble with the Marlin. Instantly, the wendigo charged for the two-legs, thinking the boomstick wasn't alive anymore.

With a grimace, Ryan triggered the longblaster at point-blank range, the muzzle-flash actually touching the mutie. The colossal .444 round punched through the creature, throwing it to the ground and coming out the back in a wide golden spray.

Moaning in pain, the wendigo moved away from Ryan, the gaping crater in its matted fur slowly closing.

"Hammer the bastard!" Ryan commanded, levering in a fresh shell and firing past the head of his horse.

As the beast roared defiantly, the rest of the companions fired their weapons, the hail of soft lead and hardball rounds driving the mutie to the surface of the ancient road. Lightening in color, the wendigo reached out a distorted hand, the claws only scratching along the rough concrete, then it went still.

"Mutie shit!" Jak snarled, drawing his blaster and putting five fast rounds into the mutie. Rolling to the side, the wendigo scampered across the highway to vanish into the forest.

"Thank God, we drove it off." Mildred sighed in relief, cracking open her blaster to replace rounds with sure fingers.

"That was just to test our defenses," Ryan said, intently studying the rustling greenery.

"Be back," Jak agreed, slamming a fresh clip into his blaster and jacking the slide.

"Hell, yes, here it comes!" J.B. shouted, squeezing the trigger of the MAC-10. As he waved about the stream of bullets, leaves exploded from the ground in a whirlwind. A clean miss. Drawing the sawed-off, J.B. fired both barrels and some bushes splattered yellow blood, the plants retreating into the gloom howling in bestial rage.

Spotting a nearby hill, Krysty saw that the greenery only reached halfway up the sloping sides, the grass at the top was dry and dead. A dead zone like that amid the lush greenery could only mean a rad pit. That would chill norm and mutie, but the dead grass around the blast crater might work for them.

Briefly offering a prayer to Gaia, the woman charged her horse up the side of the hill at breakneck speed. "Follow me!"

The rest of the companions paused for only a split second before following close behind. Rad pit or not, they trusted the woman's judgment. The companions reached the top just as the wendigo appeared from the opposite side of the highway. Its fur was now a dull black, a perfect camouflage for hiding inside a shadowy forest. As it raced across the concrete, the long hair of the wendigo rippled into a pale tan once more, with a double-yellow line running across the middle.

Taking advantage of the mutie's brief visibility, the companions paused on the crest of the hill to pound the thing with blasters. Inhuman blood exploded from a dozen hits, then the wendigo was across the highway and moving among the dead bushes, the fur already turning a mottled array of greens and browns.

"We could run," Doc suggested, feeling his belly tighten in fear. The wendigo was like a childhood nightmare come to life. None of their weapons did more than slow the beast, and if it ever got among the horses, the companions would be slaughtered.

"Get ready to move!" J.B. commanded, holstering the sawed-off to rummage around in his munitions bag. Hauling the Molotov into view, the man lit the rag fuse tied around the neck, then threw the bomb onto the dry grass. However, the Molotov missed the rock he had been aiming at and lay there undamaged.

Triggering the MAC-10, J.B. missed the bottle. Swinging his longblaster downward, Ryan shot once and a fireball erupted. Realizing what the men were doing, Mildred tossed down her bottle of shine, and Krysty ignited the flammable liquid with the muzzle-flash of her AK-47 rapid-fire. Throwing down a packet of black powder he had been saving for the LeMat, Doc set it off with a single shot from the M-16, and Jak lit an oily rag with a butane lighter and dropped it on top of a dry bush.

Crackling loudly, the flames spread across the wind-dry hilltop with surprising speed. Already nervous from the presence of the mutie, the horses stiffened at the scent of their primordial enemy of fire, rearing high before galloping away.

Rising behind the line of flames, the wendigo voiced its rage, the fur incredibly trying to match the shifting colors of the licking flames.

Snarling as if in reply, J.B. hosed the MAC-10 at the beast, most of the 9-mm rounds missing completely. As the last clip emptied, the frustrated man tossed the useless rapid-fire away and cut loose with the 12-gauge sawed-off, the spray of double-O buckshot blowing open the chest of the snarling mutie.

Taking careful aim through the smoke, Ryan put a .444 round into the creature's head. As it fell backward, the rest of the companions quickly retreated and started a second wall of fire. This was a tactic that had served them well many times before. An enraged animal might summon the hatred to run through fire once, but the second stopped them every time.

Lumbering through the wall of the flames, the wendigo paused at the second barrier, once more giving voice to its odd moaning bellow. Incredibly, the cry was answered from several locations.

"Gaia, there's a pack of them?" Krysty demanded, fighting to control her horse. They were having enough trouble dealing with just one of the big bastards!

"Aim for the neck!" Ryan ordered, shoving a fresh cartridge into the Marlin longblaster.

As the companions riddled the throat of the beast with hot lead, J.B. poured a bottle of shine into some weeds, then tossed in a road flare. Flames rose from the alcohol-soaked plants, but they weren't spreading fast enough to suit J.B., so he quickly dug out the coil of freshly made fuse. Igniting it with a lighter, the man tossed away the entire coil. It landed sputtering and hissing, the sparks setting fire to some dried leaves and another stand of dead bushes.

Tossing his other two flares, J.B. spread the blaze across their right flank, but no farther. A withered forest of sickly trees blanketed the rest of the landscape in that direction, extending to a shiny crystal pool that the Armorer instantly recognized as a glass lake, the heat-fused earth left behind after a tactical nuclear strike. His skin crawled at the thought of just what the companions might be breathing, but without a rad counter, J.B. had no way of knowing if this was a safe zone or if they were already aced. But that didn't matter, because until he started coughing blood, the man was going to fight for life.

As Mildred put short bursts from her rapid-fire into the mutie, blowing off strategic chunks of flesh from the arms and legs to cripple its advance, J.B. threw a spare box of mismatched cartridges into the blaze. If he couldn't see well enough to shoot, then the flames could do that job for him! As the brass began to randomly ignite from the searing heat, the mutie was hit several times and began to paw at the fire, its tentacles lashing about madly, trying to find the source of the noise.

"Okay, ace the bastard!" Ryan shouted, and every blaster owned by the companions was trigged again at the stationary target.

The barrage of copper-jacketed lead, dumdums,

stones, glass and nails removed most of the throat of the snarling wendigo. Mutely, it stumbled backward to land sprawling in the flames, the thick fur losing all color as it began to burn. Gushing yellow fluids, the beast flailed about blindly, rolling deeper into the blaze until it was completely engulfed in flames.

The companions cheered as the wendigo stopped moving, but then they stopped as three more of the huge muties appeared behind the firewall.

Batting away the flaming bushes, the wendigos incredibly pushed their way to the burning corpse, their own fur smoldering and sizzling like a hundred tiny fuses. The creatures nudged the corpse as if trying to help it awaken, but as their minds slowly accepted the reality of the death, the wendigos turned to face the norms on horseback and thunderously bellowed in fury, their black eyes full of raw hatred.

"Keep them on the other side of the firewall!" Ryan shouted, working the bolt on his longblaster. The weapon was slippery in his sweaty hands, and the man shook his head to clear his eye of some hair that had fallen across his face.

Taking advantage of the grouping, Doc braced himself and discharged the gren launcher. The blackpowder "shotgun" charge boomed louder than artillery, and the recoil knocked the old man backward, almost throwing him out of the saddle if not for his boots in the stirrups. The wide spray of rocks, glass and nails went high, hissing through the swirling smoke, but missing the wendigos entirely.

The wildfire was spreading rapidly now, the flames

darting in random directions, following the thickest line of weeds, as dictated by the gentle winds.

Growling at one another, two of the muties began to head left, the others going to the right in an effort to circle around the fiery obstruction.

Caught in the act of reloading, Jak almost dropped his blaster, wondering just how smart those things were.

However, the firewall was much broader now, the blaze spreading fast across the dried grasslands, the thick volumes of smoke masking the hillside. Stymied by their attempt to go around the inferno, the wendigos tried to go through the blaze, but were forced back strictly by the pain of their burning fur. Then one of the muties grabbed the charred corpse of the aced wendigo and threw it into the heart of the fire. As the flames tamped down for a moment, the wendigo scrambled over the corpse to stand triumphant on the other side.

Instantly, Krysty and Doc emptied both of the rapid-fires into the mutie's chest, the hail of rounds invoking a score of yellow spurts, but none of them lasted longer than a few seconds.

"Doesn't this thing have a weak spot?" J.B. demanded, jerking his wrist to snap closed the breech of the sawed-off scattergun.

As the indomitable wendigo lumbered forward, Mildred leveled her blaster in both hands and fired a single round into the mutie's tender nose, a known vulnerable spot for most hunting animals. Yellow blood erupted from the hit, and the wendigo keened in misery, a sound the dying mutie had never made. Mildred shot again and missed, but then Jak flipped a hand forward, and a knife thudded into the bloody nose, the blade going in all the way to the handle.

Wailing in agony, the wendigo turned away from this new enemy, and the companions cut loose in another tight volley, ripping off chunks of flesh and bone from the back of its head. As the grayish brain came into view, the mutie slumped to the ground, then rolled over, as if trying to protect itself.

Unleashing the scattergun from the back of his horse, J.B. missed again. With a wild expression, the man hopped off the animal to run closer to the regenerating wendigo and savagely kicked it over to trigger the remaining barrel directly into the brain. The grayish matter exploded a horrid goo across the flames, bubbling and steaming wherever they landed.

Watching from behind the wall of flames, the other wendigos bellowed in rage as they were splattered with the gore of their fallen comrade, then they turned to disappear into the thick smoke.

"Fuck this, let's ride!" Ryan commanded, kicking the horses into a full gallop.

Heading away from the growing inferno and the glowing rad pit, the companions streaked across the deadland on their horses, hooves kicking up clouds of dust from the sterilized ground. Casting a glance behind, Krysty saw that the two wendigos were again in pursuit, their charred fur healing as the creatures charged along on all fours, their inhuman gaze locked upon the companions. However, as the miles passed, the muties began to fall behind and soon disappeared over the horizon.

"Keep riding for as long as we can!" Mildred shouted

over the clattering hooves. "There's no telling if these things ever get tired!"

"Head south!" J.B. yelled, his eyes closed, his face scrunched. "If there's a swamp, there might be a bridge we could cross and burn behind us! Stop them from following!"

"And if there is not?" Doc rumbled, bent low over his galloping mount.

"Then we head for a redoubt that's a couple of hundred miles to the east," Ryan continued, his black hair flying in the wind. "We'll be safe inside and can jump out of this area for good!"

"But our stuff…" Mildred began plaintively.

"Forget it!" the man retorted. "What we've got now is good enough to start again!"

"Had less when first met," Jak added succinctly, moving to the powerful stride of his stallion.

"We found eyeglasses before," J.B. stated confidently. "So we can do it again!"

The rest of the companions voiced their agreement to the idea, with only Mildred and Doc abstaining, their troubled faces cloudy with private thoughts.

Chapter Fourteen

Racing through the darkness, Dunbar bent low over the motorcycle's handlebars, straining to see the road ahead in the black night.

The bike's headlight worked just fine, but turning that on would give Ryan and the others advance warning of his approach, which would defeat the whole purpose of the hard recce. He was here to find the group and bring back their heads. Armed for the mission, Dunbar had a sawed-off scattergun in a holster at his side, a bandolier of spare brass across his chest and a Browning 30.03 longblaster tucked into the gun boot alongside the yoke of the bike. There was also a bowie knife tucked into one of his U.S. Army combat boots, and a predark gren weighed heavily in the pocket of his leather jacket.

Privately, Dunbar had mixed emotions over the assignment. Ryan and the others had freed him from the prison cell, so he owed them his life. However, they attacked people in his ville. Okay, the ville people attacked first, so the friends had only been defending themselves. But then they broke down the front gate and chilled sec men. Both acts were hanging offenses. He was obliged to ace them, yet owed them his life. If there was some way to do both, Dunbar would have gladly done it, but so far no such solution presented itself. When in doubt, protect the ville, as his father always used to say. The teenager took some comfort in that, but his heart was still in turmoil, torn between duty and loyalty.

In preparation for a long trip, the sidecar attached to his hog was jammed with spare brass, fuel, food and water. There was even a rainproof poncho in case he was still hunting for the outlanders when the spring rains came. That had been a not-so-subtle reminder from the baron to bring back proof the outlanders were chilled, or not to come back at all. Period.

Two against six, Dunbar ruminated dourly. Those were not very good odds, especially considering that the friends had escaped from a locked ville with a hundred people blocking the way.

Lieutenant Fenton was driving the second bike. Incredibly, somehow, the sec man had survived the explosion in the apple orchard. If *survived* was the right word, Dunbar mentally corrected himself. Fenton had several broken bones and was thickly wrapped in bandages, until only a single eye glared out at the world. Not even the baron had been able to make the sec man stay in the ville and heal. Fenton wanted blood, and he wanted it now. Everybody knew that the man would be a wreck when the bandages came off, his once handsome face reduced to a mass of overlapping scars.

The lieutenant's sidecar was similarly packed with brass and assorted supplies, including a working rad counter. That had been a gift from the baron to help make sure that the Delta folk stayed clear of rad pits.

Slowly, the miles flashed by, the shadowy landscape rising like waves on the sea. Once they were past the apple orchards, the two sec men streaked across fields of grass. Only once did the rad counter start to click, but the glow on the horizon had already warned them of the approaching rad pit, and they wisely steered clear of the ancient nuke crater.

Reaching a stretch of predark highway, the two sec men opened up the hogs to full speed and roared along at nearly eighty miles per hour for several hours until the roadway abruptly stopped near the edge of a swamp. As they slowed, a stickie rushed out of the bushes, hooting and waving its arms. Dunbar sped away, but Fenton waited until it was almost upon him before triggering his revolver. The blast shattered the night, and as the mutie fell, the lieutenant spit on the creature, then kicked the hog alive and raced away to rejoin the sec chief.

"That was a waste of brass," Dunbar growled over the sputtering engine.

"Just wanted to make sure I could still shoot," Fenton lied, holstering the massive blaster.

Heading toward the north, the two men arched around Redstone ville and Tickle Belly Lake.

"You know, the bubbling water there is supposed to have special healing powers," Dunbar said as a suggestion. "Kinda magical-like."

"Ain't nothing gonna help but chilling me some outlanders," Fenton growled, the words muffled by the multiple layers of bandages.

Passing a rusted predark sign of a winged horse, the sec men killed their engines and coasted to a stop. Listening to the night wind, they tried to hear if anything was moving in the area.

"Can't hear a thing," Fenton said, a hand cupped to his ear. "Think our friend is hereabouts?"

"Certainly hope not," Dunbar replied, drawing the Browning from the boot and working the arming bolt.

There was a reason why very few wendigos ever bothered Delta ville. The muties were terrified of the Outer Guard. It lived in a cave in the foothills and watched everything that passed on the predark road. When the former baron had sent messengers to Redstone, they always gave a wide berth to this area, going miles out of their way to avoid the Guard. In spite of its size, the Outer Guard moved as fast as a horse, so if a man was on foot when it attacked, he was soon on the last train west. If a person was on horseback, it was an even race. And if a person was on a hog or in a wag, driving past was easy.

"Unless you're hauling an overloaded sidecar," Dunbar muttered softly, making sure the longblaster was set on full-auto. One pull of the trigger now would discharge the twenty rounds in the magazine faster than a man could sneeze.

"Yeah, I know," Fenton growled in agreement, clearly thinking along similar lines. Pulling out his own Browning, the wounded man briefly checked the weapon. "We could swing to the north, only waste an hour or so. Sound good?"

"Yeah, sounds good," Dunbar said, then stiffened as two crimson lights appeared in the darkness ahead. There came the steady whomp-whomp-whomp of something large coming their way fast.

"Too late!" Dunbar yelled, triggering the BAR. "Open fire!"

The heavy longblaster was almost torn from his grip as it cycled through the twenty cartridges, and the teen could hear the lead ricocheting off the armored hull of the Guardian.

With nothing to lose anymore, Fenton turned on his headlight and spotted a dented predark machine. Over six feet high and easily three times that in length, the armored body was oblong, similar to an egg, and there were six metallic legs coming out of the sides, giving the Guardian a definite spiderlike appearance. A pair of serrated pinchers extended from just below the feature-less face dominated by a pair of large, red crystal eyes that constantly spun in place. The sight was unnerv-ing and disorientating, which was probably the idea, since this was known to be a military war machine, an ancient guardian, although of what nobody knew anymore.

Swiveling on a belly mount, some kind of blaster aimed at the two men, and a steady rattling noise rent the air, like pebbles shaken in a tin can. But nothing seemed to happen. Whatever the weapon was, it no longer worked.

However, the pinchers did, and stomped closer. The Guardian made a pass at Fenton and then Dunbar, the scissoring metal missing them by mere inches. Then a rancid smell hit the sec men, the telltale reek of rotting flesh informing them that the Guardian had slain some-thing recently. That was when they saw the pinchers in the reflected light of the headlight, the pitted steel coated with dried blood and dangling strips of decom-posing offal.

Slamming in a fresh clip, Dunbar switched back to

semiautomatic, clumsily working the arming bolt with his left hand, to hammer the machine once more with a fusillade of 30.06 rounds. But this close, he could actually see the soft-lead bullets flatten against the domed body and tumble away like tiny gray pancakes.

Trying his own weapon, Fenton lost control of the bucking BAR on full-auto, the stream of armor-piercing rounds churning a path of destruction through the dirt, then chewing bark off a tree some fifty yards away.

Suddenly, excited hooting rose from the swamp, and the men cursed as they realized the sounds of blasters had attracted the attention of a group of stickies.

As the Guardian turned to face this new threat, Fenton drew the Webley and triggered a fast four rounds. The big bore blaster thundered into the night, the massive rounds slamming dents into the armored hull and shattering one of the crystal eyes.

Turning, the machine snapped its pinchers at the man, shattering the windshield of his motorcycle, the pinchers slamming closed only inches away from his chest.

Clawing for the sawed-off, Dunbar gave the Guardian both barrels, the double report echoing across the landscape and into the swamp. The maelstrom of soft-lead pellets blasted across the machine, deepening several of the dents and opening one like folding back a curtain. Briefly, the sec chief saw inside the machine, twinkling lights, nests of wiring, banks of electric motors and a complex array of plastic netting that pulsed with moving beams of light.

Without conscious thought, Dunbar aimed the

sawed-off and pressed the trigger, then bitterly cursed as the empty weapon merely clicked.

Spinning around and around again, the Guardian then lurched away from the two men, one of its legs impotently dragging behind.

"Come back here, ya tin fuck," Fenton growled, yanking out the spent magazine from the Browning to insert a fresh one from his ammo belt. Yanking back the arming bolt, he aimed and put two rounds into the departing machine, which only made it move faster toward the nearby trees.

"Stop wasting brass," Dunbar said, reloading the Remington scattergun.

"No, I want it chilled," Fenton snarled, firing six more times, the ricochets zinging off the domed hull to hit some rocks on the ground and throw off sparks.

"Lieutenant, I said enough!" Dunbar bellowed, using the whipcrack tone his father had taught both of the brothers at a very young age.

The furious sec man paused for only a moment. "Yes, sir," he answered sullenly, lowering the smoking longblaster.

Just then, several stickies rose from the scum-covered water of the nearby swamp and began eagerly sloshing toward the muddy shore, hooting and waving their sucker-covered hands.

Instantly, the two sec men raised their weapons to fire, then holstered them, kicked the bikes into life and drove away, leaving the shambling stickies quickly behind.

"That machine was pretty badly damaged before we arrived," Fenton said, a loose strip of his bandages fluttering in the wind. "That's the only reason we got away so easy."

"Agreed," Dunbar said over the rumbling engine. "I'd guess that the outlanders have been this way and tangled with the Guardian first."

"Pity it didn't ace 'em," Fenton muttered, then barked a laugh. "Come to think of it, mebbe it did, and the stickies dragged off the bodies for dinner!"

"If that's the case, we're well and truly nuked," Dunbar replied. "Because neither of us is ever going to see the inside of Delta again unless we have the heads of the outlanders!"

Slowing his bike, Fenton cast a glance at the dark swampland to the south. The stickies still raced after the two men, waving their arms and hooting wildly. Shitfire, Fenton thought. Even if they somehow managed to find the bodies in there, the outlanders would be stripped of any flesh by now, the skulls featureless white bone with nothing on them that could be used for identification.

"Sons of bitches better be alive in Modine so I can ace 'em myself," Fenton snarled, twisting the throttle of the big motorcycle to gun the engine and race ahead into the Stygian night.

As THE COMPANIONS rode along the rusty railroad tracks, Mildred studied the nighttime sky above, relishing the brief respite from the usual heavy cover of polluted storm clouds. A crescent moon sat high amid a sea of the twinkling stars, the heavenly orb oddly obscured by a thin fog. The physician wasn't sure if it was something in the sky or something around the moon itself.

Had the British ever built their mining base on Luna? she wondered. Were the astronauts still there, breeding and building, forging a new space-based civilization? Or had they perished after the last shipment of supplies? The history of humanity seemed to be equal parts incredible heroism and monumental stupidity. The yin and yang of life.

At least the companions were finally safe from those accursed wendigos.

There had been a predark bridge that extended over the southern swamp, the pylons thick with flowering vines that snapped at the horses and tried more than once to impale the companions with thorn-tipped roots.

Upon finally reaching the other side, J.B. had used half their remaining supply of ammunition to make a bomb powerful enough to blow the ancient structure in two. Which was good timing because as he finished, the stickies arrived in force, dozens of the horrid muties hooting insanely and waving their sucker-covered hands at the thought of a juicy feast of norms and horse flesh just waiting to be harvested.

The blast destroyed the bridge and sent the stickies hurtling away to land in a bubbling pool of toxic chems that melted the flesh off their bones. The resulting span between dry land and the ragged end of the bridge was a good hundred feet, so even if the wendigos were still after the companions, they would now need wings to continue the hunt. Nothing that walked was making it through that swamp alive.

Following the rusty tracks, the companions spent days traveling through abandoned farmlands. The houses, barns and silos had all crumbled back into the earth, the crops running wild, the fields of cotton, soybeans and clover mixing in a rather pleasing panorama of colors and smells.

"If it wasn't for the stickies, this would make a good place to settle," Ryan said, an unfamiliar touch of gentleness in his normally gruff voice. "You could build a small ville on that hilltop over there, see? It has an excellent view of the landscape, and climbing up that hill would make a ville hard to attack."

"Yes, it would," Krysty agreed, riding her horse a little closer.

"And nobody bother for years still think this mutie territory," Jak said with a lopsided grin, then laughed. "First time stickies good for anything."

"Think we'll ever find Petrov and his boys?" J.B. asked.

"Don't know," Ryan said honestly. "But we're heading east again, toward Modine, and we're close to a redoubt."

"We're still not planning on a jump," Mildred said, hugging the flaccid med kit to her chest.

"No, we're safe from those wendigos," the man growled. "But we can check inside the redoubt for supplies. If luck is with us..." He shrugged and kept riding onward.

"Not see anything like wendigos," Jak stated, stropping a knife blade on a smooth rock. "Tough."

"What's that up ahead?" Krysty asked, craning her neck.

Slowing their mounts, the companions drew blasters and proceeded slowly, moving away from one another purely as a precaution. However, that proved to be unnecessary as over the next hillock was a small farming community. Scarcely more than a village, there was a truck stop surrounded by a dozen houses and a couple of grain silos.

"I don't think this place has ever been looted," Ryan said, loosening the reins for his horse. "The stickies must have kept everybody else away."

"But not us," Krysty added.

"No wonder intact," Jak scoffed. "Nothing here worth anything."

"Millie, think there might be an eye doctor here?" J.B. asked.

"There might be." She smiled. "There just damn well might be!"

As the companions rode closer, they noticed the village was in poor shape, with most of the homes collapsing inward upon themselves. There were wags on the streets and telephone wires overhead, but the little town reeked of decay, the canvas awnings of the stores tattered, and the few intact windows were so thickly encrusted with grime they were a murky opaque in color, a nondescript shade of forgotten.

Checking for ammunition first, the companions discovered that the police station was burned to the ground, most likely from a lightning strike. Only a few scattered pieces of the foundation showed through the accumulated piles of dead leaves and dying ivy. The windows of the pawnshop were intact, but the roof had collapsed, and now a small jungle of wild plants grew amid the display cases.

On the street, the cars and trucks sat on their rims, the rubber tires long crumbled away. If there had been drivers behind the wheels, the bodies had also gone the way of all flesh, destroyed by time itself, instead of the savage hand of man.

"There's nothing here to scav," Ryan muttered, looking around the place. "We might as well continue on to the redoubt and see if we can find any supplies there."

"Quiet," Krysty snapped, pulling her rapid-fire from the gun boot. Just then, the woman jerked her head up and drew both blasters to fire at something moving fast in the sky overhead.

Chapter Fifteen

The night was warm, the rain long gone, and the breeze from the north, carrying the smell of the Cobalt Mountains, was rich and heavy with pine and distant snow.

Sitting inside the rim of a broken fountain, the Pig Iron Gang was cooking dinner over a campfire. The ancient granite reflected the waves of heat from the small fire, making them quite comfortable inside the basin. Above them, the smoke curled along the bronze statue of some predark sec man carrying a muzzle-loading longblaster and wearing a coonskin cap.

Looking over his roasted leg of dog, Petrov Cordalane blinked in surprise. "Say that again," he ordered, tossing the partially eaten food over a shoulder and wiping his mouth clean on a sleeve.

"I can read it," Thal said, shaking the journal in one big hand. "I cracked their code!"

Stretching for what seemed like miles around the gang were the crumbling ruins of the predark city of Modine. Great towers rose tilted into the cloudy sky, every window gone or splintered into a spiderweb of crazy cracks. Covering the streets and sidewalks was a thick layer of rubbish, most of it glass, but also a lot of rusting metal in the most amazing variety of shapes and sizes, along with a host of plastic things that nobody had any idea about whatsoever. The ancient rubble was yards deep in some areas, piled up against the charred buildings like windblown leaves. Different size wags were everywhere, ripe for the looting, the engines still intact and untouched. Some were colored like chunks of the rainbow, while others were huge and gray, massive machines of rusty armor, supporting a blaster so big it had to have taken two strong men to load in a brass. Tricycles and toilet seats, tea kettles and turbines, Modine was the richest predark city west of the Missy Sip. Hundreds of people had to have come every year to try to scavenge something of value. Only the presence of the wendigos kept most folks at bay, including those annoying barbs, but the Pig Iron Gang knew how to trick a wendy, and so had safe passage through the ruins. That made Modine the perfect hunting ground. All they had to do was grow a little moss, poison a few ponds, then wait for the feebs to arrive.

"What's it say?" Rose asked, rubbing a slice of apple on her own roasted leg of dog meat.

"There's a calendar in the front of the book," Thal said, not answering her question. "Which was odd, because all of the other printed pages are gone, torn out, see?" He riffled the ragged edges of the missing pages. "So I started thinking, why keep this one page unless it was important somehow?"

"Paper is only important in the lav," Rose replied.

"Anyway," Thal continued, "underneath the calendar was the only thing in the book not in code, one sentence." He waited. Nobody said anything. "'The quick brown fox jumps over the lazy dog.'" Thal grinned. "It was us eating dog that made me think of it. Dog, that's the key."

"Has he been smoking any zoomers?" Petrov asked, glancing sideways.

"If so, he ain't been sharing it with me," Rose mumbled, her mouth full.

"Someone told me once that sentence has every letter in the alphabet," Thal explained, feeling like he was trying to push a wet rope. "So I started exchanging letters with the garbled stuff, and nuke me, it suddenly made sense!"

"Okay, Thal, you're the baron of all whitecoats, congrats." Charlie sighed, placing aside his cup and lighting a cig. "So what's it say?"

Angling the journal for some better light from the campfire, Thal pursed his lips, then haltingly began. "Greetings, my name is Mildred Wyeth, I am a physician and was cryogenically frozen in December 2000, only to awaken a hundred year later in Deathlands."

"This was writ by someone who was frozen?" Petrov asked in a whisper, staring at the big man. "A freezie?"

"Guess so," Thal said excitedly from behind the book. "Now listen up, you gleebs, here comes the good part." The man cleared his throat. "I will be putting down my innermost thoughts on these pages, as honestly as I can, to help me sort out the…ah…transition from the past to this monstrous new world."

"Blah, blah, blah, the freezie prefers the predark world to working for a living," Petrov scoffed. "Probably too ugly to be a gaudy slut. Why should we give a damn about this drek?"

"…I will also be putting down any, and all, useful information that I know," Thal went on, "from safe zones where a person can seek refuge, such as Two-Son ville in the NewMex desert south of the Great Salt, to villes to avoid like Rock ville east of the Ohio River. Also, how to spot a rad pit, how to kill the worst of the mutants—that's old talk for muties—the formula for black powder and how to process it into the much more powerful gunpowder, basic chemistry, some electronics and all of my vast medical knowledge."

"A phiz-zish-son. That be a healer?"

"Appears so."

"Blind NORAD, and we left her by the waterfall for Big Joe to sell to the slavers!" Charlie growled, exhaling a long stream of smoke. "A predark healer! We could have gotten anything we wanted from a baron for her, any nuking thing we wanted!"

"I heard of a coldheart named Fitzwilly sold a healer slave to a trader for a war wag," Rose added excitedly. "A whole damn war wag! Blaster, brass, juice and everything! Now he rolls under a different name, Broke-Neck Pete, and has barons kissing his arse for the things he brings in for trade."

"You mean like the stuff we have here in Modine," Petrov said very slowly, tasting each word. "The drek that's piled yards deep for a mile in every direction."

Licking her lips, Rose could only nod, while Charlie gave a long, low whistle. Wealth beyond their dreams lay about them piled in heaps, ripe for the taking, if they had a war wag to ferry the stuff to the East Coast barons, those were the richest. More brass and better food than they could ever hope to barter from the traders, and without the constant danger of the fragging slavers trying to toss the gang into their damn wooden cages.

"Does the book tell the location of her cryo-whatever unit?" Petrov asked eagerly, cracking his knuckles. "That must have been where she got that implo gren and these fancy blasters."

"Not yet." Thal sighed, closing the journal with a thump. "I've only done the one page, and that took me most of today. But there's a map in the back of a place looks like a bomb shelter. A huge one, five stories deep, mebbe more."

Petrov felt as if he had been hit with lightning. *Jackpot!* "Then stop yammering at me and get back to work," Petrov commanded, with an imperial wave of the hand. "We'll do the rest of the hunting and the cooking. Your job now is decoding that book, and nothing else."

"No prob. Sure could do with a cig," Thal said, his words thick with meaning. "That'd help a lot."

Without a comment, Charlie removed the hand-rolled smoke from his mouth and passed it over.

Smiling, Thal took a long drag, then opened the journal and started counting letters again, flipping back and forth from one part of the journal to another.

"What do you think we'd find in that bomb shelter?" Rose asked, her fingers toying with the pretty sextant hanging between her breasts.

"Our future," Petrov whispered, lost in thought, stirring the campfire with a green stick. Just then, the clouds parted to bath Modine in silvery moonlight as the hot embers rose in a swirling cloud to fly into the nighttime sky and disappear from sight.

THE SOUND of Krysty's blaster was still ringing in their ears when a spear slammed into the ground among the companions, a scalp dangling from the wooden shaft as decoration.

"Barbs!" Ryan cursed, hauling out the Marlin.

At the word, hundreds of people silently rose into view from every building in the little town. Each of them was dressed in simple buckskins and carried a long spear. Most of them wore bandoliers hung across their chests, the leather strips supporting blasters of every kind, wheelguns, autoloaders, derringers, zipguns and a couple that Ryan couldn't identify. From their travels, the companions knew that the barbs didn't use the blasters, only their deadly spears. They collected the weapons as trophies, to show their chills, the same way some coldhearts did ears or fingers.

Tense minutes passed while Ryan and the chief barb did nothing. With weapons in hand, neither moved or said a word as they faced each other. Slowly, the minutes crept by before the chief barb broke the imposing silence.

"You must leave," the chief barb said in a deep and commanding voice. "With the destruction of the swamp bridge, the unstoppable Great Ones will be forced to make their nest here, in our holy place."

Unstoppable…wendigos?

"Why not chill them?" Ryan replied simply.

"Impossible!" a female barb yelled. "Nothing can stop a Great One!"

"We done," Jak stated with a shrug.

A low murmur of confusion swept through the huge crowd, and the chief barb looked hard at the albino teenager before nodding. "I hear truth in your voice," the man said slowly. "Tell us how this was done, and you shall have safe passage through our lands for a day."

"A month and a day," Doc said.

Puzzled, the chief barb frowned.

"He means for a moon," Mildred translated, nudging the old man with an elbow.

A moon and a day? The chief barb dismissed that with a wave of his hand. "No, you ask for too much!"

"We don't know what to ask for," Ryan said, controlling his temper, "since we don't know the extent of your land."

The crowd smiled at that, and the chief barb snorted a laugh. The outlander was wise. "We rule from the swamp to the Cobalt Mountains, and from the glass lake to the black doors of Horseshoe Canyon. All of that belongs to us." The barb expected the outlanders to be impressed, but their silence was heavy, their features stiff from the effort to remain neutral. So, they had seen the black doors, eh? Few outlanders had and lived to speak of it. The Great Ones guarded the doors like their cubs. Yet those were to the north, and the outlanders came from the west. Interesting, the chief barb thought.

"How long would it take to reach Horseshoe Canyon?" Krysty asked, keeping the interest out of her words. Black doors, could that be the entrance to a redoubt?

The barb almost smiled at that question. "Two suns."

Which meant the earlier offer of one-day safe passage was merely a trick to get them out of the town, Ryan realized coldly, so that the companions could be attacked somewhere else. Perhaps these were the descendants of the original farmers and still held the land in reverence.

"Then again, perhaps we'll stay right here," Ryan said, patting his horse. "This is good land. We might farm, raise families and never leave."

"Sacrilege!" a barb screamed, advancing a step and raising his spear to throw.

The crowd gasped in horror at the action, when there came the crack of a blaster and the wooden shaft of the spear exploded as it flew out of the barb's grip. With a cry of pain, the barb cradled his bleeding hand, his fingers bristling with splinters.

"I could have removed his head," Mildred said, holstering her smoking blaster.

"But you did not," the chief barb murmured. Was it from fear of their numbers? No, he saw no fear in these six, unlike the four that had passed through earlier on their forbidden machines. They had reeked with nervous sweat, and it was only the speed of the iron horses that allowed them to escape alive.

"We don't chill unless it's necessary," Ryan stated, crossing his arms.

"Nor do we," the chief barb replied, turning. "Chal-ka! Who is your worst enemy in the tribe?"

"Tal-hala," the wounded barb muttered uneasily, his gaze shifting to a beautiful woman who scowled at him in open contempt.

"Since he is no more, his widow, Da-sha, is now your wife for the next winter."

"No…!" the barb started, then bowed his head in shame. "I hear and obey. Her pots will be full of meat, her bed warm."

"Then your sin is forgotten," the chief barb said ritually, and looked back at Ryan. "You knew we do not chill here." He didn't phrase it as a question.

"We're still breathing," Ryan said in explanation, "and you had the drop on us. Fair and square."

Saying nothing for a few minutes, the chief barb thrust his spear into the soil. "Safe passage for a hand of days, no more."

Five days to leave territory only two days wide. "Fair deal," Ryan said, pulling his knife.

Walking closer, the chief barb also drew a knife and in unison the two men cut their own palms, then clasped hands. The entire tribe thumped the ground with the blunt end of their spears in approval.

"I am Hoal-thar, and this is the tribe," the chief barb said, reclaiming his hand and sheathing the bloody knife.

"The name's Ryan Cawdor." He introduced the rest of the companions.

"So, tell me, Ryan of the One-Eye, how did you slay a Great One?" Hoal-thar asked, binding his palm with a strip of cloth.

"Fire. They can't regen from fire very quickly," Ryan answered, doing the same with a handkerchief. "Move fast, and they fall."

Another low murmur swept the army of barbs at this pronouncement, but this time their faces were stern and disapproving.

"That is a forbidden word," Hoal-thar growled, tightening the crude bandage until his skin turned white from the pressure.

"Nothing is forbidden if there is no other word to use," Doc spoke up again.

The tribe made various noises at that, and the chief chuckled. "Your wrinklie is wise."

"What can you tell us about those black doors?" Ryan asked.

Suddenly, someone on a rooftop screamed, and a barb vanished from sight only to reappear a second later, the two halves of the body sailing away in opposite directions.

"A Great One!" a barb yelled in warning, pulling back his arm to throw the spear, then pausing, unable to break the ancient taboo on chilling.

Bellowing, a wendigo rose into view and swatted the barb aside, the man flying off the rooftop to land on the street below with a sickening crunch. Snarling defiantly, the barbs raised their deadly spears, then lowered them again, their faces clearly showing the internal struggle between wanting to fight and breaking the most sacred of all laws.

Seeing their indecision, Ryan made a fast decision. "Ace it!" he shouted, levering a round into the Marlin.

Opening fire with their blasters, the companions hammered the wendigo with hot lead as the huge mutie jumped off the roof to land in the street, the impact cracking the pavement for yards. Their bodies trembling from the effort to do nothing, the barbs could only watch in impotent rage.

Constantly jerking from the arrival of the bullets,

yellow blood everywhere, the wendigo slowly stood to
stumble toward the companions in an awkward gait, its
broken bones audibly grinding back into place.

Chapter Sixteen

Shutting down their sputtering bikes, the Pig Iron Gang checked their blasters before stepping off the hogs and walking toward the rocky cliff. Some pebbles were kicked ahead of the gang and tumbled over the edge to disappear. It was almost a full minute before they hit the ground below and bounced off the jagged boulders into the sluggish river of blue water.

"And there it is, just like Big Joe said." Petrov chuckled, resting the plastic stock of the Steyr on a hip.

"I guess for once the son of a bitch wasn't lying," Charlie said, a cold grin slowly forming.

Clutching the book, Thal merely grunted in agreement.

"Amazing," Rose whispered, extending the Navy telescope to its full length. "Simply amazing."

Looking down into the craggy abyss of Horseshoe Canyon, the four coldhearts studied the colossal pair of black metal doors. This time of year, the Cobalt River flowed gently through the box canyon, green plants growing along both of the rocky banks and surrounding the single pillar of red stone that rose from a small island in the middle. During the spring, the melting snow from the Cobalts made the river a rushing torrent that flooded the little canyon nearly to the top, the northern water foaming from the punishment it received racing into the curved box canyon, only to rush out again toward the east, moving even faster.

Over time, the brutal currents had to have shifted enough of the loose stones to uproot a boulder, and as it shifted position it revealed a pair of the black doors. The metal appeared to be new, without a scratch or a flake of rust, as if freshly forged only minutes earlier. Yet they had to have been hidden before skydark, over a hundred years before.

Swinging up the Steyr, Petrov looked through the telescopic sights, sweeping along the murmuring river until finding the black doors. A warm breeze ruffled his clothes as the coldheart studied the metal barrier carefully and then the nearby rock formations. Aside from the black doors, there was nothing unusual about the rocky pillar. A couple of small trees tried to grow out of the sides, and a stingwing had a nest situated in the branches of a yucca tree at the very top, the nearby rocks littered with the gnawed bones of hundreds of small animals.

"If there's a keypad down there somewhere, it's bastard well hidden," Petrov announced gruffly, lowering the longblaster. Then he petulantly raised it again and fired. The stingwing jerked from the arrival of the 5.56-mm copper-jacketed round and collapsed into the nest. Instantly, the newborn stingwings began tearing their mother apart into bloody gobbets.

"The book says it's there," Thal stated confidently, hugging it closer.

"Well, I can't see the damn thing!"

"Not from here anyway," Rose countered, double-checking with the Navy telescope. There was no sand or even dirt near the doors to hold any footprints. A dead juniper bush stood in front of the portal, which meant that either nobody had been there for at least a day or the doors slid aside, instead of swinging out.

"Ain't no choice," Charlie said, pulling a piece of smoked fish from a pocket and starting to gnaw on it. "We gotta go down there and check up close."

"There could be all sorts of traps to chill the curious," Rose warned, checking the rad counter clipped to the lapel of her jacket. Thankfully, the device was silent.

"No, that isn't a shatterzone," Petrov stated. "The blast craters and skeletons would only reveal where the door had been hidden. That is, before that boulder moved."

The rest of them nodded in agreement. With the boulder in place, there would have been no way to tell the doors were there, unless you were standing on the island only a few feet away. They knew the predark military had been crazy, but not stupe.

"How did Joe find them again?" Charlie mumbled around the fish.

"Hiding from some trader named Roberto. He sold the guy a bag full of diamonds that were actually something called quartz, and the damn trader went ballistic! Over diamonds."

"What good are they, aside from putting into a scattergun for shrapnel?"

"Dunno, but that Roberto acted like he'd been sold a bag of fake brass, and that's a fact."

"So, Big Joe never got inside?" Rose asked.

"Nope. Oh, he tried to blow his way in using black

powder and even something called TNT, but the doors never budged, never even shook hard." The coldheart frowned. "Then again, Big Joe never knew to look for a keypad."

"I tell you it's down there somewhere," Thal reiterated stubbornly, tucking the book away inside the canvas med bag.

"Well, I don't see any way down from here," Rose stated, glancing over the ancient stones. "We'll have to circle around to the flatlands and travel up the river."

"Without a boat?" Charlie asked, tightening the belt on his bearskin coat. "Gonna carry us on your back?"

"The water isn't very deep here, only downstream where we crossed a few days ago," Thal answered, then his eyes went wide. "Down! Everybody get down!" he cried out, dropping flat.

The others swiftly followed suit, then crawled forward on their bellies to peek over the edge of the cliff to see what had startled the man.

"Son of a bitch, it's the Guardian!" Charles whispered in astonishment.

Down in the canyon, a droid was sloshing through the shallow river, the five legs kicking up rippling wakes. The rusty chassis of the machine was battered and dented, an eye was missing and one leg was dragging along behind, tufts of grass and a tree branch caught in the crook of the bent metal.

"What do ya think it's doing here?" Rose asked in a hushed whisper, working the bolt on the Uzi rapid-fire.

"The same thing we are," Petrov growled in reply, titling back his fedora.

Going around the curve, the Guardian went straight to the island and stood before the black doors. Nothing seemed to happen, but a moment later, the doors ponderously slid aside, revealing a smooth tunnel brightly illuminated with lights. As the damaged machine stumbled inside, the doors rumbled closed again with a dull boom.

"Well, that nukes this idea!" Rose growled, rolling onto her back to face the sky. "Only a feeb would attack the Guardian. Even one as beat-up as that!"

"Not necessarily," Thal said, removing his wool cap to scratch his bald head before pulling it back into place. "One of the levels in the book is marked as a garage, with a machine shop. The Guardian is probably going in there to fix itself."

"How is that good news?" Charlie stormed.

"Because it'll probably leave here to go back to the swamp and stand guard again."

"And if it doesn't?" Charlie retorted hotly. "What if the triple-cursed thing is settling in for good, making this its new home?"

The giant man scowled at that possibility, but could offer no reasonable rebuttal.

"Your call, Chief," Rose said, sitting up and turning to look into the canyon again. "Should we wait to see what happens, or do we go in now?"

"Neither," Petrov said, slowly standing. "We go down right now, but even if we find the keypad, we don't go inside. We knock on that black door until the Guardian comes out to see what's going on." Rummaging about in the munitions bag, the coldheart unearthed a pipe bomb. "Then we blow it to hell and claim the bomb shelter for ourselves!"

CUTTING LOOSE with all of their blasters, the companions maintained a steady barrage of lead into the lumbering wendigo, smashing the leg joints and shooting out the eyes as fast as they were being regenerated. But even then, the fur kept changing color to match whatever it was near—the street, a bush growing out of a pothole, the rusted wreck of the predark wag.

Stepping in close, Ryan viciously slit the mutie's throat. Yellow blood gushed out to cover the man, and using all of his strength, Ryan tried to remove the head. But the neck bones proved to be impossible to cut through and the one-eyed man had to step aside fast when the gurgling creature lashed out with its tentacles.

Raising his spear to throw, a barb then turned away in shame and cast it onto the ground. With tears of frustration in his eyes, the barb looked at the ancient metal signpost that marked the city limits. It was thirty feet away. A child could throw that far before they were weaned! Now it was as distant as the moon. Standing in the middle of the street, a female barb slumped her shoulders in defeat, while another male softly began to hum his death song. Unable to fight and unwilling to run, there was nothing else for the tribe to do but stand and perish.

"Medusa, call me Perseus!" Doc shouted, bracing the M-16/M-203 combo against his leather saddle. Impatiently, he waited until Ryan was clear before triggering the reloaded shotgun shell. The deafening discharge forced the horse to stumble sideways and filled the street with a billowing cloud of dense smoke.

For several long moments, nobody could see the wendigo, then the cloud slowly dissipated, and the headless beast was still standing, thick golden blood pumping from the severed arteries in the neck. New muscle fibers were rising from the body in what could only be an attempt to regrow the destroyed head.

"Son of a bitch!" Mildred whispered, lowering her rapid-fire. "That…that's impossible!"

"Nothing impossible!" Jak snarled, putting five rounds from the booming Magnum blaster into the belly of the beast. The massive .44 rounds slammed the wendigo to the ground, gushing blood, and the filaments noticeably slowed in their work.

"Keep pumping in lead!" Ryan commanded, using the Marlin longblaster to blow off a knee. "Hoal-thar, help us ace this thing!"

"We cannot fight here. It is holy land," Hoal-thar said softly, his face bright red with shame.

Blindly struggling forward, the wendigo bumped into a barb and smacked the male aside with a paw full of claws.

Vivisected, the barb fell to the ground, his intestines slithering out of his body like greasy rope.

"Then give us wood!" Krysty snapped, slamming a fresh magazine into the AK-47. "Find a hole and fill it with wood, anything you can find! Is that permissible, the stacking of wood?"

"Yes, it is!" the chief barb said with growing excitement, then the man cupped a hand to his mouth and cut loose with an undulating war cry.

Surging into action, every member of the tribe rushed into the nearest building to come right back out again carrying a table, or a chair, sometimes both. Using his spear to point into the exposed basement of the old police station, Hoal-thar directed the hasty construction of a huge stack of flammable material.

As Krysty, Mildred and Doc maintained a steady pounding of the wendigo with their rapid-fires, Ryan knotted a long rope into a loop, while J.B. and Jak used their butane lighters to set some spare clothing on fire, then tossed it into the basement, along with the last of the shine and black powder. In only a few moments, the dry wood was ablaze and began growing into a bonfire.

Jumping onto his horse, Ryan lashed the rope around the pommel, rode toward the sightless mutie and threw the crude lasso. He caught a flailing arm and kicked the frightened stallion into a gallop. The Deathlands warrior knew that this trick had better work because at the rate the companions were using brass, they were never going to get another chance. This was it, all or nothing. Live or get aced.

Softly in the distance, another wendigo sounded a long, plaintive cry, sounding eerily like a wolf howling for its mate.

Unexpectedly jerked off its feet, the regenerating wendigo was brutally dragged down the street, patches of fur ripped off the monstrous body to leave a gory yellow trail along the cracked span of pavement. Riding pell-mell past the police station, Ryan cut the rope loose as he reached the mailbox and the mutie rolled along the ground to stop at the edge of the blazing-hot basement.

Even as white bone started to form a face amid the pulsating muscle tissue, the creature flinched from the growing waves of heat and started to move away.

Running up the street at full speed, J.B. insanely charged the wendigo and thrust his sawed-off right into the ragged belly. "Regen this, nuke sucker!" he snarled, and fired both barrels.

Thrown backward from the double blast, the wendigo stumbled over the rim of century-old masonry and fell sprawling into the inferno. Instantly, the sizzling fur turned fiery colors, and the mutie tried to claw its way out of the banked holocaust, the ancient brickwork coming out of the walls under the raking claws.

Rushing closer, the companions tied rags around their mouths to help them breath in the thick smoke and triggered their blasters into the mutie, blowing off fingers every time it tried to get free. Thrashing about mindlessly from the intolerable pain, the wendigo turned to battle the flames, punching and clawing at the unseen enemy, its tentacles lashing out in every direction. The regeneration of the head slowed as the skin blistered and charred, the raw hide splitting to reveal the flesh and bone underneath. The creature fell to the ground and didn't rise again, succumbing to the hellish embrace of the growing bonfire.

"Okay, it's aced." Ryan exhaled, tossing in the tattered head of the mutie.

"It would seem you spoke the truth, Ryan of the One Eye," the chief barb muttered, staring in frank wonder at the burning corpse. "I did not think it was possible to stop a Great One."

"Keep some pits stacked with wood just outside

the town limits, and they'll be easy picking from now on," Krysty added, removing the magazine from the AK-47 to check inside. Five rounds remained. Gaia, she thought, that had been close. Too damn close.

"Understood," Hoal-thar whispered, as the rest of the tribe hesitantly gathered around the crackling fire to peer down into the flames. Most of them smiled broadly, but a few of the barbs walked away to return with more wood and added it to the conflagration, not quite satisfied that the Great One was truly on the last train west.

"We have no way to thank you for this," Hoal-thar said simply, closing his empty hand into a tight fist. "We cannot even allow you more time to cross our lands. A deal once bound in blood cannot be changed. That is the law!"

"Then consider this our gift, sir," Doc rumbled, sliding his right hand into a pocket. "The enemy of my enemy is my friend, correct?"

The tribe of barbs murmured their approval over the sentiment. Suddenly, Da-sha pulled a rusty wheelgun from her bandolier and cracked open the cylinder to spill the .38 brass onto the street. There were two spent shells and four live.

"We collect blasters, not brass," the barb declared, tucking the blaster away once more, then pulling out a .22 zipgun and next a 9-mm Luger.

Standing nearby, Tal-hala nodded in approval and looked at the female with newfound respect.

Soon, the entire tribe was dropping clips and opening breeches, generating a small mound of ammunition in every imaginable caliber.

Waiting until everybody else was done, Hoal-thar then added his own contributions to the pile, a hundred spent rounds, fifty live and a U.S. Army gren with a double-red stripe around the canister.

"Dark night, that's willy peter!" J.B. stated, pointing a finger. "White phosphorous! It's hotter than a hundred bonfires! You might wanna keep that. It will fry a wendigo like a trout on a spit!"

"We cannot use tech," the chief barb stated solemnly, taking the gren and pressing it into the hand of the smaller norm. "But take it with our blessings."

Down in the basement, a burning table loudly cracked in two, sending a flurry of hot embers swirling into the sky. As if in reply, the other wendigo howled again, sounding much farther away than before.

Gathering around the mound of brass, the companions picked out the live rounds and pocketed them to check over later to make sure they were still in working condition. They would have preferred to do it immediately, but somehow they felt that would be seen as an insult. These barbs were touchier than a sweaty stick of dynamite.

"Your spears have been replaced, that is only proper," the chief barb said formally, as if speaking from memory. "But now you must leave, outlanders. Go, and find your friends in the Horseshoe Canyon, but never enter our lands again!"

Tucking a handful of .44 Magnum rounds into a pocket, Ryan arched an eyebrow at that statement. "Our friends who ride on two-wheels?" he asked in a measured tone.

"We do not speak of such things," Hoal-thar stated, thumping his spear on the sidewalk.

"But we still have your permission to reach Modine?" J.B. probed, pouring a fistful of assorted brass into his munitions bag.

"Once you are past the Horseshoe Canyon, it is of no concern to us what you do," Hoal-thar said, looking directly at the man to see if he understood what wasn't being said.

"As you command, Lord," Ryan said, placing a hand on his heart.

The chief barb gave no verbal response, but he flashed a very brief smile before turning and walking out of the predark town with the rest of the tribe close behind.

ONCE PAST the city limits, the companions picked up their speed and vanished into the overgrown farmland.

"Petrov and his gang are at the canyon," Krysty said excitedly, her hair flexing and curling. "Think they know about the redoubt?"

"How could they?" Mildred asked, feeling herself break into a sweat.

"Dunbar had said they were going to start up a new slave trade in Modine," Ryan said, brushing back his hair. "That canyon would be an ideal spot to grow their bastard moss out of sight of any passing trader or travelers."

"Okay, how do you handle this? Straight on, or a nightcreep?" J.B. asked, cracking open the sawed-off to yank out the exhausted cartridges.

"Still got that skin of poisoned water?"

With a jerk of his wrist, J.B. snapped the blaster closed. "Nope, lost it with the van."

"Then we just ride until we find them, then ace them on sight," Ryan snarled, walking over to reclaim his horse. The animal was chomping on the grass in front of what had once been a public library. Only the sign remained.

As the companions climbed onto their horses, Doc did so using only his left hand. Only Mildred seemed to notice the fact, but said nothing.

"Stay razor, people!" Ryan commanded, tucking the longblaster back into the gun boot. "They've got the advantage on us with those bikes. But once they're within range of this longblaster, they're meat in the ground!"

"Got Steyr," Jak reminded, scratching his horse behind an ear. The animal was clearly uneasy from the smell of the burning wendigo, but at his gentle touch she whinnied and stomped her hooves in pleasure.

"Not for long they don't," Ryan promised, kicking his stallion into a sprint and then a full gallop.

Racing out of the predark town, the companions gave their mounts free rein, and the horses moved fast along the ancient road, eagerly leaving the ruins behind, as the smoke from the grisly bonfire in the police station rose upward to spread across the cloudy sky.

Chapter Seventeen

Smacking aside a hissing alligator, a female wendigo suddenly stopped wading through the steaming swamp-land and became alert to a terrible smell on the wind. She instantly recognized it as smoke from the burned flesh of her mate. Fire! That was the only thing her species would try to avoid. Nervously, her fur rippled through a wide spectrum of different colors at the thought of the all-consuming destroyer.

Bawling in fury, the alligator charged once more, its teeth snapping, its deadly tail swinging back and forth like a killing pendulum. Annoyed, the wendigo simply grabbed the reptile in both clawed hands and ripped it apart, the beating heart and lungs splashing into the scummy water.

Casting aside the pieces of the twitching corpse, the wendigo started to slosh directly toward the awful death smell, but then paused as she remembered the destroyed strip of sky-ground that used to arch over the pool that ate flesh. The two-legs had destroyed that. Now the only way to reach that section of land was by following the road of water. But that would take until dark to reach, and by then the two-legs who burned her mate might be gone. The idea of the two-legs escaping her wrath made the mutie insane with rage, and she cut loose a roar that made everything in the swamp go immediately silent.

Fuming in frustration for a minute, the female reached down to grab the bloody carcass of the gator, then began sloshing toward the north. The wendigo would eat while she walked to the road of water, trusting the ever faithful wind to tell her where to go next and what to kill.

WITH A LOW RUMBLE of working hydraulics, the blast doors to the Horseshoe Canyon moved aside, and a Guardian stepped into the bright sunshine. The armored hull sleek and smooth, painted and polished. The six legs were working in perfect unison, and two red crystal eyes scanned the riverfront hostilely.

More importantly, there was a fully functioning Bedlow needler hanging from the belly mount. The ferruled barrel was barely thicker than a finger, but fully capable of silently emitting a stream of a hundred 1-mm steel slivers per second.

Striding onto the pebble shore, the Guardian barely registered the snap of the breaking twine stretched across the opening of the redoubt. As it looked down, expecting to see a snapped twig or broken stingwing egg, the canyon walls shook from a powerful explosion. With a grinding noise, the huge boulder rolled forward with surprising speed and smashed into the machine, driving it into the loose stones and rolling over it.

Pinned underneath the boulder, the Guardian flailed its crippled legs, then with a sad ratcheting noise went completely still.

"Told you that would work," Charlie boasted, pulling

out wads of waxed cloth from both ears as he rose from behind a blossoming juniper bush on the shoreline. "If it looks like a fragging spider, then chill it like a spider. Stomp on the bastard with your boot until it stops moving!"

"Speaking of moving..." Thal began, pointing a finger.

In a low rumble, the blast doors were already starting to close, the entranceway getting narrower by the second.

With a snarl, Petrov hurtled himself forward, charging up the sloping beach. The distance was less than a hundred feet, but by the time the man reached the doors they were almost closed, the opening only a few inches wide, impossible to get through. Risking everything, Petrov shoved his arm into the diminishing crack, skinning his knuckles, the squeeze was so tight. As the cold metal touched the coldheart's arm, he braced for the terrible onslaught of pain.

The cold metal tightened slightly on his arm, cutting off the circulation, then the imposing pressure eased, and the massive portal thankfully began to cycle open once more.

"My grandy told Big Joe about this," Petrov said, his body visibly relaxing. "These automatic doors got some kind of sensor thing that stops it from crushing an unconscious sec man lying in the way."

"You're just triple-damn lucky the sensor thing still worked," Thal said, looking down the tunnel. The floor and walls were made of the same smooth material, without any sign of age, wear or even corrosion.

"No guts, no glory." Petrov chuckled, massaging his

undamaged arm. Lining the ceiling, fluorescent lights glowed brightly, their soft hum barely discernible over the murmur of the nearby river. Electric lights! The coldheart was very impressed. He'd only occasionally seen that kind of illumination before, aside from the headlights on wags and such.

Behind the gang, the Guardian crushed under the boulder rattled softly, then went still again, hydraulic fluids leaking onto the ground like thin blood.

"Well, you sure enough got balls," Rose muttered, resting the Uzi on her shoulder. "Big, fat, hairy balls."

"You can load that into a blaster and fire it," Charlie agreed, adjusting his glasses.

Just then, the blast doors began to ponderously close once more.

Hurriedly, the companions stepped into the tunnel and moved away from the entrance. The doors closed with a dull boom, and the gang stood there for a few moments listening intently for any sound of movement down the tunnel. But there was only a deep silence, heavy and imposing.

Checking over their weapons, the gang started along the tunnel, then almost jumped as hidden air vents in the walls began blowing a warm breeze on them. It tasted oddly metallic, kind of flat, almost as if the very air had been scrubbed clean.

"Bomb shelter, my arse," Petrov muttered, slinging the longblaster over a shoulder and bringing up the S&W M-4000. "This is more like a predark mil base!" The long-range Steyr had many uses, but the inside of a building was scattergun territory.

"Bet there are a hundred of the implo grens in here

somewhere!" Charlie whispered, licking his thin lips. "Mebbe even nukes!"

"What the frag are you going to do with a nuke?" Rose snorted in disdain, the rapid-fire tight in her hands.

"I can think of a few things," the man replied, his face shiny with dreams of destruction.

"There could also be a hundred more of those Guardians," Thal commented. "So watch your six, and shoot anything that moves!"

"Anything that comes our way," Petrov corrected, working the pump action on the scattergun to load a cartridge for immediate use. "Spend the brass and save your ass. That's an order!"

Nodding assent, the Pig Iron Gang moved in a tight group along the tunnel, then turned the last corner and entered the garage level of the redoubt. Dozens of wags were parked in neat rows, regular wags, armored transports, an APC with an electric minigun on top and even a tank, a loose tread lying uselessly on the floor. But aside from a few deflated tires, the wags were in fine shape, the windows intact, the paint still bright with color, the trim shining in the reflected light of the fluorescent tubes overhead.

The sight of that many predark vehicles in perfect condition made the gang stop, then they cursed at the sight of the crippled Guardian standing at a tool bench on the far side of the cavernous room. The damaged leg had been removed and was clamped into a vise while snakelike tentacles from the dented machine did something inside the tube with bright flashes of a blue light.

Nuking hell, the machine outside wasn't the old Guardian fixed, Petrov realized in shock, but a replacement!

Moving fast, Thal lit a pipe bomb and whipped it over the rows of wags. The bomb landed on the tool bench with the fuse sputtering loudly, and the Guardian had only a second to register the fact before a massive explosion engulfed that side of the garage. It vanished inside the blast as a maelstrom of loose tools flew across the room to shatter hundreds of wag windows in a deafening cacophony of destruction and send a tidal wave of glass hurtling at the four coldhearts....

BACK IN THE fetid swamp, a group of stickies attracted by the smell of fresh blood rose from the slimy muck alongside a fallen tree to converge on the slain alligator and gleefully devour the assorted gobbets of flesh, hide and bone. Hooting in delight over the marvelous feast, the muties then followed the lumbering wendigo, happy to consume whatever else the giant being cast aside as offal.

RIDING THEIR HORSES along a shallow river, the companions had separated, with Jak, Doc and Mildred on the north side of the waterway, Ryan, Krysty and J.B. on the south bank. Each group was closely studying the ground for any sign of Petrov and his gang. Unlike hoofprints, the tire tracks of a motorcycle were very difficult to completely erase by simply dragging a leafy tree branch along behind.

"They here," Jak declared suddenly, pointing at a tiny

puddle of water with a rainbow sheen. "That engine oil! Some bike must leak not know about."

"More the fools they," Doc said, the reins held tightly in his left hand.

Just then, everybody pricked up their ears at the sound of an echoing blast. It quickly faded away, leaving behind only the gentle sounds of the murmuring water.

"Was that thunder?" Mildred asked suspiciously, glancing skyward. But there were only the usual clouds of black and orange, the occasional flash of heat lightning softly crackling inside the roiling banks of pollution.

"Sounded more like a gren or pipe bomb," J.B. noted, brushing a hand across his hair in lieu of straightening his missing hat.

"Think Petrov is trying to blast his way into the redoubt?" Krysty asked, using an oily cloth to wipe down one of the newly acquired 7.62-mm rounds before thumbing it into an empty magazine for the AK-47 rapid-fire. Unless properly maintained, old brass could jam in a weapon, easily taking off a finger or ending your life.

"I wish them good luck with that endeavor," Doc retorted scornfully. "Those doors were built to resist a thermonuclear detonation. I doubt very highly that even a thousand pipe bombs would so much as scratch the surface!"

"Mebbe so, but I had an implo gren in my bag," J.B. countered thoughtfully, "and there was no sign of it being used at the Boneyard."

"Implo work on blast doors?" Jak asked with a scowl,

leather reins in one hand, the S&W handblaster in the other.

"Hell, I don't know. Nobody knows how the things work, not even Millie, so how can I know what they won't do?"

"Fair enough," Ryan admitted, then stopped talking to scowl at a clump of bushes located underneath a yucca tree.

Slowing his mount, the one-eyed-man rode to the plants and slid off the saddle. The other companions saw nothing unusual about the flowering plants, but Ryan drew his knife to slash something inside the bushes, and they sprang apart to reveal a canvas lump. Yanking it off, the man exposed four motorcycles. They were parked close together, the engines ticking softly as they slowly cooled.

Rushing over, J.B. checked for any traps and easily disabled a mousetrap armed with a razor blade hidden under the curved dashboard for unauthorized fingers. It was crude, but effective.

"Clear," he announced, going directly to the saddlebags and ripping one open to check inside. The bag was packed with supplies, smoked meat, bedrolls, a frying pan, even some blasters and spare brass. There was even a leather bag packed full of damp moss. Unfortunately, his glasses weren't present.

Looting the other bikes, the companions filled their pockets with ammunition, and J.B. took possession of four Molotovs. The mixture seemed a little thin, but the rags were properly soaked in machine oil. Yeah, these would do just fine.

There had even been a couple of rounds for the

AK-47's gren launcher, but none of the companions had one of those stubby blasters attached to their rapid-fires, and the Russian shell was much too small to use in the 40-mm launcher that Doc carried. J.B. tucked them into his munitions bag anyway. Even without a blaster, the 30-mm shells had a host of different uses. At the very least, he could remove the C-4 plastic explosives from the warheads and make a triple-powerful pipe bomb.

"Any sign of the rest of your stuff?" Mildred asked hopefully, dropping the clip of an AK-47 to check the brass inside. Satisfied, she tossed the rapid-fire away and tucked the magazine into a pocket for later use.

"Nothing they stole is here," J.B. answered, checking the storage compartment hidden underneath a hinged seat. "Want me to ace the bikes?"

"Just disable them," Ryan decided, throwing away a .44 Magnum round that had a spot of corrosion on the bottom. "We might need them later."

Drawing her Brazilian revolver, Mildred pretended to check the ammunition while riding closer to Doc until their legs bumped.

"Yes, madam?" he asked, without looking up from his work.

"Want me to wrap that?" Mildred whispered, spinning the cylinder. "I have enough strips of cloth to do a good job."

"What are you talking about, dear lady?" Doc asked, feigning confusion.

"I saw you favoring that hand back in the village," she replied, closing the blaster to face him directly. "Firing that goddamn 40-mm launcher as a shotgun broke your wrist, didn't it?"

"It is merely sore, at worst, a mild sprain, I assure you," Doc demurred uneasily.

Reaching out, Mildred grabbed his hand inside the pocket and squeezed. Doc grunted but didn't turn white or gasp outloud.

"Fair enough. A sprain won't get infected," Mildred said, sitting back in the saddle. "Just don't use it again, or else the recoil of that blunderbus will snap those bones like breadsticks."

"Like…what was that again?"

"Matchsticks."

"Ah."

"Done," J.B. announced, dropping the spark plugs into his bag and tucking the toolbox back where he found it originally.

Personally, the man would have preferred to ride a bike instead of a horse. He got along much better with machines than animals. Unfortunately, a Harley made a very distinctive sound. The signature rumble of the big flathead engine would instantly tell Petrov and his gang of coldhearts who was coming. Stealth was more important than speed at the moment. Besides, a quiet hunter ate meat every day, as the old saying went. Wise words.

Closely studying the landscape up ahead, Ryan easily found the entrance to the box canyon, the gentle river flowing in from one side of a redstone pillar and out the other.

"It's my turn to take point, lover," Krysty said, loosening the blaster in its holster for a faster draw.

"Nobody is on point this time," Ryan countered. "Everybody off your horse, and let's find some rope!"

That confused the companions for a moment, then grinning widely they got to work. Lashing the pommels of the saddles together, the companions walked the tethered horses along the river until they reached the fork. Smacking the animals on the rumps, they sent the horses trotting upstream while they crossed to the island.

Keeping a careful watch on the top of the cliffs on the opposite side of the river, the companions proceeded slowly along the base of the pillar, half expecting to be attacked by snipers at any second. However, nothing moved in the curving canyon aside the rustling green plants that grew in abundance along the rocky shore. Minutes later, the riderless horses came splashing back into view from around the curve.

Catching one by the reins, Ryan led the animals onto dry land and checked them over for any wounds, but they were completely undamaged.

"No shots fired, or any cursing," J.B. muttered, twisting his hands on the sawed-off scattergun. "Which means they're either not here, aced or asleep."

"Or inside," Mildred stated.

"And exactly how would they manage to do that?" Krysty asked pointedly.

"Always plan for the worst to happen," Doc said, clearly quoting from something.

Nodding to that, Ryan passed the horses to Jak and started along the base of the pillar once more, working the bolt on the Marlin to chamber a round.

Moving past an outcropping of the strange redstone, the companions stopped at the sight of a crushed droid pinned underneath a huge granite boulder. It didn't take them long before they discovered the burned remains of a string trip wire that led directly to a section of the rocky ground churned by a powerful explosion.

"Yep, it was one of my pipe bombs," J.B. stated, lifting a twisted piece of melted metal. "I recognize my own work."

Fireblast! Ryan thought. The coldhearts were inside the redoubt. They had to have aced the droid and slipped past the blast doors before they closed. It was the only possible answer.

Checking for any more trip wires or land mines, the companions moved across the sloped shore to reach the blast doors. Even though he knew it was useless, Ryan pressed his ear against the cool metal to try to hear inside, but there was only the drumbeat of his own pounding heart.

Going to the hidden keypad, Krysty checked for traps before tapping in the access code. As the blast doors rumbled aside, a thick black cloud rolled out, and the companions were assaulted by the strident clanging of a fire alarm. How could the base be on fire? There were automatic suppression systems built into the ceilings and walls! Then the companions heard the rattle of a rapid-fire and muffled voices shouting orders.

"The horses go first," Ryan commanded.

Forcing the reluctant horses into the redoubt, the companions followed close behind, squinting to see through the billowing smoke, their blasters at the ready. It didn't matter if they were about to tangle with Petrov and his coldhearts or somebody else entirely. There were intruders inside a redoubt, and that meant it was chilling time.

ABANDONED ON the rocky shore, the crushed droid crackled with a surge of electricity from its emergency reserves and managed to feebly wiggle a couple of its legs on the downward side of the hill. As the loosened stone rolled away, the boulder resting on top of the machine shifted position slightly. Weakly, the droid nudged some additional stones away, and the huge boulder moved a little bit more....

Chapter Eighteen

Halfway down the smoky tunnel, the horses balked and refused to go any farther. Reluctantly, Doc took the coiled bullwhip from his side and lashed the animals to make them continue. The old man hated to do that, but it was a simple matter of the horses or the companions. Galloping away from the stinging lash, the horses disappeared into the billowing cloud.

Separating, the companions stayed to the walls to keep out of the way of any outgoing lead. Whatever was happening in the garage was in full swing, and they easily recognized the sound of their former weapons—the bark of the Steyr, the chatter of the Uzi and the unmistakable boom of the black-powder LeMat.

Just then, the fire alarm went silent and the companions quickly tucked their weapons under clothing a split second before a sticky white foam gushed from the ceiling to cover everything with a soft blanket of fire retardant. As the deluge stopped, several voices were raised in jubilation down the tunnel.

"Yee-haw, that got the nuke sucker!" a man called out in victory.

"Shut up! Thal, grab that sledgehammer and pound the son of a bitch flat!" a gruff voice commanded. "I never want to see this bastard thing walk again!"

"My pleasure, Petrov," a man said in a low bass.

"Hey, where the fuck did those horses come from?" a woman demanded. "Did the doors open again?"

Softly, the companions could hear the frightened animals running about, bumping into what sounded like several parked wags, and the constant crackle of breaking glass.

"You were the last one inside, Rose," Petrov growled accusingly, his voice fading away only to come back strong. "Nuking hell, it's a feint! There's somebody else inside!"

Knowing better than to rush toward an armed enemy, the companions stayed exactly where they were, waiting for the coldhearts to come to them. But then they heard a sizzling noise and a lead cylinder clattered onto the floor at the mouth of the tunnel.

Instantly, J.B. triggered both barrels of the sawed-off, the blast sending the pipe bomb rattling back into the foam-filled garage. A moment later, there was a resounding explosion and the sound of ripping metal.

Using the blast as cover, Ryan charged around the last corner of the tunnel and hit the wet floor to roll behind the destroyed remains of a sleek sports car, the fiberglass chassis splintered into jagged pieces.

Rising into a crouch, the one-eyed-man saw four people frantically reloading blasters near the smoldering wreckage of a droid. Swinging up the longblaster, Ryan aimed and fired in one smooth motion. But the smoky air threw off his aim, and the largest man flinched as the big Magnum round only scored his cheek and smashed into the empty Peg-Board wall, blowing it apart. Retardant went flying everywhere.

"Bear!" a tiny blonde woman screamed, then brought up the Uzi to trigger several bursts. "Eat lead, ya nuking bastards!"

Ducking low once more, Ryan levered in a fresh cartridge, then fired at the clock on the wall. As the glass covering shattered, it drew the attention of the coldhearts, and the rest of the companions charged into the garage, taking cover behind windowless wags.

Kicking some foam-covered glass out of the way, Krysty dropped prone and tried to find the boots of the coldhearts through the maze of tires. But there were just too many wags in the way for her to see that far, not to mention the white mounds of drying retardant.

As a horse scampered past, J.B. crawled behind a civilian wag and cracked open the sawed-off to yank out the spent cartridges and shove in two fresh ones. Then he looked at Ryan. The two men nodded at each other, and J.B. triggered a blast directly into the ceiling, as Ryan stood and fired the Marlin once more. But the coldhearts were gone; only the sound of breaking glass revealed their movements behind the banks of speckled cars and trucks.

Stepping out from behind a tank, Charlie cut loose with both of his blasters, the copper-jacketed .38 rounds cutting down two of the horses.

Popping up, Mildred sent a long burst from her rapid-fire, the hardball rounds punching through the sheet-metal bodies of the civilian wags and ricocheting off the armored chassis of the APC.

"Give us back our blasters and stuff, and we'll let you walk out of here alive!" Ryan shouted, standing for only a heartbeat to put a round into a pressurized tank of an acetylene-gas welding torch. A hole appeared in the container, but there was no explosion.

Shitfire, an empty! Ryan cursed.

"Come take it yourself!" Petrov answered, shooting the Steyr into a fluorescent light fixture. Breaking free from its moorings, the rack of glowing tubes came hurtling down to loudly crash on top of a sleek limousine, sending out a corona of sparkling debris.

Getting the bead on the female coldheart, Mildred started to shoot when a running horse got in the way. She withheld until it was past, and by then the coldheart was out of sight behind a Hummer dripping with chrome.

Creeping behind an SUV covered with military decals, Jak grunted as a shard of glass stabbed into his arm right through the deerskin jacket. Keeping both blasters in his hands, the albino teen used his teeth to extract the sliver and spit it onto the sticky floor. Then he shifted to the right and triggered both weapons in a brief flurry of mixed blasterfire, hammering one of the elevator doors. The soft lead rounds ricocheted off the predark steel, and there came an answering curse of pain from one of the hidden coldhearts.

Sneaking a peek around the tail fin of a civilian Chrysler wag, Ryan found himself locking gazes with Petrov, doing the exact same thing from behind a VW minivan. A split second passed, then they both drew weapons and fired. The S&W scattergun boomed, a hail of double-O buckshot hitting the Chrysler to blow off a fin and send a hubcap skittering away. Ryan answered with the Marlin, the Magnum round plowing completely through the lightweight VW minivan and coming out the other side, the denting sheet metal shoving Petrov onto the glass-covered floor. Bleeding from a dozen cuts, Petrov ran for better cover, firing the scattergun blindly as he darted between the parked wags.

Suddenly, everybody began shooting at the exact same time, metal crumpling and glass shattering, with ricochets going everywhere. Frightened horses whinnied at the exchange and tried to get out of the way by clambering over several wags to reach the relative safety of the fuel pump in the far corner.

As the barrage paused, Petrov pulled out another pipe bomb and lit the fuse. It took two tries because of the flame retardant drying on his hands, but finally he got it sizzling.

Recognizing that sound all too well, Ryan shouted, "Incoming!" and dived behind a U.S. Army 4x4 truck.

Whistling sharply, Petrov tossed the pipe bomb to Thal, who relayed it to Charlie, who whipped it forward, then ducked. The cylinder hit the littered ground hard, sliding through the broken shards to bounce off a tire to roll another ten feet before coming to a halt under the APC.

Slapping hands over their ears, the companions opened their mouths to save their eardrums. But the blast still sounded louder than doomsday, and the armored personnel carrier actually lifted a few inches off the concrete before crashing back down. The rear door burst open and out tumbled several skeletons, clutching rapid-fires and wearing military-grade body armor. Charlie made a grab for the armor and nearly lost his arm.

Smiling grimly as he reloaded his blaster, Jak paused and heard an unexpected noise from the direction of the access tunnel. Then a sucker-covered hand appeared around the corner, followed by a misshapen head.

"Stickies!" Jak shouted in warning, triggering both his weapons.

Spinning, Ryan snarled a virulent curse at the sight of the muties, then fired the Marlin from the hip. The first stickie jerked as the massive Magnum round took its life, but the hardball round continued onward to punch through two more stickies before stopping inside the fourth. However, as they dropped lifeless to the floor, a mob of stickies came charging out of the tunnel, waving their arms and hooting loudly, their primitive minds overexcited by the sound of the blasters.

Using both barrels. J.B. triggered the sawed-off, and two stickies went flying to hit the wall in bloody chunks. But more of them poured out of the tunnel in a seemingly endless stream.

Firing the LeMat into the hooting mob, Thal missed the first few times, the vicious recoil of the Civil War handcannon almost more than he could handle. Holstering the Colt, he got the LeMat under control and aced three more muties before they reached the rows of parked wags.

Well trained to defend themselves, two of the horses reared on hind legs to paw at the horrid muties, crushing the skull of a female and shattering the shoulder of a male. Then another horse screamed as a stickie grabbed its shoulder to rip off a strip of flesh. Bright red blood gushed from the injury, and the horse stumbled away as the happy stickie hooted in delight and began to feast.

Moving behind a pickup truck, Krysty sprayed a volley of 7.62-mm rounds into the stickie, fountains of crimson spurting from the line of holes across its chest.

Shooting through a windowless civilian wag, Rose used the SIG-Sauer to avoid attracting attention. Modified several times by J.B. over the years, the built-in sound suppressor—when it worked—reduced the muzzle-blast to a mere cough. Craning its neck for a look around, a stickie jerked from the impact of a 9-mm Parabellum round into its chest and went tumbling, only to reappear a second later, its left arm dangling limply, but otherwise unharmed.

Triggering the M-16 rapid-fire, Doc mercilessly hosed the heads of a pair of stickies, acing both the male and female.

"Have some of this!" Charlie snarled, alternately firing the hammerless S&W revolver and the Czech ZKR. A stickie had its face torn off, another merely wounded, and the rest escaped unharmed.

Whooping like a daredevil, Jak moved among the wags and trucks, both of his blasters booming death. Muties fell, pumping life fluids, and soon the albino teen was splattered with gore.

By now, the garage was almost completely clear of smoke, the constant flow of sterilized air thinning the dense clouds to a patchy haze. However, the drying foam still lay in a thick blanket across everything, and walking was a dangerous proposition. Every step meant a boot could slip, and a person would fall onto the layer of broken glass.

Fumbling to insert a clip into the Steyr longblaster, Petrov worked the bolt just in time to shoot an advancing stickie in the chest. Hooting loudly, the mutie threw itself at the man, but Petrov neatly pivoted away from the rush and fired another 7.62-mm round directly into the back of its head. Blood and teeth hit the floor a split second before the aced mutie did, the last hoot cut off in the middle.

Dropping a spent clip from her rapid-fire, Mildred reached for another, then realized that she was too slow. A stickie was upon her, both of the killing hands reaching for her face. With no other recourse, the physician rammed the barrel of the assault rifle forward like a spear, the Russian steel stabbing deep into the mutie's belly, invoking a plaintive howl. Uncaring, Mildred twisted the shaft to enlarge the wound before yanking it free. As the stickie stupidly began to examine the wound, Mildred quickly reloaded, worked the arming bolt and put a burst of rounds into its face, blowing away most of the forehead.

Drawing his blaster, Ryan fired three quick rounds into a stickie starting to climb straight up the wall. As it died, the creature let go with its hands, but the sucker-covered feet stayed attached. It flopped backward to hang upside down, pale blood dripping onto the broken glass and cars below.

Holstering the LeMat, Thal switched to the Colt Python and began to fire steadily at the companions and the stickies.

Catching a brief glimpse of her med bag, Mildred

almost rushed toward the big man, but a stickie blocked her way, and she wasted precious seconds acing it.

Jumping into the back of a pickup truck to avoid the deadly hands of a stickie, Krysty swung the stock of her longblaster and smashed it in its face. Hooting in pain, the mutie turned to shamble away, and the woman ruthlessly shot it in the back of the head.

Snapping the sawed-off shut, J.B. crouched behind a sleek sports car, watching the floor. As soon as he saw sucker-covered feet, he stood to fire both barrels, one to the chest, the other to the face. The stickie staggered backward, a tattered ruin. But three more stickies arched around the frantically reloading man and took off among the rows of windowless cars, constantly hooting.

"Shut the frag up!" Rose yelled, waving the Uzi around, the stream of 9-mm rounds randomly slapping into wags, horses, the aced droid and numerous vehicles. A military tire deflated, only to automatically seal the hole and reinflate itself with quick-hardening foam.

Trying for Petrov, Jak fired his two blasters but only caught a stickie, the mutie doubling over to expel the ghastly contents of its stomach onto the drying retardant. The smell of the two was beyond description, and Jak gagged, trying not to vomit.

Unexpectedly, the sideview mirror on a nearby Corvette exploded, one of the coldhearts mistakenly shooting at the reflection of the teenager. Returning to the attack, Jak felt a surge of adrenaline and such minor considerations as nauseating smells were temporarily banished from his mind.

Leaping on top of a wag, a stickie crouched as if to jump on Ryan, and the one-eyed man fired both blasters, the combined discharges sending the mutie flying away to smack into the side of the APC, its bones audibly breaking.

Firing his scattergun one barrel at a time, J.B. chilled two more stickies, then knelt to reload when he saw a section of the empty access tunnel move.

J.B. squinted hard and fired a single barrel. Something bellowed in pain, and piss-yellow blood hit the wall to reveal a familiar outline. Dark night, he thought.

"Wendigo in the tunnel!" J.B. shouted, firing again, trying for the head. But against the smooth monotone walls of the redoubt, the creature was virtually invisible, and the spray hit nothing this time but empty air.

Chapter Nineteen

Reloading even faster than before, J.B. wondered if the wendigo could have herded the stickies along like advance troops to weaken the enemy. He hoped not, because if the mutie was that smart they were chilled already.

Just then, the bedraggled Walker droid limped into the garage, propelled by a single working leg. The mystery of how the stickies got inside the redoubt solved, Ryan carefully aimed the longblaster and put the last Magnum round into the machine. The titanic bullet punched completely through the crippled droid, sending out a spray of wires and gears. Once more, the droid went still, and hydraulic fluid dribbled from a score of cracks in the deformed chassis.

Triggering his rapid-fire in single shots, Doc maintained a steady discharge, while Mildred reloaded. Then she started shooting while Doc reloaded. Moving and fighting in tight unison as if they had been doing it for a hundred years, the former school teacher and the physician began to slaughter the remaining stickies.

Closely watching the dirt floor, Jak saw some of the retardant move, and he promptly triggered both of his blasters, aiming high. Hit both times, the wendigo roared, its fur rippling with colors and corporate logos as it ran along the line of cars and trucks.

"Did...did they say a wendigo?" Charlie asked in a tight whisper, frantically shoving fresh rounds into the Czech ZKR.

"Yeah, they did," Petrov growled, casting away a spent rotary clip for the Steyr. "Okay, new plan. Let's get the frag out of here."

"Are you crazy?" Charlie demanded, closing the cylinder. "We'll never get past these people. Not to mention the stickies and wendy!"

"Not even gonna try," Petrov replied, glancing sideways. "They can dance with the muties forever for all I care. We'll take the stairs and leave by the back door. Thal found it on the map, fifth floor, little room with six walls. That's the secret exit."

Tucking the hammerless S&W revolver into his gun belt, Charlie grinned widely. "Now you're talking!" Sprinting low and fast around the tank, the coldheart snapped off a couple of shots from the Czech ZKR at the companions while passing by the elevator bank. Krysty cried out as her rapid-fire was torn from her grip, and Doc jerked from the passing of lead so close to his cheek that he briefly felt the heat.

Putting two more rounds into a stickie that was blocking his way, Charlie grabbed the handle to the stairwell door, then foolishly paused to yell for his friends to follow. A longblaster cut loose, and the coldheart jerked from the passage of the 7.62-mm round through his body, his lifeblood splashing on the wall. With a gurgling sigh, Charlie slumped to the floor, the Czech blaster tumbling from his limp fingers.

Happily lunging for the body, another stickie began to messily feed, when Rose stepped out from behind a military wag and chilled the mutie with a tight burst from the Uzi.

Putting two more 12-gauge cartridges into the wendigo, J.B. dived over a chilled stickie and landed in a mad scramble, his boots slipping on the foamy floor. Bellowing loudly, the furry mutie chased after the two-legs, backhanding a civilian wag out of the way.

As the wendigo strode forward, J.B. reached the fuel pump in the corner. Hoping it was primed, the man yanked off the nozzle and squeezed the release lever just as he thumbed a butane lighter into action. The rush of gasoline ignited into a column of flame, and J.B. swept the makeshift flamethrower over the wendigo.

Engulfed in flames, the creature howled in agony, its tentacles lashing about to smash the hood of a wag and rip the light fixtures from the ceiling. Grimly, J.B. maintained the stream of fire, even though his hand was already beginning to feel uncomfortably warm on the metal nozzle.

Grabbing a detached car hood, the wendigo raised it as a shield, and J.B. simply shifted the stream of fire onto its exposed legs, the thick fur instantly catching on fire.

As the snarling wendigo raised the shield to throw at the man, Ryan stepped into view and sent five thundering rounds from his handblaster into the beast.

As the howling wendigo fell to the floor, every stickie in the garage started to hoot insanely as they converged on the area, eagerly trying to reach the stream of pretty, pretty fire.

Trapped in a corner, J.B. desperately switched hands

again, trying to hose both the onrushing stickies and the wendigo.

Seeing this as the perfect chance to escape, Petrov rummaged in the munitions bag for any more pipe bombs, but only found a couple of road flares. Twisting off the top, he scratched them alive, then tossed the flares inside a nearby stack of spare tires, the rubber old and rotting. At first, the material simply melted a little, then the softened tires burst into flames, issuing an amazing amount of thick, black smoke. Instantly, the remaining coldhearts broke cover and charged for the stairwell door.

Finished reloading, Ryan took aim and blew a chunk out of the groin of a stickie, then kneecapped the wendigo. But the huge beast had slithered to the corpse of a horse and it didn't stop eating, its clawed hands dripping gore as it ripped the horse apart. Already it seemed larger and more heavily muscled, the missing patches of fur coming back with astonishing speed.

Just then, the rest of the companions arrived from amid the rows of vehicles, their blasters unleashing a withering hail of death. Caught between the fire and the blasters, the stickies were ruthlessly slaughtered, torn asunder and roasted alive.

When the last hooting mutie fell, Ryan and the others turned their full attention to the wendigo. As their bullets tore away chunks of its hide, the creature stood and bellowed with new strength, then J.B. set it ablaze once more.

By now sweat was pouring off his face, and J.B. held the nozzle with both hands, the tendons in his neck protruding from the awful strain of keeping the agonizing grip. There was a faint smell in the air of roasting pork, and J.B. knew that was him starting to cook.

Appearing out of nowhere, Jak grabbed the hot nozzle, his hands wrapped in the deerskin jacket. Thankfully, J.B. relinquished control to the albino teen and stepped back from the fiery torrent, carefully flexing his blistered palms in a mound of cool retardant.

Standing, the wendigo roared with renewed life, and Doc swung up his rapid-fire to jam the stock against the armored side of the APC, gritted his teeth and pulled the trigger. The strident boom of the shotgun blast torn the mutie apart, and it slumped to the floor.

Stepping in close, Ryan kicked the head free, and Mildred shot it twice, then Jak covered the creature with fire, sweeping the stream back and forth, until the wendigo was a blazing inferno. Sluggishly, the mutie tried to rise, but Krysty emptied the clip of her AK-47 into its tattered chest, and the wendigo dropped to the floor, unmoving.

Jak released the nozzle with obvious pleasure. The teen was drenched with sweat, the deerskin jacket giving off the appetizing aroma of a venison roast.

"Well, I don't trust this tricky bastard as far as I can throw an APC," J.B. growled, pulling out the WP gren. "Start running, people! It's going to get mighty hot in here!"

Hopping over the aced stickies, the companions charged through the rows of battered cars. When they were far enough away, J.B. yanked the safety pin, released the arming lever and tossed the canister on top of the burning wendigo. Then he turned and raced through the maze of wags as fast as he could.

Circling the tank, J.B. found the rest of the companions waiting there. He started to say something when an incandescent light grew from the other side of the armored machine, and a searing wave of unbelievable heat filled the air of the garage. The fire alarm clanged for only a moment before cutting off, overwhelmed by the volcanic heat of the military gren. Then the ceiling cut loose with a fresh deluge of retardant foam, but it seemed to have no effect whatsoever on the hellish corona of the white phosphorous.

However, over by the door to the stairwell, the burning stack of tires went out, the thick cloud of dirty smoke washed clean from the atmosphere.

Staying on the lee side of the tank, the sopping-wet companions sloshed through the descending foam to reach the body of the coldheart. Moving fast, they stripped the corpse of its possessions, returning everything he carried to the original owners.

"Where did the rest of them go?" Krysty growled, her hair flexing wildly. The woman was disgusted at the filthy condition of her bearskin coat and hammerless S&W Model 640 revolver, but was delighted to have the items back.

"Took stairs," Jak stated, indicating the footprints disappearing in the downpour of retardant. There were only three of his leaf-blade throwing knives on the coldheart, but it felt good to him to have some familiar steel in his belt again.

Across the garage, some of the fiberglass wags were

beginning to melt, then the fuel pump exploded into a geyser of flame, that cut off instantly as the safety valve engaged. Slowly, the glare of the white phosphorous died away, and as the heat diminished, the foam cut off.

"Where do you think they went?" Mildred asked, checking over the Czech ZKR blaster before tucking it into a pocket. The Brazilian Taurus was a good gun, but nothing beat the perfect balance of the ZKR. To the physician it was like the difference between an ax and a scalpel.

"They're probably going down," J.B. said, vigorously cleaning his glasses on a shirttail, looking for an exit. Sliding his glasses on, the man blinked, then smiled broadly.

"Now, let's get back the rest of our stuff," the Armorer declared, slapping Ryan on the back.

"SHITFIRE, BEAR, there's no exit tunnel in here," Rose snarled, looking around the antechamber of the mat-trans unit. "There's nothing here but something that looks like somebody's idea of a shitter!"

"Sadly, you seem to be correct," Thal muttered, curiously stepping into the unit and glancing around. There was a keypad on the wall, but he knew better than to fool with one of those, especially in a mil base, and quickly stepped out of the unit.

Oddly, the big coldheart thought he had heard a thumping noise come from the floor just before he did, but as he listened intently, the sound didn't come again. Bad plumbing?

"You're right, this is a waste," Petrov said, turning around and heading for the door. "Let's head for the basement."

"And if there's nothing there?" Rose demanded, starting across the antechamber.

"Well, then we go back to the garage and finish off those bastard outlanders!"

"Now you're talking," Thal grumbled, touching his bloody cheek.

Stepping through the door, the coldhearts stopped talking as they crossed the room full of comps. The blinking lights on the complex control panels frightened them quite a lot, although nobody would admit it.

Back in the outer hallway, Petrov took the lead and marched directly for the stairwell, when they heard a musical ding. At the far end of the hall, the elevator doors opened and out rolled a thick cloud of smoke, then blasters started firing nonstop.

Diving for the floor, the coldhearts returned fire, crawling forward to find cover inside some of the offices along the way. Then the elevator doors closed, and it began moving again.

"Guess we scared them off," Petrov said, not really believing it himself. Then he caught a whiff of the smoke. Rubber. The elevator had been full of burning wag tires. But that didn't make any sense…unless the blasterfire had actually just been some spare brass stuffed into the rubber before it was set ablaze. It was a diversion!

Spinning, the leader of the Pig Iron Gang started to shout a warning to the others, when the door to the stairwell slammed open and out poured the companions with every weapon firing. Snarling in rage, Petrov got off a single shot from the scattergun, then something slammed into his chest and pain filled his world, but not for very long.

Epilogue

Arriving at the ruins of Modine, Dunbar and Fenton parked their motorcycles near a wild tangle of jungle that had once been a public park, then took a moment to top up their gas tanks from their jerricans.

"Where do we start looking for Ryan and his gang?" Dunbar asked, flexing his aching hands. Riding a hog always looked like fun, much better than a horse, but it was hard work. A man could rest on a horse, even sleep a little, and trust that the animal would stay alert and not ride off a cliff. That wasn't true for a machine, and his entire body ached from the rough ride through the rocky terrain of the badlands. They had been chased by barbs for almost an entire day, those triple-cursed spears coming uncomfortably close, before finally leaving them behind in the dust.

Not bothering to answer, Fenton dismounted his bike, dragged out the canteen marked with a strip of duct tape and took a long drink.

"Careful now, that's potent stuff," Dunbar warned, stretching his back muscles.

But the words weren't heeded, and Fenton continued to swallow mouthful after mouthful of the jolt-laced shine until he dropped the empty container to clatter on the street.

"Blind NORAD, I needed that," the lieutenant said

in a perfectly normal voice. "That was fragging wonderful! The baron's healer was right. I don't feel any pain now! None at all! Nuking hell, I don't…" Trembling slightly, Fenton sighed deeply, the sound fading away until there was only silence. He dropped to the ground.

"Lieutenant?" Dunbar asked, climbing off the hog to rush over and check the motionless man. But it was as he expected. Fenton was gone, chilled by his uncontrollable need for revenge, for honor, for…everything.

"Goodbye, old friend," Dunbar whispered, bending to gently close the one eye staring out of the bandages.

After burying the body in a patch of daisies, Dunbar transferred the extra fuel and brass to his sidecar and drove off toward the east. Hunting for the companions alone in the ruins would be madness, and there was no way he could go back to Delta without proof of their deaths, which left only a single option. On the ride from the Boneyard, Ryan had mentioned his home ville of Front Royal back east. That sounded like as good a place as any for the teenager to begin again. Everybody needed sec men these days, and if the hog held together that long, it would buy him a house and a horse to start a new life.

Kicking the Harley alive, Dunbar drove out of the ruins, heading toward the unknown.

RECLAIMING THEIR belongings from the aced coldhearts, the companions did a fast recce of the redoubt to make sure there were no stickies, droids or wendigos hiding anywhere. But the base was deserted. Hoping for the best, the companions checked the armory, but as usual, that was completely empty, the shelves covered with a thin layer of dust.

After Mildred used her med bag to patch their wounds, the companions went directly to the jump chamber and sat on the floor. After a few seconds, there was a thumping noise from below, the strange electronic mist swirled up to engulf the friends and the universe fell away as they were instantly transferred to another redoubt somewhere.

Moments later, the exhausted people awoke, gasping and wheezing. But after a few minutes, they struggled erect, left the chamber and did a recce of the new redoubt. This one was also deserted, but the armory had a few weapons and ammo left. Other stores revealed food, medicine and clothing. A bonanza of supplies!

Enjoying a hot meal for the first time in weeks, the companions then settled in separate rooms for some sleep after a hot shower. The next day, they would check outside to see where they had arrived, but tonight, they would rest.

Pretending to fall asleep, Mildred waited until J.B. was softly snoring before easing out of the bed to pad into the bathroom for some privacy. Cutting out the first few pages of the journal, which she had recovered from Thal, she ripped the sheets into tiny pieces, then flushed them down the toilet. At last, all evidence of her mistake was destroyed.

Certain aspects of life in Deathlands just shouldn't be committed to paper, she realized.

Sleep was a long time in coming, but when it finally did, her dreams were pleasant and untroubled.

The
Don Pendleton's
Executioner®
ENEMY AGENTS

American extremists plan a terror strike....

When California's Mojave Desert becomes the training ground for a homegrown militia group with a deadly scheme to "take back" America, Mack Bolan is sent in to unleash his own form of destruction. But first he'll have to infiltrate the unit and unravel their plot before it's too late.

Available in June wherever books are sold.

GOLD EAGLE®

TAKE 'EM FREE
2 action-packed novels plus a mystery bonus

NO RISK
NO OBLIGATION TO BUY

GEII

James Axler
Outlanders®

TRUTH ENGINE

An exiled God prince acts out his violent vengeance…

Cerberus Redoubt, the rebel base of operations, has fallen under attack. The enemy, Ullikummis, is at the gates and Kane and the others are his prisoners. The stone god demands Kane lead his advancing armies as he retakes Earth in the ultimate act of revenge. For he is determined to be the ultimate god of the machine, infinite and unstoppable.

Available August wherever books are sold.

AleX Archer
TEAR OF THE GODS

The early chapters of history contain dangerous secrets…secrets that Annja Creed is about to unlock.…

A dream leads archaeologist Annja Creed to an astonishing find in England—the Tear of the Gods. But someone knows exactly what this unusual torc means, and he will do anything to get his hands on it…even leave Annja for dead. Now she is fleeing for her life, not knowing the terrifying truth about the relic she risks everything to protect.

Available July wherever books are sold.